DANA'S

DILEMMA

A Dana Morgan Mystery

Connie Terpack

DANA'S DILEMMA
A Dana Morgan Mystery

This is a work of fiction. All of the characters, names, incidents, organizations, and dialogue in this novel are either the products of the author's imagination or are used fictitiously

iUniverse books may be ordered through booksellers or by contacting:

iUniverse
1663 Liberty Drive
Bloomington, IN 47403
www.iuniverse.com
1-800-Authors (1-800-288-4677)

ISBN: 978-1-4620-3405-5 (sc)
ISBN: 978-1-4620-3406-2 (ebk)

Printed in the United States of America

iUniverse rev. date: 09/01/2011

Acknowledgements

Many thanks and deep appreciation to my friend, Cynthia, for her tireless help and editing skills.

Much love and appreciation to my son, Shawn, for his computer skills and patience in teaching me how to use my laptop.

Many thanks to my friend, Deborah, for her support and editorial skills.

To my sister Pat

PROLOGUE

"Okay, ladies, time for recess. You know the drill!"

The inmates at the medium to maximum security prison in South Carolina, quickly lined up at their cell doors, some mumbling under their breath, and others silently following orders but with looks ranging from boring to hateful. They knew the punishment for moving too slowly. The guards stared harshly at each prisoner as if daring them to make a mistake, or give them any meager reason to dole out some form of punishment.

Each prisoner focused straight ahead except Harry Drago, aka Dragon Man, because of the large dragon tattoo on his left forearm. He looked at the guards and sneered, adding an extra touch of love with the second finger of his left hand held up high, revealing his dragon tattoo in its full glory. The dragon's long pointed red tongue licked at the back of his wrist with drops of bright red blood dripping from its fangs. Its large bluish-green scaled body covered most of Drago's forearm ending with the crimson red pointed tail snaking all the way up his upper arm. Its blood-tipped curved claws were sharp and ready to snatch anything within its reach. The eyes were red and black with a thin arc of silver. One would almost swear they moved, ever watching for its next prey. It was a magnificent tattoo.

Dragon Man had been born Harry Drago forty-nine years ago to loving parents. He was fourteen and the oldest of five when his father died of cancer. To support his family, he had turned to a life of petty crime and quickly moved on to armed robbery and murder, becoming one of the toughest criminals to catch. Drago's gang was ruthless. If you were not in his gang, you were not in any gang. At his arrest, Drago admitted killing only three people, but during his illustrious career he had terrorized hundreds, leaving at least thirty-six dead in his wake. The fact that they had mostly been small time criminals or other gang members was, in a perverse way, appreciated by the legal system. Finally, Drago had been caught and four years ago sentenced to life without parole. It was something to be proud of that he was in their prison. His reign of terror had covered ten counties in three states.

None of the other prisoners would dare do what Drago got away with. The head guard snorted at Drago and ignored him. The last guard that had punished Drago ended up dead from a car bomb. No evidence had been found to prove that Drago or any of his former gang had anything to do with it, but the police were crediting him with the crime nonetheless. Bombs were known to be one of Drago's favorite ways to eliminate his enemies. The guards, as well as the other prisoners, believed the talk and Harry Drago's legend grew as the gossip circulated around the prison.

When the guard was satisfied that all the men were ready, he nodded to the guard in the booth and a buzzer sounded. The cell doors slowly slid open clanking loudly into place. All five prisoners darted into the hall, quickly forming a straight line, only to wait again.

Immediately six fully armed guards tromped in and surrounded the prisoners, one in front, one in back and two along each side. It was almost overkill for only five prisoners, but these five were considered highly dangerous. They marched in double time down a long hall to the side door. They continued to march in place, eyes facing forward, while they waited to be scanned before the door opened to the fenced-in yard for their daily outdoor exercise. The escort guards watched as the prisoners entered the secure yard then disappeared back inside, their duty done.

Once outside each man migrated to his favorite spot. The tower guards watched them as the prisoners leisurely settled in. John Andrews was a big guy, six feet four inches, around three hundred pounds and all muscle. He seemed to enjoy hurting people just for fun. Over his four year crime spree he had murdered ten people and crippled eight others. He always left a smiley face sticky note on each victim. He had been there only three weeks and would be leaving next week when there would be an opening on death row for him. Everyone kept their distance from him. Even Drago seemed a little leery of him. He never revealed what set him off nor why he stopped.

Vaughn Allans specialized in robbing banks. Eight people died in the process of his stealing three and a half million dollars from five banks. He was elusive and able to vanish until his next job. Unfortunately for him, he accidently killed an off-duty police officer during his last robbery so the man hunt was doubled. That one mistake had finally cost him his freedom. As it turned out, he robbed as a man but lived as a dowdy, old wealthy widow woman. He was only five foot nine inches tall so it was easy for him to look shorter when he walked hunched over a cane.

Brian Shawnly was the oldest at fifty-nine and had served the longest, twenty-six years. He had been head honcho until Drago moved in and there was obvious enmity between them. Drago's reputation gave him power that Brian did not like.

Blaine Sevans sat on one of the benches nearest the entry gate and started reading a well worn letter like he did every day. He was the youngest of the bunch and the only black prisoner in their section. Last month marked one year served with forty-nine more to go. He had gotten that letter his first week and guarded it like a precious jewel, reading it over and over. No one else ever got to see it.

Letters and visits were scarce in this sector. Family and friends tended to forget their loved ones incarcerated here. A letter was usually a big deal for them. A phone call or visit was almost a sacred event. Watching from the safety of his guard shack, Parish North, twenty-four and relatively new to the team, recalled the day last month Drago had received a letter. He tore it open while walking to a bench and started reading it. A moment later he placed his hand on his chest, fingers splayed wide apart and plopped down on the bench. His mouth was wide open like he was gasping for air. The letter shook in his other hand. The guards had all been informed of the signs and symptoms of a heart attack and that Harry Drago was a prime candidate for one. CPR directions were posted in the guard rooms and on their cell block. To them, it looked like Drago was having a heart attack. The guards had all come to alert with three running out into the yard, not knowing if this was some sort of ruse or if he truly was having a heart attack. By the time they reached him, they realized he was simply genuinely happy. He stood shouting, 'I'm a daddy! I've got a little girl!'

Parish had watched from the shack as Drago, without any objections, let one of the guards read his letter. He looked proud with his chest out and chin up as he handed the guard the single page missive. His younger sister had written to tell him that his second wife, Lisa, had a little girl about two years old. She did not know what her name was or exactly where they were staying. She saw her and the child at the Ladybug, a dress shop for toddler to preteen girls. His sister was talking to another woman and she overheard the woman mention the child's father was in prison and she would never get to know him. Drago knew the girl was his because the age fit with his last conjugal visit.

There were no letters today. The guards relaxed as all the prisoners looked like they were behaving. "Think it'll rain today?" Parish asked his fellow guard, Hayes Spencer, as he turned from the window to light a cigarette. "We sure could use some to cool things off."

Hayes glanced up from his report into the pale blue cloudless sky and answered gruffly, "Ya think? Those are some mean storm clouds up there."

"Well, you don't have to be so nasty about it."

"I know you're still fairly new, but you've got to remember to keep your eye on the prisoners all the time. You've spent three minutes getting a pack of cigarettes out of your jacket pocket, lighting up, and staring up at the sky."

"They're not doing anything."

Hayes slapped his pen down on the paper and rolled his eyes upward as he shook his head, muttering under his breath, "Lord, give me patience." He took a deep breath and patiently responded, emphasizing each word, "But you never know."

Defensively Parish retorted, "I thought the guys in the rifle towers watched them and there's Jose and Mike over in the other guard room."

"The rifle towers watch outward, not just the yard. There's five mean prisoners in there that need every eye on them. I wouldn't care if they killed each other, but I like my job. You can't trust them. Like I've said before, you never know what they might do. I need to do this monthly report. While I'm busy with it, you," Hayes stood and jabbed his thick pointer finger into Parish's chest for emphasis, "are supposed to watch the prisoners."

Petulantly, Parish put out his cigarette and sat down in his desk chair, swung to the side of the desk and put his feet up on it. He grabbed his half finished can of soda and sullenly stared out the long window. That window gave him an unobstructed view of the yard from top to bottom and side to side. The outside thermometer registered one hundred and three degrees. There was no shade. He almost felt sorry for the prisoners sweltering in the heat, but they had requested yard time today.

Parish did not like working with Hayes. He was an okay guy and knew his stuff, but he always saved that monthly report for the last day which put him in a bad mood. Hayes tended to be disorganized, but Parish only got into trouble whenever he tried to subtly organize him. It seemed Hayes could not function with planning ahead. He had pitched a fit the one time Parish had most of the information needed for the monthly report penciled in by the third day of the month and it was not due until the tenth. He had shown it to Hayes and was taken aback by his reaction. Hayes tossed it in the trash can after barely a glance, telling him his info could not be accurate since not everyone had time to put together their facts. It was a simple report and only two other people had to submit their share. In the year that Parish had been there, not once had they ever taken past four days of the new month to give Hayes their information. It had taken Parish only twenty minutes to do it, yet Hayes would spend an hour or more working on it. Parish often thought that was what made Hayes angry—that he knew how much time Hayes wasted.

The phone rang. As Hayes reached for it he told Parish, "After I finish this report I'll give you a break."

"Yeah," Parish responded without turning his head. Hayes did not mind when they were alone not being called *Sir*, so Parish did not bother to add it to the sullen *yeah*. He watched the prisoners as they sat around. It was too hot to do anything else. In the time he had been here, he had already nicknamed most of them. Drago was the only exception. He already had his own nickname and Parish half thought he had given it to himself because of the dragon tattoo, wondering if he had picked a dragon because of his last name. Parish chuckled to himself and thought *If his name had been McFly, would he have had a fly tattoo?*

Drago had a letter which he carefully folded and put back into the pocket of his orange jumpsuit after reading it. Parish was curious to know if that was the same letter Drago had received last month or a new one. Something seemed different about his attitude since getting that letter. It made him happy and proud for a few days followed by a regretful sadness. Today there was something different again, but Parish could not put a finger on it.

Vaughn liked to jog around the enclosure so he became the Jogger. Today he did only one lackadaisical run around the yard then stood by the fence doing some stretching exercises and watching the other inmates. Parish figured it was too hot for him to jog. After a while he sat on one of the benches and was soon joined by Drago. Even though Parish could not hear them, it was obvious they were talking. Those two had never spent much time together before. It was unusual, but not alarming.

At six foot four and almost three hundred pounds, John Andrews got the nickname of Big John. With his youthfully innocent face, Parish considered 'Gentle Giant' for John, but discarded that because of his violent past. Faces could be very deceiving. Most likely that was how he lured his victims into thinking he was harmless in spite of his size. John had been a model prisoner here. Parish had never seen him act aggressively or threateningly to anyone.

Brian Shawnly was Grandpa with his premature gray hair and slight pot belly. He looked like an innocent, sweet old man. He had beaten his first wife and she divorced him. He had beaten and killed his second wife then two days later killed his sister-in-law—all because he thought his wife was cheating on him with someone her sister had introduced her to. During the trial, he found out the man he overheard them talking about was a character on a soap opera and he broke down. People that knew him said he changed after that. Parish did not see anything special about him. He was quiet and did not joke much with the others, but he did not know what he was like before. Brian was talking with Big John. Nothing unusual or alarming there either. Those two normally got along.

Blaine was the Letterman and always sat alone. His reputation had preceded him and no one wanted to be around him. The other inmates kept a safe distance. Blaine was anti-gay and enjoyed slicing the throat of anyone he thought was gay. He had killed ten men, four of which were not homosexuals. He did not like his first cell mate, a tough former gang member who was too mouthy to suit him, so Blaine sliced across the man's jugular with a sharp, rough thumbnail. It was not enough to kill him, but it was enough to create sufficient blood to earn Blaine some time in solitaire.

Understandably, Vaughn kept as far away from him as possible in the confines of the prison. The other guys made sure Blaine knew they were all straight, but, just the same, they avoided him as well since they had no idea what set him off. It was the same week that Blaine returned from solitaire that he received his letter.

It had changed him drastically, going from lead dog to the whipped puppy. Blaine guarded it like a precious jewel, growling and threatening anyone who got near him when he was reading it. Parish figured Blaine had to have that letter memorized by now. He had never gotten another one. Parish wished he could read that letter.

Parish sipped his soda, enjoying the air conditioned comfort of the guard shack. He never revealed his silly nicknames to the other guards. He was making personal notes about their behavior for his thesis in Criminal Psychology. He had another year to go before he graduated with his Bachelor's degree then he planned to apply to the FBI.

The prisoners talked, lay on the benches, or walked around slowly. Everything was like it was any other day. It was almost time for them to go back in when Parish noticed that two of the prisoners' demeanors had changed. He had let his mind wander too long thinking about his own plans and almost missed the subtle change.

Maybe there was something to what Hayes was saying. Things can change in the blink of an eye. Parish sat straight up then leaned forward, almost appearing relaxed with his forearms resting on his thighs, but his eyes and mind were alert, watching. *Okay, what are you guys up to?*

Dragon Man and John were somewhat enemies. Normally they did not sit or stand together. Whenever they were in the yard they had always been at opposite sides of the yard. Now they were within arm's length of each other—not necessarily alarming, just very unusual. *That could be bad.*

Quickly, Parish scanned the entire group of prisoners, noticing something else a little odd. All of them were facing away from the guard shack, except Blaine, who was still focused on his letter, running his fingers over the worn paper, and not paying any attention to what was happening around him as always.

Maybe it was nothing, but Parish kept watching. He was not ready to say anything to Hayes yet, but something did not seem right. His teen years had been spent with the Torres gang. You had to develop a sixth sense about things or you did not live long.

Nothing changed for a moment. Yet something was not right. Parish was sure of it. He felt as if there was something that should be setting off alarms in his head, yet nothing looking seriously amiss. He looked over at Hayes who was on the phone again, but continued writing as he talked. He knew if he interrupted Hayes, he would be reprimanded. Parish decided to watch.

Parish's glance moved from inmate to inmate, trying to read their body language, trying to figure out what was bothering him. Grandpa was talking to Dragon Man. Again, that was not that unusual, but they were not the best of friends. Grandpa lost his seniority to Dragon Man and he was not happy about it. *Why are you two talking? What are you talking about?*

They had less than five minutes before it would be time to go back inside. Nothing looked amiss, but Parish felt strangely on edge. His instincts were warning him that something was wrong. Yet his eyes and brain were telling him everything looked normal–almost. *Maybe I should interrupt Hayes and ask his opinion. Nah, he'll think you're an idiot.* Suddenly, Parish saw one small hand signal, a sign to fight, and jumped to his feet as he hollered, "Hayes!"

In the next instant mayhem ruled the yard. Big John and Brian attacked Drago. Drago was no match against the two of them. They dragged him down. Big John stomped hard on Drago's right lower leg then grabbed his foot and twisted it with a sudden jerk.

Big John smiled in satisfaction when he heard the bone crack.

In spite of the grimace of pain on Drago's face, one would almost swear he was smiling too.

The fight ended in less than thirty-seconds. The guards raced out and had them subdued in record time even though there was no one to subdue. The inmates cooperated fully, yet the guards still used their fists and clubs to make sure they behaved.

Drago, holding his leg, rolled on the ground moaning. "My ankle! My ankle!"

Parish kneeled beside him to check his condition. It did not take a medical degree to tell that it was broken. It was already swollen and oddly twisted. "Don't move. We'll get the medics here to help when the other inmates are put back in their cells. What happened?"

"Ooohhh," Drago groaned, "I don't know. I guess he doesn't like me."

"I don't doubt that, but I saw the hand signal. What were you trying to do?"

Drago stopped moaning long enough to give the officer a sideways glance, "I don't know what you're talking about."

"Yeah, right. I grew up in a gang. You gave the signal to start the fight."

"I did, did I? How about that. I was just flexing my fingers. I got arthritis, you know."

"Like I'm supposed to believe that."

"Hey, I'm in pain here and you're delaying my treatment!" Drago yelled.

"Nope. Can't do a thing 'until it's safe." Worried that this trauma might be enough to set off a heart attack, Parish asked, "You're not having any chest pain, are you?"

Glaring at him hatefully, Drago spat out, "No! Are you hoping my heart gives out?"

A distant voice yelled, "Clear!"

A moment later the medics came running out.

CHAPTER 1

Six Weeks Later

It was a fairly deserted part of town known as Towers End because of its forest of electrical towers. Most phones, radios and televisions did not work within a two block radius around the group of towers. Reception was spotty for the next two to three surrounding blocks. Not even the gangs liked this area. There were only two old house trailers making up this poorest of poor neighborhoods.

One old trailer sat on a large corner lot with more dirt than grass in an unkept and cluttered yard. Scattered remnants of rusty bent wire and broken wood posts accented with tall grass and weeds at their bases remained where an actual fence once stood. A small girl with wispy long blond hair held a rag doll as she swung on a rusty swing. She wore a faded flowery yellow dress tied in the back. Red and white flip-flops covered her dusty feet. It was a picture for *Poverty USA*.

Megan Smith stopped swinging and looked up in the sky. It was a clear blue with a few thin white clouds, a beautiful summer day. Megan skipped to her picnic table, kicking up little twirls of dust as she went. Her table was a battered, chipped concrete display table with a hole in the center which Megan's mother had filled in with a flower pot full of colorful plastic flowers.

"I'm getting hungry. I think it's time for lunch. Don't you think so?" She set her doll in her plastic highchair. "Now you sit here until I get back, Mary Alice." The rag doll silently stared at Megan with her large black button eyes.

Megan climbed the crooked, loose block steps. She was careful like her mother always told her to be. The blocks did not wiggle under her insignificant weight like they did for her mother's slender form.

The door was slightly ajar. Her mother always left the door unlatched so Megan would be able to open it. Everyday Megan was afraid that Tom would lock the door and she would be stuck outside for the whole day with nothing to eat. Before stepping inside, she peered around the edge of the door frame.

It was dim and cool inside. Tom was sitting on the couch in front of the loud television. His head was thrown back and his mouth was gaping open, making silly snoring sounds.

Stepping quietly, Megan went to the kitchen. She was glad Tom was sleeping. She did not like it when he yelled at her, and he yelled a lot. Sometimes he slapped her, but she would not tell her mother because she was afraid to. Her mother had told her they had no place to go and had to put up with Tom for a little while longer until she could make other plans.

Megan had seen on a television show that some people slept in a box in a dirty alley if they had no where else to go. She wondered if she and her mother could find a box big enough for both of them. What did you do if it was raining? Where did you go to the bathroom when you lived in a box? Could you make mac and cheese? That was her favorite, next to a peanut butter and jelly sandwich. There were always big rats scurrying around the boxes. Would they be able to find a place to sleep where rats wouldn't eat her?

Megan took her bathroom break while she was there then tiptoed back to the kitchen. It was hard for Megan to pull open the heavy refrigerator door. She slid the foot stool out from under the table and put it near the front of the old refrigerator. She stepped up on it and with both hands pulled on the refrigerator door handle. Once the door was open, she let it barely close, jumped down, pushed the stool clear with her foot then opened the refrigerator door all the way.

Her mother had her lunch packed in a cooler bag sitting on the lower shelf. Megan was proud of her pink fairy lunch bag. It was what she would use in a few months when she started going to the big school. Her mother told Megan she could use it during the summer if she was careful with it. Megan promised she would be very careful.

She had turned five in April and had been going to a special school because of her learning disability and speech impediment. Megan liked her special school and was a little afraid to go to the big school.

Just as quietly as Megan had entered the house trailer, she left and returned to her doll. Megan set her lunch bag down on her little table. "We'll have water now and save our juice for wa-," frustrated Megan stomped her foot and finished by loudly over pronouncing, "later."

She picked up the glass coffee carafe with the small crack near the top and carried it to the garden hose. Because the spigot knob was loose and easy for her to turn, it constantly dripped water. It had not rained in five weeks and the ground was fairly dry and dusty except where a small puddle formed from the constantly dripping spigot.

Megan straddled the puddle as she carefully filled the carafe with the sun warmed water. Megan did not want any mud getting into her water. It was heavy and she had to carry it back holding it with both hands.

"I was careful with the water this time, Mary Alice." Megan poured some water into her doll's tiny plastic cup. She gave a little giggle, "That muddy water we had w-last time was nasty." She stuck her tongue out as she set the carafe down. "Now, you wait for me."

The zipper stuck on the lunch bag. Tears stung her eyes as Megan struggled to unzip it. She reached in with her small hand, but could not pull anything out through the narrow opening. "Mary Alice, we may not get to eat lunch today if I can't fix this."

The tears started to fall and her shoulders slumped as she talked to her doll. "Mommy says I'm a big girl now. She says I'm smart, too." Megan sighed, "I can't sit here and cry, can I?" She put her face inches from the zipper and studied it intently until she finally saw the problem. With her slender fingers she pulled and tugged until the caught thread finally came free so she could unzip it.

"Mommy will be so proud of me!" she said to her doll with a huge smile on her face. "I'm not stupid like those mean kids say, w-right, Mary Alice?" She paused as though her doll had agreed with her. "Just because I can't talk w–oops–right." She corrected herself again. "I can say your name w-right and that's what counts. Names are important. Titles are important, too."

She took out her tin cup and set it in its proper place on the table. "Oh, it's cold, Mary Alice! That'll help make the water cold." Reaching in again, she retrieved a small plastic plate, then her peanut butter and jelly sandwich, spoon and, lastly, a cup of chocolate pudding. She neatly arranged her place setting like her mother had shown her. Megan peered inside and saw a few carrot sticks in a sandwich bag along with a box of juice. "We'll save the juice and carrot sticks for w-later this afternoon, okay?"

Megan shared a corner piece of bread with her doll and placed it on the plastic saucer attached to the tiny tea cup. Megan ate and chattered nonstop. Mary Alice sat perfectly still and did not eat her small morsel.

After finishing her meal Megan rinsed off her doll's plate as well as her own at the hose spigot then carefully repacked her dirty dishes in her lunch bag. "The sun's so hot, it made the water too hot today. Let's go swing some more."

She raced to the swing set and stopped, "I know. Let's go down the slide! You like the slide."

Megan quickly climbed to the top of the ladder and sat down. Her dress covered her bottom until she started to slide. She screamed in pain as the hot metal burned her legs on the way down.

With tears streaming down her cheeks, Megan stood at the bottom of the slide and twisted around to see the back of her legs. They were both red with a little bit of blood oozing down the back of her left calf.

Sniffling, Megan told her doll, "I need a Band-Aid." She hugged her doll tightly, "I wish Mommy were here now. We can't ask Tom for help. He's mean and would laugh or make it hurt more." Megan held her doll up to her face and buried a sniffle in her red yarn hair.

Megan started walking towards the trailer then remembered she had to take her lunch bag inside. Still sniffling she walked over to her table and picked up the bag. "I think I'll stay inside now. We can hide in my room and play quietly. Tom won't know we're there."

Slowly, and quietly sniffling the whole time, Megan climbed the steps into the trailer. She stopped her soft crying long enough to peek in and see what Tom was doing. He was still sleeping. Walking softly, she put her lunch bag on the table for her mother to clean and repack for tomorrow's lunch.

Without realizing it, Megan set the bag too close to the edge and it fell onto the floor with a soft plop, but, as it fell, it accidently knocked off the tripod of three empty beer cans which made a loud clatter when they hit the tile floor, bouncing and rolling around.

"Uh-oh!" Megan softly exclaimed before clamping her hand over her mouth. She looked up at Tom who was roused from his nap.

He jumped up and reached her in a few quick long strides, yelling loudly as he moved. "What do you mean, Brat, making all that noise and waking me up!" He raised his hand as if to slap her.

Megan cringed and quickly ducked under the table. "I'm sor-wy," she whispered hugging Mary Alice tightly.

"You better be!" He lowered his hand. "Quit talking like a baby! Clean this mess up and get out of here." He hiccuped loudly and called her names as he went to the bathroom, "Brat, Baby, Brat. Nothin' but a big baby." He laughed as he closed the door.

Megan picked up her lunch bag. This time making certain it was far enough back on the table. The beer cans she threw into the trash can, out of habit counting each one as she tossed it in. Eager to get to her room, she walked down the hall, stopping just before she reached the bathroom door. For a moment she watched the door. It stayed closed. Megan hesitated a moment more to take off her flip-flops so she could run as quietly and as fast as possible past the bathroom to her room.

Sometimes Tom would open the bathroom door and trip her in the hall or throw something at her. Usually it was a wet towel or one of his dirty shirts. They did not hurt, but sometimes they were stinky. When he was in one of his mean moods, he would throw a bottle of shampoo or his shoe, anything he knew would hurt but not leave much of a bruise. He always laughed. He thought it was amusing when he hurt her.

Megan fairly flew down the hall to her room. She tossed herself on her bed and cried for her mother. Mary Alice never complained when she got wet with Megan's tears. Megan talked to her doll in a whisper between her soft sobs, "I wish my real daddy didn't get dead. I don't remember him much, but I remember he was kind and loved me. He would've hugged me and made my boo-boo feel better."

Megan cried herself to sleep.

CHAPTER 2

TV News Commentator: *"The police are still searching for Harry Drago, better known as Dragon Man because of the large dragon tattooed on his left forearm. He escaped while being transported from his doctor's appointment back to the prison over a week ago. One of his gang members, a Thomas Roads, was found yesterday but was accidently shot as the police were closing in and died on the way to the hospital. Detectives have talked to Mrs. Lillian Drago, his mother, and his first ex-wife, Tisha, but they both have denied any knowledge of his whereabouts. They have been unable to locate his second ex-wife, Lisa. At this time, it is unknown if she is with him or not. The police are on the lookout for other gang members and say they have no other leads at present.*

"In the local news there has been a rash of convenience store robberies in the East End and South End areas. Jimmy Ponti, a known member of Drago's gang, was caught after robbing the convenience store on Meyers Street in the South End. His face was hidden from the store security camera when he shot the clerk in the upper chest. Fortunately, the clerk, who is only nineteen years old, will survive. The bullet punctured a lung, but was not fatal. As luck would have it, the clerk, a Miss Nita Stewart, had put her own web camera on the shelf behind her which gave a better angle than the security camera. His face was in full view of her camera. According to her report there was a 'really cute guy' that came in every day between two-fifty and three-fifteen. She put the camera there to record his picture so her friend, Joyce, could see the man. Nita Stewart turned the camera on a few minutes before the thief walked in." The newscaster smiled, *"So cute criminals beware."*

The camera cut to the female commentator. *"Thank you, Tad, but I have to admit, I do find him kind of cute myself. Can I get an eight by ten made of his face?"* She laughed as she adjusted her papers. *"Now for a truly unusual theft. Yesterday, Mrs. Clara Brown, who lives near Towers End, hung her laundry on the clothes line in her back yard in the morning. Later that afternoon, when she went to take them down, she could not find any of her husband's clothes. Missing were two pair of denim blue coveralls, three pair of new white undershorts, and four white tee shirts. No one saw anyone take the clothes, but the police have a vague idea of the size of the criminal since her husband is five foot, ten inches tall and weighs two hundred pounds.*

Sheri pulled into the dirt driveway and turned off the car. She did not see Megan and scanned the yard again, more carefully this time, as she walked to the door carrying a small bag of groceries. "Megan, Honey, Mommy's home!"

Silence only answered back. Unless it was raining, Megan was outside. Rarely would she go inside and chance an encounter with Tom. Sheri could not wait to move out. She looked over into the neighbor's yard. It was as empty as her own.

Sheri went inside and glanced into the living room. No Megan. Occasionally, Tom would let Megan watch cartoons while he slept. Tom was snoring with his empty beer cans stacked on the floor beside his feet. There was only a three-can pyramid. *Slow day,* Sheri thought to herself as she walked to the kitchen. The television played loudly as usual.

She set the grocery bag down on the table and felt the stickiness on the floor on the soles of her tennis shoes. Sheri turned the oven on to preheat for the pizza she had bought for dinner. She noticed the floor had dried splotches of something on it. She looked in the sink and on the counter, then she saw the beer cans in the trash. *Ah, not so slow a day.*

Not wanting to wake Tom yet and put up with his beer-breath kisses, she did not call for Megan. She would walk to her bedroom, and, if Megan was not in there, then she would wake Tom in a way he would not like at all.

Sheri walked to Megan's bedroom and found her sleeping on her bed. She looked so sweet and innocent. Sheri brushed the loose wispy blond curls from her eyes. "Hey, Sweetie, Mommy's home."

Megan mumbled in her sleep and moved her legs. Sheri decided to let her sleep until the pizza was ready and moved her legs to pull the cover over her. She gasped when she saw the few spots of dried blood on the sheet.

Her first instinct was to kill Tom if he was responsible for hurting her little girl. Sheri leaned over and kissed Megan's cheek. Softly she said close to Megan's ear, "Megan, wake up. Tell Mommy what happened." She gave Megan's shoulder a little shake.

Megan sleepily opened her eyes. She smiled happily and gave her mother a huge hug. "Mommy, I'm so happy you're home!"

Megan started crying again and Sheri held her and rocked gently. She was dying to know what happened, but she knew Megan needed her 'cry time'. There were a few times Megan had caught Sheri crying after her husband died. She had given her a hug saying, "That's okay, Mommy. You need some cry time, too." Sheri did not believe her daughter was as mentally disabled as the professionals thought.

"I went down the sw-slide and it burned me."

Sheri gave her daughter another hug. "Honey, I'm so sorry. Didn't you ask Tom to help?"

"No, he scares me." Megan was not going to tell her mommy what he did do.

"Well, we won't have to put up with him much longer." Sheri looked toward the empty doorway before continuing in a whisper, "I met a really wonderful man at work. He's a lot like your real daddy was. He's sweet and kind. He walks with a limp because he was hurt fighting in a war. His name is David and he has a little girl who's about three years old. Do you think you'd like to be a big sister?"

"I could teach her how to swing and have a tea party?"

"Yes, you could."

"That would be great." She turned around and grabbed her doll. "Won't that be wonderful, Mary Alice?"

"Let's get your legs fixed up. I brought home a pizza."

"Hurray!"

Sheri washed both wounds and put a little Aloe gel on each. "The boo-boo on your left leg is too big for a Band-Aid. I need to wrap a bit of gauze around it, okay?"

"Okay."

"You've been so good. I have a special treat for this weekend. It's a secret. You can't tell Tom or Mary Alice."

"I won't tell Tom, but Mary Alice is my best friend. She won't tell anyone."

"Tom might hear you talking to Mary Alice. You can't tell Tom about the man I met. We have to keep it a secret for a few more days."

Tom yelled from the kitchen, "Pizza's almost done!"

They looked at each other with surprise. "How about that?" Sheri said with more amazement than question.

Pain forgotten, Megan skipped to the kitchen while Sheri followed quickly behind.

"This is a great treat," Sheri smiled but still remained cautious. She never knew what to expect. Tom's mood fluctuated as often as the wind depending on how much beer he drank. She wondered about what drugs he might also use, but was afraid to ask.

"Yeah, the smell from whatever is stuck on the bottom of the oven woke me up. I decided to pop the pizzas in while you two had your little girl chat."

"It was more than a chat. Didn't Megan tell you she got hurt on the slide?"

"No," he looked at Sheri and continued speaking with a mouthful of pizza, "the little angel didn't say a thing." He reached over to pat Megan's head, but Megan ducked back from his hand. "She's a trooper."

Sheri's noted Megan's dodge. Her heart ached that they were still here and glad it would not be for much longer. Megan was such a bright happy little girl. She did not want Tom's abuse to take that away from her. Last month Megan confided in her that Tom called her a brat or baby all the time. Tom never called Megan names or mistreated her when she was around. Sheri knew there had to be another reason Megan was afraid of Tom. She did not believe name calling was the only reason. Megan would not lie about him being mean, but she wondered if Megan was telling her the whole truth.

While they ate, Sheri worried that he might have overheard her tell Megan about David. He was not acting any differently at the moment, but she had known him to do this before. Polite one minute and a raving maniac the next. Anytime he was drunk, or even occasionally when sober, a simple off hand comment meant as a joke could send him into a rage.

Tom had hit her once when he had been blind drunk. Luckily for her, he had been too drunk to have much force behind his fist. After he swung, he fell to the floor passed out cold, and Sheri had left him lying there. He had clipped her enough to bruise her eye. The next day when he saw the swelling and purplish discoloration, he expressed concern. He did not remember hitting her and was very apologetic. She told Tom that if he ever hit her again, she would press charges and it would be the last time he would see her.

Sheri told Megan the truth about how she had gotten hurt and they shared some crying time together. That incident instigated Sheri's plans to move. She did not want to stay with him living in fear of being beaten again, and she knew it would happen. She had heard it too many times on all the talk shows. Tom behaved for a few weeks by drinking a little less, but he was back to a six pack a day by the end of the month. If she had known he was an alcoholic, she never would have moved in with him.

It was fate that about the same time Lily mentioned wanting a person to share a large four bedroom house with her. Sheri liked to be independent, but most rent was too high for her meager salary, or the cheaper places were no better than where she was now minus the drunk Tom. Lily's need was like an answer to her prayer. They discussed their plans and Sheri secretly started saving money. Her parents were willing to give her money for the deposit which was a big help. She just had to save for her share of the first month's rent.

Tom was pleasant for the rest of the evening. He got Megan a popsicle to enjoy while she watched her cartoon show. Sheri was convinced he had overheard her and all hell was going to break loose after Megan went to sleep. Sheri wished she had somewhere she could go with Megan tonight.

About eight-thirty that evening, Tom came to Sheri and wrapped his arms around her as she was washing the few supper dishes. Very sweetly he asked, "Could I borrow your car to run up to the convenience store. I want to get a pack of cigarettes. I'll be back in a few minutes." He kissed her cheek. His breath was minty instead of smelling like stale beer and cigarettes.

She was sure he was up to something, but was glad to get him out of the way for even a few minutes. Sheri pulled the keys from her pocket and handed them to him. "There's not much gas." She hoped he would take the subtle hint to put some gas in it for her. Lately, his money had been going for his beer and cigarettes. He had given her only eighty dollars for groceries last week and nothing the previous two weeks. For the past two months since he'd lost his job, she had to pay the whole amount of the trailer rent instead of half or they would have been out on the street. Tom did not seem to care about anything but his beer and cigarettes.

Sheri sat with Megan in her lap watching cartoons until nine o'clock. "You get to skip a bath tonight because of your legs. After you wash your face and brush your teeth I'll read you a story."

Despite having a nap earlier Megan was still tired enough to go to bed at her usual time. Megan picked her favorite book about a fairy princess which she had probably heard a hundred times, but never tired of. Sheri curled up beside Megan on her bed so Megan could see the pictures. Megan was sound asleep before the story was half finished.

Tom returned about eleven-thirty. Sheri had washed the few dirty dishes, watched a little television, and was ready to crawl into her bed when she saw the car's headlights shine around the gaps in the bedroom drapes. He would have seen that her bedroom light was still on, so she could not pretend to be asleep.

They had not shared the same bed since she moved in except for the occasional times they had sex. He had more of a drinking problem than he cared to admit which caused an erection problem. Tom was rough and quick when they had sex and, since there was no 'love' in their lovemaking, Sheri never fussed about the infrequency of their sexual activity.

Sheri was relieved not to have to worry about coming up with excuses all the time. The few times they did have sex had been very disappointing for her. She wondered if she wasn't being unfair and unconsciously comparing him to her husband who had been excellent in bed.

Sheri and David had not had sex yet. She felt a thrill whether it was simply holding his hand, being in his arms, or kissing him. Sheri smiled as she reached to turn out the light. It excited her to simply be in the same room with David stealing hidden glances at each other during work.

She wondered if she would compare David to her first husband, Kevin, but Sheri did not think so. Were other women prone to do that? David was loving and kind like Kevin. Whenever they were ready to have sex, she was sure it would be wonderful because it would be between two people in love, not just a physical act to satisfy a craving like it was with Tom. He did not care if she was satisfied or not, and she usually was not.

Tom knocked softly on her door. "Sheri, can I come in? I have something for you."

Sheri groaned, wishing she had been faster and had turned out the light before he had returned. He did not sound drunk so she took a chance and opened the door. She stood partly behind the door using it for protection.

He was smiling and holding a small bouquet of plastic wrapped flowers. He stretched his arm out, wearing a lopsided smile, and presented the flowers to her. He was cute when he smiled. That was one of the things she had liked about him when they first met.

She took the flowers and buried her nose in the colorful petals. The fragrance was light and pleasant.

"How sweet. Thank you." Sheri smiled and kissed him on the cheek. This was more like the Tom she had first known–impulsive, sweet and loving. Had it all been an act or did something happen that changed him? Sheri used to blame herself, although, she had no idea what she might have done to have caused it.

"They didn't have any flowers at Carson's. I had to drive to three different stores before I found some. Before you ask, I did put a few bucks of gas in your car." He put his hands on the door frame and leaned inward. "Can we sit down and talk?"

"I guess," Sheri answered somewhat hesitantly. She put on her robe and slippers. *What's he up to?* Sheri wondered as she followed Tom to the living room, still wary that he might hit her. She stopped at the kitchen and got an old vase from under the kitchen sink to put the flowers in. Sheri set the flowers on the counter then went into the living room. Tom was sitting on the worn couch, allowing room for her beside him. He patted the empty space beside him, but Sheri ignored him and sat down in a chair opposite from him. He looked a little disappointed.

Hesitantly he started, "Before I tell you what I wanted, oh, heck, Billy gave me an application to the garage where he works. I start Monday." He gave a little smile.

"That's good. I'm glad. I can put Megan in a daycare. That's not much notice." Sheri got up.

Tom grabbed her hand. "Wait. There's more. I know I've been difficult to live with."

Slowly Sheri sat back down. This time beside him. She felt like she could have interrupted at that point and told him precisely how difficult he had been, but she kept silent. She wanted him to continue. She did not want this to turn into an argument.

"I know I've made your life miserable."

7

Sheri bit her tongue to keep silent.

"I can't take back any of the bad stuff I've done." He smiled shyly. "I was kinda hoping you would stop me and say, 'Aw, it wasn't that bad.' I guess that tells me it was. What I'm trying to do is say I'm sorry. Can we start over? I'll go sober. I don't want to lose you."

Sheri did not know what to do. Her first instinctive response was *Too late,* but she kept her mouth shut. He wanted a second chance. Could he do it? Should she let him have another chance? What about her feelings for David? He claimed to love her and she remembered her feelings in the beginning. It hadn't been the wild and crazy kind of love she had had with her first husband, but it was a comfortable somebody-to-take-care-of-me feeling.

Her feelings for Tom had changed, from like to dislike. He had his moments, but she did not think she could trust him to stay straight. This just wasn't fair! Why did he have to decide to go straight now! Was he serious? Would it last longer than a day or two?

Slowly, anxiously, Tom rubbed the palms of his hands on his jeans while he waited for Sheri's reply. Sweat ran down his brow as he went on to explain, "I watched a talk show about alcoholics today that made me realize what I'm doing to myself, you," he hesitated, "and my family. All the guests on the show were former alcoholics. I know you've preached to me before, but today they said some things that made a difference." He took her hands gently in his, again with that silly endearing grin she found so irresistible, "Don't think I'm crazy, but I had a wild dream while I slept after the show. That scared me into wanting to go straight."

Sheri did not believe him, but decided to agree with Tom for now. She could not move into the rental until the twelfth of next month anyway. Tom needed her, but that was not love. She loved David. Tom was not worth throwing away everything she had with David. Tom would fall off the wagon again and he would hit her again. His sister had told her how he had tried to sober up before and failed. She would not desert Tom now. She would make sure he got the help he needed before she moved out.

Sheri feared if she told Tom the truth now, he would beat her or not get the help he needed. Better to play along. Later, she and Megan could walk out, after he had already started getting help. She could never live with herself for being the cause of his staying drunk. She would help him until next month when she was ready to move. If she was lucky, Tom might find someone else. After all, she had found out she was his fifth or sixth live-in girlfriend in the past three years.

Sheri smiled and squeezed Tom's hand. "I'll stay and help. I still care about you." That much was true and she could say it with sincerity.

Tom grinned widely and wrapped her in his arms. "Thank you."

Sheri wrinkled her nose at the strong smell of beer on his breath as he lowered his head to kiss her.

CHAPTER 3

Thursday Morning
Police Precinct

"Why me?" Officer Dana Morgan questioned Captain Ed Wells. Her tone was level, but the belligerence gave it an uneven, raw edge. She had been on the force for four years, and this was the first time she had ever questioned one of his orders. Captain Wells was a bit surprised to say the least.

He was trying to cut her some slack due to the recent stress she had been under. Her partner had been killed less than four months ago then just two weeks ago she had been wounded in the leg. That had been a minor wound and easy to get over, but he knew she blamed it on her own carelessness. The captain also knew she was having a hard time getting over the loss of her partner and was beginning to wonder if she needed counseling.

When Dana had first graduated from the academy, he thought it would be great to have father and daughter working together. They only had each other now since his wife divorced him and moved out west. He had been there for Dana when her brief marriage fell apart. It did not matter that he tried to convince her she was too young to marry him anyway. He divorced her to marry an older wealthy woman, only to die in a plane crash three months later.

Captain Wells knew he was fortunate to have Dana, even as head strong as she was. She had been there for him when he had his mild heart attack three years ago and was supposed to be taking it easy. She hired a Mexican woman to come in and take care of the house and laundry two days a week. Dana kept him up-to-date on the cases so he would not fret over not knowing about their progress.

He had not realized how hard it was for him not to play favorites. He did not want to put Dana in dangerous situations, even though it was her job. He was proud of his little girl. *You're a fine officer, Dana Girl, even though sometimes you can be a big pain in my butt,* he thought with an inward smile.

Captain Wells pushed himself up from his chair. That effort caused a nasty twinge of pain in his back reminding him he needed to retire, and he plopped back down into the well worn, brown leather chair. "For the third and final time–he needs a partner and you need a partner. I've been going easy on you these past few months, it's time you bucked up." That was too blunt and maybe a little cruel, but necessary.

Dana stood, leaned across the desk, putting the palms of her hands on the cluttered piles of papers for support, which put their faces only inches apart. She spoke with heated emphasis, "I don't need a partner. I can manage fine without one. Maybe if I had one of those fancy rigged cruisers, it would be like having a partner–the kind that doesn't talk back or argue with you." *Or die on you.* The unwanted thought buzzed through Dana's brain before she realized it. *Now is not the time for regrets and thinking of what could have been. Get back on focus.*

Dana straightened up and put her arms akimbo. It was the same defiant gesture she had used since she was five years old. "I don't want to work second shift. It's not fair! It took me nearly two years to get on day shift. What about my promotion? Am I going to stay a lieutenant until I'm forty like Uncle Charlie did?"

"Don't get your panties in a wad. It's not permanent. Just give me a few months to get him oriented to the area and the people." Captain Wells had to bite his tongue. It would be so simple if he could tell her the truth, but if she knew she might act differently and Nick did not want that.

9

"Don't treat me like an idiot! I know all about those so called 'temporary' shifts. James stayed on nights 'temporarily' until his baby was in junior high. How long do you consider this to be temporary?"

"Like I told you, just a few months. I'm not sure. He's a Yankee. Maybe he'll be a fast learner."

"What about Peters? He's always late for his day shift. Give him second shift." Dana glanced down at the schedule changes he had given her. "You're even taking away my weekend. I had plans for this weekend!"

Captain Wells heaved a sigh, rubbing the dull ache that was starting across his forehead. "I expect you to follow orders. Would you rather I fire you?" He held his breath, hoping, and earnestly praying she did not take him up on his hasty, offhanded offer. There was a lengthy pause that Dana filled with a glaring look and crossed arms, and probably a tapping toe if he could have seen down over the edge of the desk to her feet. That was her favorite pose as a young girl when she did not get her way, and it only got stormier as she grew older.

Fearing she might give him cause to do something more drastic like unpaid leave or termination, the captain hastily continued, "Report back here tomorrow at two o'clock or consider yourself fired. End of discussion!" His patience finally gone, his last words were measuredly emphasized, "Now get out of my office! Get back to work!"

"I'll get out, but I don't have to like it." Dana mumbled as she left, ignoring the looks of sympathy her coworkers sent her way. She had always thought him to be fair-minded in spite of the family relationship. Now she was having second thoughts. This had come out of the blue. There had been no warning or discussion. Not that she expected or wanted any preferential treatment, but a heads up would have been considerate. Now she had to call Myra and Lori to cancel their weekend plans.

As she walked through the building and out to the parking lot to her patrol car, Dana continued to fume inwardly. *I hope I passed that FBI test so I can move on. He can't treat me like this. Peters or Carter should get the evening shift, not me. I have more seniority. I wonder when I'll hear about the test results. Once I hear, I'm out of here. He'll miss me when I'm gone. Then he'll be sorry. Dad or no Dad.*

Captain Wells was sorry he could not tell her more. Dana was fairly young on the force, but she was bright and had become one of the best officers he had seen in years. He was proud of her. She was up for a promotion and he was not going to hold this little tete-à-tete against her. At least not yet anyway. As hard as it was, he could not play favorites.

Megan's House

"I don't want to wear jeans, Mommy," Megan whined as her mother helped her dress.

"I know, Dear, but you need to protect your sore leg. It's still a little red and I don't want it to get any worse. Maybe tomorrow you can wear a dress again. Does it hurt much?" She helped Megan slip her tee shirt over her head.

"No," she answered with her little hip wiggle.

"It may rain today so be careful." Sheri lowered her voice to almost a whisper, "Tom has been behaving lately, but if you have to come in, I think it would be better if you stayed in your room and read. Just keep out of Tom's way. Okay?"

"Okay, Mommy." Megan picked up Mary Alice and hugged her tightly. She did a little wiggle trying to get comfortable in her jeans. She loved her dresses and hoped she could wear them at the big school, too.

Mother and daughter sat quietly at the kitchen table eating their bowls of cold cereal. Mary Alice sat at the edge of the table leaning against the wall silently staring at the duo with her large black button eyes. Tom stared at the television while eating his bowl of cereal as he sat on the faded and well worn couch with his legs propped up on the chipped coffee table.

"I put an ice pack in your lunch bag so you can leave it on the table and not have to struggle with the refrigerator. I made you a peanut butter and jelly sandwich today. There's a banana, two sugar cookies, jello cup and gummie fairies."

"Oh, thank you, Mommy. I love you."

Sheri smiled at her daughter. "I love you, too. Monday you'll have to start going to daycare again. Tom's got a job."

"Will it be at the lady with the red hair?"

"Mrs. Johnson? Yes, if she has room. Why?"

"I like her. She's fun. Do you know, she can count all the way to one thousand? That's a bunch."

"Yes, that is. How far can you count?"

"We pw-practiced and practiced until I could go to one hundred." Megan giggled and stretched her arms out wide.

"That's a lot, too. I'm proud of you. I'll call her today while I'm at work. I don't have much time to arrange things. I may try to take Monday off." Sheri glanced at the clock. "I have to go."

After quick hugs and kisses, Sheri took Megan's hand and they headed outside. Sheri gave her daughter another hug and kiss. "Tom's not hit or touched you like we talked about?"

"No, Mommy."

"I don't know if I'll work over tonight or not."

"Mary Alice and me will be okay." After another hug and kiss, her mother finally got in the car to leave. Megan ran to the middle of the dirt road, waved and watched until her mother disappeared from view on the main road.

"It's warm today, Mary Alice. It's not as hot, but we won't go on the slide anyway." Megan over emphasized the word 'slide' to pronounce it right. "Whew, Mary Alice, talking right is hard work."

Several times Megan walked to the corner of the yard and watched for cars coming down either road, but none came. She could see many cars on the busy streets at the far ends. It was exciting when they drove down her street and waved at her. She hoped she would never see those mean teenage boys again.

"Mary Alice, we've only had four cars come by this whole week." She held up four fingers so her doll could count them. "Even the pow-police car has come by only once." Megan looked around. She saw no sign of Tom, but still she whispered to her doll, "Mommy says we may move. I hope there'll be more cars to wave at the new house." She put her finger to her lips, "Don't tell Tom. It's a secret."

Megan continued playing. "I'm bored. I wish I had someone to pw-play with today. Tom was good w-last night, but he still scares me. I know he scares you, too, but don't worry. I won't let him hurt you."

She moved from the swing to the sandbox to the monkey bars. Megan would never go into the woods that were just beyond her swing set even though there was no fence to stop her. They were dark and too scary. She knew that bad things happened to people that went into the woods. That's what they always showed in the movies Tom watched.

Megan played hard all morning and never noticed the man watching her near the edge of the woods. Leaning on his cane, Drago stood still and remained camouflaged by the shadows and trees.

Harry Drago watched the little girl get water from the garden hose and put it in the coffee carafe. That was the very thing he needed. His friends had managed to steal a coffee maker when he first escaped, but he had broken the glass carafe two days ago. Drago missed having his coffee and decided there was no need to go without it since a replacement was available. Hers was perfect. He would wait to get it when she was not around. He did not want to alarm the little thing. She was so petite. He wondered if his own daughter would be like that when she reached five. He smiled at her lengthy discussions with her doll.

He enjoyed watching her and could not wait to see his own baby. He guessed she would be around two or two and a half years old. Drago was eager to find her and tired of hiding out. Living in a tent had turned out to be the safest place he could have thought of. He had a small television and radio combination to keep track of the law's efforts to find him and a coffee maker. One of his gang brought food and water, but the visits had become fewer and farther in between due to so many of them being killed or imprisoned. He used the battery powered generator sparingly, most often in the mornings to make his coffee.

He knew the police would have checked all his old haunts and anticipated they would still be watching both of his ex-wives. Drago smiled with satisfaction at how well his scheme was working. The cot was not the most comfortable bed, but he was still free, and he was positive the police had no clue as to his whereabouts.

He was hoping that soon the police would start looking further out, preferably in the next state. It was hard to take care of his personal business. If they did not move on soon, he was going to have to create a major distraction. Drago thought about how much explosives he had left and what would be the best target.

Drago's leg started to hurt from standing so long and he wished he had something to sit on. His broken leg was healed, but it still hurt to stand for long periods or walk more than eighty feet. Maybe it had been too soon, but he had to make his escape the day he got the cast off or he might not have gotten another chance.

"Mary Alice, I'm getting hungry." Megan shaded her eyes with her hand and looked up into the overcast sky. "I can't see the sun. I think we'll eat now."

Drago watched Megan go into the trailer. He looked around before cautiously moving out of his hiding place. His eyes glanced in all directions as he slowly advanced. He had taken only a half dozen painful steps when Megan came back out carrying her lunch bag. As quickly as Drago could with his cane, he hobbled back into the safety of the shadows of the woods.

Methodically, Megan carefully unpacked the items in her lunch bag, putting each one in its proper place on the table. Again she shared a tiny corner of her sandwich with Mary Alice who sat in her highchair and, as usual, left her portion untouched.

Drago was delighted to see a coffee cup that he could use, too. He was reusing a plastic cup that was getting rather nasty after a week's repeated use without the benefit of being washed. The little girl's cup was the metal lid from a thermos bottle which was good enough for him. He was glad his efforts to steal the carafe had been thwarted or he would have missed getting the cup.

He had to laugh at himself. He was used to a life of relative wealth and luxury. Now he was living in a tent with a battery powered generator, wearing clothes stolen off a clothesline, eating food from the soup kitchen, and planning to steal from a little girl. Maybe he would see about leaving her twenty dollars later on her table so she could buy herself a fancy little tea set.

He wished he could hear the little girl's conversation with her doll. He wondered what his own little girl would be like at that age. He wondered what color her hair was. He was angry that his wife had never said a thing to him about being pregnant. How could she have kept that from him? If his sister had not written him about his baby, would he have found out?

No one would believe that for such a tough guy, he was such a softy for kids. He already had two teenage sons and a twenty-one year old daughter by his first wife, but they had no interest in him anymore. All they wanted from him was his monthly support check. To have another little girl by his young, new wife was almost a miracle. It surprised him that she filed for divorce without wanting any child support. She had to have known she was pregnant when she filed.

A chill breeze kicked up and a few fat rain drops fell. Drago moved back a little into the shelter of the trees, but stayed where he could still see Megan.

"I think we better go into the trailer, Mary Alice," Megan shivered as she gulped down the last bite of her sandwich. She tossed her spoon and empty plastic pudding cup into her lunch bag. A gust of wind blew the empty sandwich bag off the table. Megan chased it down and stuffed it hastily into the bag, zipping it partly shut. "That'll keep you from getting away again," she giggled. "It's getting cold and starting to rain." She smiled broadly, reaching for the cup to put it in her bag. "Did you hear me, Mary Alice? I said everything right."

Suddenly, a loud boom of thunder echoed around her. She dropped the cup and it rolled, coming to a stop against the flower pot in the middle of the table. A bolt of lightning struck one of the towers near Megan. She screamed, grabbed her doll by the arm, and ducked under the concrete table.

The rain started pouring down fast and hard; the storm clouds eager to release their burden.

Megan cried to her doll, "I got to get my lunch bag!" She held Mary Alice tightly as she tried to feel for it with her hand from under the table, but finally had to give that up and venture out into the downpour. She popped up from underneath the table, quickly found the bag, and snatched it off the table just as a gust of wind tried to take it from her grasp.

The wind picked up, as though angry with Megan for taking its trophy. The clouds opened up, letting loose a torrential downpour. Megan ducked back under the table, huddling with Mary Alice and her lunch bag. The coffee carafe, her cup, and half-eaten cookie were left behind in her haste.

The fierce storm raged around Megan's little shelter. Another boom of thunder startled her. With each clap of thunder and each lightning strike, Megan cried and screamed, squeezing Mary Alice tighter and tighter. The wind splashed little waves of muddy water over her feet.

Shivering, Megan said to her doll, "We've got to get in the tw-railer. I'm cold and I bet you are, too." She looked out at the never ending rain which seemed to have let up some. "I wish I had an umbrella." Megan started to run. Halfway there she slipped and fell face first into a large mud puddle.

Drago, drenched himself and unable to get to his tent before the sudden downpour started, watched from the meager shelter of the trees and ached to go help her, but knew that he must not be seen. She might tell someone about the man with the dragon on his arm that came to her rescue. No one forgot his dragon tattoo.

Megan got up, picked up her doll and lunch bag, and continued running. Her tears blended with the rain drops washing down her face. Tom was sleeping in front of the television, as usual, even though the screen was only static noise and snow. Megan went to the bathroom to wash up.

She shivered as she washed her face. Her mother had put a small mirror on the sink for Megan's use. All Megan washed was her face and hands. She did not care about her muddy feet. Shivering with cold, Megan could not do anymore.

Megan went to her bedroom and took off her wet clothes. She did not want to parade naked down the hallway in case Tom woke up. After putting on dry underpants, she crawled under the covers to get warm and pulled the covers over her head to keep the thunder away. In a moment she was fast asleep. Soaking wet, Mary Alice was left lying on the bedroom floor.

Megan awoke to a bright sunny afternoon. She heard the rumble of a car engine and kneeled on her bed to look out the window. "Ha, Mary Alice. We missed those mean teenage boys. I know I heard their car." She looked up and down the road, "Guess what, Mary Alice, the sun's shining and no mean boys! We can go out and play!"

With a shiver of horror, she remembered the first time the mean boys had thrown some ripe tomatoes and stinky water with stringy stuff on her. It was cooked cabbage, but Megan had never had cabbage before. The female police officer had come almost right behind them so they took off in a roar and a dust cloud.

She looked at the clock on her little pink and white dresser. Megan studied the position of the hands intently. "It's past three o'clock, but not yet three-thirty. Mommy will be home at five-thirty. We slept a long time."

She picked up her doll. "Oh, Mary Alice, you're all wet and muddy. You must be cold. I'll wrap you up in your blanket until Mommy gets home. She says you like to go in the washing machine for your bath."

Megan took the dress she had worn yesterday out of the clothes hamper in the corner of her room. "I think it looks all w-right, don't you think, Mary Alice? I can't put those jeans back on." She slipped her muddy sandals back on her feet ignoring the dried mud covering her toes.

Uncertain of what to expect once she left the safety of her bedroom, Megan walked cautiously and softly down the narrow hall toward the front door and Tom. She hoped he was still sleeping.

Tom was in the kitchen, humming as he made himself a sandwich. Megan tried to make herself very small and sneak past him, but he heard her. "Whatcha doing, little Brat?"

He was talking goofy. Megan knew when he talked like that he could be either nice or mean. She had not figured out what made the difference. Timidly, she answered as she tightly squeezed her doll, "Nothing. I'm going outside."

"Well, good riddance, Brat." He tossed the damp dish towel at her then laughingly staggered with a can of beer in one hand and the sandwich in the other to the living room.

Megan ducked. The dish towel hit her harmlessly on the shoulder and fell to the floor. She picked it up and put it on the counter, giving him a glaring look which he did not see. She wanted to get a juice drink box, but was afraid to ask since the mean Tom was back. She decided she would have to drink water. Then she remembered her lunch bag. She looked inside, but the juice and pudding cup were gone.

"I ate those," Tom chuckled from the couch, accented with a loud belch.

Megan thought about getting one out of the refrigerator, but she did not want to be around Tom any longer than absolutely necessary. He might get really mean and hit her. "Water will be okay until Mommy gets home, Mary Alice. It won't be long now," she whispered reassuringly to her doll.

Megan stopped when she got to the bottom of the steps and looked around. The yard was all mud and puddles of water. "There's no pw-place to pw-play, Mary Alice. Let's go get a drink."

She maneuvered carefully around the deep puddles to reach her table. The cookie she had left behind was now a few crumbly specks tucked in the coarse holes and crevices of the concrete. The coffee carafe and cup were no where to be found.

Megan looked on the ground, under the table, and on the other concrete bench. Two curved benches came with the table, but she never used the other one. She walked around the table checking out each puddle to see if they had fallen into one of them. Megan, checking the ground as she walked, went over to the hose to see if she had left it there.

She looked by the swing set and in her favorite hiding spot under the trailer. Slowly, Megan walked around the yard, her young eyes carefully scanning every inch. She went around a second time, even looking in places she knew she had not played in.

"Mary Alice, do you think the wind blew them away?" Megan looked along the edge of the woods, not daring to go in. Finally, she gave up and went in to tell Tom.

Her fear was momentarily forgotten as she stood in front of Tom. Her missing tea set was important. Tom looked up at her with bleary eyes, a bit surprised by her boldness.

"My tea set's been stolen!" Megan announced. "I can't find it anywhere. I've looked and looked."

Tom slurred, "Whatcha bothering me for? Go tell the police." His head lolled back in a drunken stupor.

Megan left and headed for the giant weeping willow tree in the far corner of the yard. She knew there she would be out of sight of the trailer. She looked in awe at a huge branch of the tree hanging down across most of the road. Without having to duck, petite Megan walked under the canopy of leaves. She giggled to Mary Alice, "We may see some fairies. It's so pretty under here."

She exclaimed, "Oh! Oh!" as she hurriedly danced out from under the branch and the surprise shower of cold water droplets falling from the wind blown leaves. Laughing, she said to Mary Alice, "That was fun. Let's do it again." Megan ran back under the canopy of leaves and waited for another shower of rain drops. Giggling joyously, she ran back out. "That's enough. Mommy will get mad at us if we're all wet when she gets home. Let's go wait for the police lady."

She looked back and saw only green leaves. Still feeling a little bit afraid that Tom might somehow find her, Megan held her doll tightly. Mary Alice never complained no matter how tightly Megan held her. "Mary Alice, the police lady did not come yesterday. I hope she comes today. We've got to get her to stop." She stood on her tiptoes and bent around trying to see through and around the leaves. Satisfied at last that they were well hidden from view, Megan whispered to her doll, "Tom can't see us. If he saw the pow-police lady, he might get mad and shoot her like he said he would the last time she stopped to talk to us. She's sweet. I don't want her to get hurt.

"Mommy says I'm smart and getting to be a big girl. When I learn to talk w-right, they won't pick on me anymore and call me stupid. W-right, Mary Alice? I'm not stupid. I talk right sometimes. I hope those mean boys don't come back while we're waiting. I bet they stole my tea set."

She stood talking to her doll for a long time. When Megan got tired of standing, she sat on the cracked remains of the sidewalk. "I'm getting tired. Maybe she's not coming today." She sucked in her breath and worriedly asked her doll, "Do you think Tom shot her aw-already?"

Just then she heard the sound of a car approaching and looked up. Megan jumped up, exclaiming excitedly, "I can see the lights on top. Hurray! She's coming!"

The police cruiser approached slowly. Officer Dana Morgan saw the little girl standing on the crumbling curb and was not sure what to make of that. She came down this road as her last run nearly every day, but this week had been unusually busy, so she had been by only once. It was isolated enough that she liked to check on a few of the older residents in the area since phone service was so spotty. This block was the worst area with only the two house trailers remaining. When you turned the corner and went up one block, you were in the old pottery mill section. If you went down the other street, you found yourself in a decent but poor neighborhood with a dozen homes.

Without reliable phone service no one wanted to live here. Abandoned shells of house trailers dotted unkept overgrown lots. Dana scanned the area. Everything looked normal except for that tree branch and the little girl. It was unusual for Megan to be here. She always stayed in her yard and always in a flowery dress. Only the color changed. She wore pastel shades of blue, pink, yellow and green. All of them were noticeably well worn and faded. This dress looked particularly dirty and wrinkled which was not normal. Her dresses may have been frayed, or a few were too big for her, but they were all relatively clean minus the dust from recent playing. This one looked like it had been fished from the bottom of the dirty laundry pile.

Dana stopped. Before getting out she made a note about the tree blocking the road, knowing it would not get top priority. The county might get around to checking on it after the tree rotted of its own accord.

This was near the end of her shift, but that would not have stopped Dana from helping someone. As she was getting out of her vehicle, she scanned the area again. It was not uncommon to use a child to put an officer off guard. Tom Jenkins was often drunk and disorderly, but was he up to something else, Dana wondered. The willow tree worried her, but she did not see any

noticeable signs of someone lurking among the leaves. She unsnapped her holster and kept her hand resting lightly on the butt of her weapon to be on the safe side.

"Hello, Megan," Dana greeted still standing beside her vehicle and glancing around. "Are those boys giving you trouble again?" The first time she had met Megan she was driving down this way, not too far behind a carload of teenage boys, when she saw the car stop and Megan race to the edge of the yard. One boy stretched out through the window in the back to throw several handfuls of something over the roof of the car at Megan. Several other hands stretched out quickly, throwing cupfuls of stuff on Megan. Dana had been too far up the road to make out exactly what they were throwing. Curious and knowing they were up to no good, she put her blue lights on and gave the siren a short burst. That was all the encouragement the boys needed. They gunned the car's engine and raced off, making a little fantail of dust in their wake. She raced after them and managed to get their license plate number before losing them after the railroad crossing. She went back to help Megan.

What Dana found when she reached Megan tore her heart out. Little Megan was standing in her yard with her arms out to the side, like a scarecrow, and tears streaming down her face. They had thrown some ripe tomatoes mixed with rotten stewed cabbage on Megan. Dana used some wipes and her own bottled water to wash Megan's face and hands. She gave Megan a hug, unmindful of how messy that got her uniform. She kissed Megan's cheek which still tasted of bitter cabbage and stewed tomatoes before walking with her to help open the trailer door so she could go in to wash and change.

Suddenly, Tom greeted her at the door with a volley of profanities that made Dana's ears burn. Megan squeezed past him and raced into the trailer. Dana pulled her weapon when he would not shut up and put his hands in view where she could see them. He continued his tirade, slurring his words and belching loudly, while Dana repeated her orders. His was far from polite conversation and she was unable to get a word in edgewise. She had to yell her orders over the top of his profanities.

She kept her pistol aimed at him while she glanced around for cover. There was none close by. If she turned her back to run, and he had a weapon, her back would be a large open target. How drunk was he? Could he hit the broad side of a barn, let alone her back? No sooner had Dana told Tom that he was under arrest and started walking towards him that he collapsed onto the floor. Dana had waited a moment, watching for movement, before slowly approaching him with her pistol still at the ready.

By that time Megan came out freshly washed and dressed. She looked down at Tom then at Dana. With a quavering voice she asked, "Did you shoot him?"

Dana quickly holstered her weapon, "No, Sweetie, he passed out."

"Are you still going to put him in jail?" Megan asked as a single tear rolled down her cheek. "What happens to me? Mommy won't be home for hours. I can handle him. He'll sleep until Mommy gets home."

Lost in her thoughts, it took Dana a second to return to the present and she was a bit surprised to see Megan in a different colored dress. Dana laughed inwardly and almost missed hearing Megan's whispered answer, "No, Ma'am." She had to think back to her question.

Megan was happy the police lady remembered her name. Names were important. She had been too upset the first time they had met to remember the police officer's name, but she had stopped a few times and told her name was Dana. Megan thought she should know her last name, but was never able to see it on her uniform. The police lady would stop, roll her window down, and rest her arm on the edge which blocked her view. She never stayed longer than a minute, just to say hello, ask if everything was okay, and say goodbye. Today Megan looked carefully at the big blue bar with black letters on Dana's uniform. She smiled at the simple letters, M-O-R-G-A-N. Saying words might be hard for her, but that word was easy since it was almost like her own.

Megan's eyes dropped and she watched Dana toying with the gun in its holster. Holding onto her doll tightly, Megan now felt very small and afraid again. Her bit of bravado about her missing tea set evaporated in front of the police officer's weapon.

"Are you okay?" she asked, noting the change in Megan's demeanor. She wondered if Megan had been abused or molested. Other than the dried mud on her feet she looked all right. She was not sure if the dress had dried blood or mud.

"Yes, ma'am," Megan answered softly, adding her little hip wiggle.

"Do you need any help?" Dana looked around again. Her senses were telling her something was not right, but she saw nothing. The woods were quiet. There was nothing moving about in the field across from them except two stray dogs. Old Man Murphy was still in the hospital so it could not be him. Then she had to laugh at herself again, she only got that prickly feeling when there was danger. Mr. Murphy was not a danger at eighty-six years old and with only one leg. Tom had caused a few fights in town. "Tom okay?"

"Yes, ma'am."

"Is your mommy okay?"

"Yes, ma'am. She's at work."

Suddenly there was a loud rustle of leaves not caused by the wind. Dana grabbed Megan and crouched with her beside her cruiser at the same time pulling her weapon. Two doe broke through the brush and raced across the road.

She waited a moment longer to see if any more deer followed before standing. Dana chuckled as she re-holstered her weapon, "Something sure had them scared. Well, since everything is all right, I'll be finishing my rounds. They've changed my shift and route. This is the last time I'll be coming around here."

"Oh."

Dana started back around towards the driver's door, but stopped when Megan's timid voice asked, "Does that mean you can't help me today?"

On alert again, Dana quickly turned around. "What kind of help do you need?"

"My tea set's been stolen."

"Ah, a crime," she smiled, figuring it was probably the wind from the storm that blew her tea set away, unless she could get lucky and arrest those teens for stealing. "That's right up my alley. Let's go take a look." Dana started walking, not realizing that Megan did not follow.

Panicked Megan cried out, "No!"

Automatically, Dana unsnapped her holster before she even thought about doing it. "Why not?" What had Megan so panicked? Dana scanned the area again as she walked around the willow tree so she could see the house trailer. Nothing stood out, but she still felt that prickly feeling on the back of her neck. Dana rubbed her neck trying to make it go away.

Oddly, the feeling persisted, in spite of no signs of trouble. She looked up and down the road. Everything looked peaceful and freshly washed from the storm. Why did she feel like they were being watched?

"Tom said he would shoot you."

"Well, that is a problem," Dana, smiling, relaxed somewhat and walked back towards Megan. "Does he have a gun?"

"Yes, ma'am." Megan's voice got softer as she squeezed her doll tighter and did her little hip wiggle. "He was gonna shoot my mommy with it, but he didn't. That's why we're still staying here."

Dana did not think Megan had been physically abused, but realized she was probably getting some sort of mental abuse from Tom. Now Dana had the desire to shoot Tom herself, but knew better. Tom had never caused any real trouble, mostly drunk and disorderly conduct. He was just a lousy man and she did not like him.

Dana bent down and smiled at Megan. "I need to look around for clues about your tea set. I'll be careful and I'll leave my cruiser here where he can't see it." Dana locked her cruiser. "Didn't you tell me that Tom said to tell the police about your missing tea set? If he says anything, you can tell him you were just following his orders."

Megan frowned as though she was considering all her other options. She liked the police lady especially when she smiled. Megan held her doll out in front of her. "What do you think, Mary Alice? Will that be all w-right? The po-police w-lady has a gun to shoot back." After a moment's pause Megan looked up at Dana and boldly answered, "Okay." Megan smiled at her doll for almost getting her words right.

Together they walked around the broken willow tree into the yard. Neither one of them saw Drago watching them from farther down the road. He sat on the remains of a stone wall behind some overgrown hedges, well hidden from their view. With the sun mostly to his right, Drago hoped the lens of his binoculars did not pick up a glint in the late afternoon glow. He had pulled his pistol from his pocket when she unholstered her weapon, thinking that he had given himself away. It was with great relief that he saw the deer, too. Drago had no qualms about killing a police officer, but he did not want to have to kill a child, and he would have had to kill Megan.

When the police woman and Megan disappeared around the tree, he started back to his camp. For some reason he had second thoughts, and decided to take the trail that led to Megan's trailer. He had been too far away to hear but an occasional word or two of their conversation and wondered why she had stopped for Megan. He needed to find out what was going on.

CHAPTER 4

"Where did you have it last?" Dana asked.

Boldly Megan marched to her small picnic table. "Right here. I left my pitcher and cup on the table when it started raining. I'm glad I took my lunch bag inside so they couldn't steal that."

Dana walked around the table and looked in all the same places Megan had. None of the mud puddles looked deep enough to hide a plastic teapot. Dana expected some part of it would be sticking up, a handle or a curved spout. "Where else do you play?"

"On the swings, under the trailer and on that pile of rocks," Megan pointed to the places she meant.

Dana walked around, curious that not even pieces of a tea set could be found. It dawned on her she might not be looking for a normal plastic tea set. "What does your tea set look like?"

Megan turned her doll around. "Mary Alice, show the pow-police lady the picture." Megan pulled a tattered Polaroid out of the doll's large front dress pocket and handed it to Dana.

Dana looked at the photo of a smiling Megan proudly sitting next to her doll with a coffee carafe and a thermos cup on the table in front of them. There was a cupcake with five candles stuck in it at crazy angles. She thought it was kind of sad that there were no other children or adults present.

"My mommy let Mary Alice and me have our own party for our birthday. Then Mommy and me had a party. I got two parties when I turned five." Megan held up her hand with all five fingers extended so Dana would know how many five was.

"Wow, that was great. I've never gotten two birthday parties. I'm not having any luck finding your tea set. You're going to have to tell your mother to buy you a new one."

Megan heaved a huge sigh for her tiny frame. "Another criminal gets away."

Trying hard not to laugh, Dana could not hide her smile. "I'm sorry. I just don't see any clues. Maybe Tom took it inside. I'll go in and check."

Megan raced to the bottom of the steps and put her hands out in front, waving frantically to stop her. She kept her voice low so Tom would not hear her, "No, I don't want Tom to shoot you." She added forlornly, "I didn't see it when I was in there, but I wasn't looking for it. I remember leaving it outside."

"You don't talk to strangers, do you?"

"No, ma'am. My mommy says I'm not supposed to talk to strangers or get into their cars."

"Good girl."

"I did hear a car that made a growling noise come by after the storm, but I was inside and didn't see it."

"Too bad. Let me look around again."

"There are those mean boys that come around in a blue car that like to throw garbage at Mary Alice and me. That car didn't sound like theirs. I mean it was almost the same, but not the same."

Dana sighed, no matter how long she did this job, she'd never understand why people did the mean things they did. Smiling at Megan she said, "I'm glad those boys didn't get you today. I promise I'll question them and make sure they didn't steal your tea set. Let me look around again. See what clues I may have missed."

Holding her doll, Megan sat on the trailer steps silently watching. Dana walked along the scrap of fencing closest to the house trailer when she stopped. Megan looked, but could not see her tea set there and went back to talking to her doll.

Dana looked along the fence line. There were little piles of litter trapped in the weeds–bits of Styrofoam and plastic, numerous pieces of paper and one disposable diaper. No tea set.

She made a few notes in her notebook and turned around, staring at the rest of the yard. Nothing else stood out. Then she realized she had not looked around the rock pile. Dana decided to check that area out before calling it quits. If she had to, she would buy Megan a real play tea set.

Still watching the ground, Dana was within a few feet of the rock pile when she stopped. She stared at the partial shoe print impression left in the mud. "Have you seen any strange men around here lately?"

"No, ma'am."

That prickly feeling on her neck was back and stronger than ever. She scratched her neck to make it go away. No luck. Dana thought she could have scratched deep enough to draw blood and it still would not have made any difference. Something was definitely not right. Again, she unsnapped her holster and kept her hand resting lightly on the butt of her gun. She stared around the yard, turning slowly as she looked. She looked across the road into the empty field and over at Mr. Murphy's place.

Nothing stood out. Nothing seemed out of character.

Now she was sorry she did not have a partner. This could not wait. The storm had been heavy enough to have washed away all the prints, so these had to be very fresh. Dana looked at her watch and realized her shift had ended fifteen minutes ago.

Dana talked into her shoulder mike. "Officer Dana Morgan reporting in. I'm off duty, but I need back up. I'm at Towers End Road and Denver Street.

There was too much static interference to make out the whole dispatcher's message. Dana only heard "…okay."

Dana asked for the dispatcher to repeat her message and waited a minute. There was no response. Deciding it would be okay to check things a little way in, she clicked off her radio so she could quietly follow the tracks. If the escaped convict was nearby, she did not want a sudden burst of radio noise giving away her location.

Dana though to herself as she followed the muddy impressions; *For weeks now we've been looking for you, Harry Drago, and you've been under our noses the whole time. That star print on the heel belongs only to convicted felons. It has to be you.* She saw six more partial prints by the time she reached the edge of the woods and stopped to take a deep breath. *Jim, I need you, Partner. Why'd you have to die on me?*

Dana had been so focused on finding more boot impressions that she had not realized Megan was following her until she began asking questions.

"What are you looking for? I don't see my tea set." With fearful awe she asked, "Is it in the woods? Do we have to go in there?"

Startled by Megan's unexpected voice, Dana jumped. "Honey, I may have found the man that stole your tea set. He's real mean. I think you better go back to your trailer and sit on the steps until I get back."

"Yes, ma'am," Megan sadly returned to the trailer. She sat on the bottom step and watched the police officer slowly disappear into the dark woods. Megan grumbled to her doll, "Why would a grown man be that mean to steal a tea set from a little girl? He must be really bad."

Harry Drago was watching when Dana noticed his boot print. He could not hear her talking, but he guessed what she saw. He had hoped the heavy storm had washed away any evidence of his presence, but he had to wait until the worst of it had passed before heading out of hiding to steal the carafe and cup. If his leg had been in better shape, he would not have needed to, but he could not chance falling in the mud and re-injuring it. It hurt bad enough now.

He had not known when anyone might come out of the trailer, so after he put the stolen items in his tent and took a powerful pain pill, he went back and brushed away his prints. Drago thought he had gotten most of them, especially those close to the trailer, but apparently he had missed more than he realized. He must be getting sloppy in his old age.

He watched as she slowly followed another print toward the woods. He moved further into the shadows and unsnapped his knife sheath. He did not want the little girl coming in and was glad the officer sent her back. Drago knew that only one of them would be coming out of the woods alive and it was not something a little girl should see.

Dana lost sight of any more prints as she entered the dimness of the woods, but she did notice a number of small branches had been cut back, creating a path. It struck her as odd that there was such a well worn path that led to the forest of electrical towers. She shined her light around and picked up another partial heel impression in the soft earth. *The right heel impressions are deeper than the left. I'm guessing, Drago, you're walking with a limp.* She stopped to listen. Birds, crickets, even a couple of dogs barking were easy to hear. More distantly, she could occasional hear traffic sounds—horns blaring or big trucks crossing the railroad tracks. *I should be hearing sirens by now. Why's my back-up taking so long? Maybe they're coming in silent.*

Also, Dana was wondering if they would think to go into the woods, or if she should head back out and wait for them on the road or in her cruiser. Dana knew it had to be Harry Drago, and he was someone she really should not go up against by herself. Another print caught her attention and she kept going, ignoring the few stray briars that combed through her hair or tugged at her uniform pants. Suddenly Dana came to a small clearing.

She stopped and looked around the area. It was lovely enough for a picnic except for the remains of an old house destroyed by fire. There was very little left of it. It was a large pile of grey rotting boards, a moldy toilet, and scattered, broken pieces of black roof tiles. A large variety of weeds and young trees were growing among the debris anywhere their roots took hold.

In the clearing the lush short grass looked like it had been freshly mowed, so Dana could not see any more prints. Even her shoe prints faded as the grass sprang back into place. She walked around one more time. The path that had been so clearly marked was now a mystery. There were no cut branches or any boot prints to indicate where to continue.

She went to the wooded area opposite from the burned home. None of the leaves or twigs on the ground looked like they had been disturbed anywhere. With the limp Drago had, she expected he would have made a trail a mile wide going through here. Dana ran up the small hill behind the house ruins hoping it would give her a better view.

She saw more overgrowth, trees and the array of electrical towers. Then something odd stuck out. It looked like a canvas triangle. *The top of a small tent? Has Drago been hiding out in a tent all this time?* Dana asked herself. She knew she could not take him alone and called again for back-up with her shoulder mike before running back down the little hill.

Knowing they would never find her this far in the woods, Dana wanted to get back to her cruiser and, remembering the tangle of overgrowth of briars along the road side, decided to head back the same way she came in. It would be easier and faster.

That prickly feeling would not let loose of Dana's neck and she rubbed it repeatedly while she walked through the clearing. She had just reached the edge of the thick brush when she caught a movement out of the corner of her eye. She ducked and turned which probably saved her life.

The knife blade intended for her throat missed. Off balance, Dana clipped the heavy set man under his jaw with her fist. He merely snorted at her puny effort and struck her right arm with his wooden cane.

"Ow," Dana made a guttural cry. The sharp blow hurt worse than she expected. The numbing pain forced her to drop her arm.

Drago was fast with his knife. Before Dana had a chance to draw her pistol, Drago sliced across her right upper arm. It was not a deep wound, but several thin lines of blood started running down her arm. Drago followed through with a punch to her jaw.

Dana's world spun for a minute. Drago's knife continued to draw blood before she had a chance to strike back as he sliced through the light weight fabric of her summer uniform across her right thigh. Again, she could tell it was not a deep cut, but it still hurt badly enough.

She retaliated with a quick upper cut to his jaw using her left fist. This time she had more power behind her punch, but it still did not seem to phase Drago other than to give her time to get a second punch in. She hit him in the kidney area. He grunted and his knee bent slightly, but he was not going down easily. She had believed they were fairly well matched for hand to hand combat. She was five foot seven and in good physical condition. He was five foot eleven with a bad leg and about forty pounds overweight. His agility surprised her.

She grabbed his knife hand, fighting to relieve him of the weapon. Dana bent his wrist backwards until he finally let go of the pocketknife. She threw it as far away as she could. Drago did not bother to chase after it.

As Dana started to pull her pistol Drago punched her in the gut. He put his whole strength behind the punch. Her head spun, sweat beaded on her forehead as she gasped in and out, wanting to throw up.

Between gasps she managed to get out, "You don't give a girl a break, do you?"

"You're a cop, not a girl. You're playing in a man's world now. Come on. Give it like a man."

Dana's leg came at him, fast and energetically. Surprisingly, Drago was faster and ducked so that her high kick hit his shoulder only a glancing blow. "You move faster than I anticipated." She figured with his age and extra pounds he would be a tad sluggish. She could tell that he was in pain.

Panting heavily, he answered, "Your move wasn't very original."

"I'll try to do better. Let me remind you, you're under arrest for assaulting an officer for starters."

Hoping to catch him off guard, Dana did a quick change of balance to her other foot and kicked her right leg at him. His cane whipped around and struck her right leg in several places. The pain was sharp and intense when he hit her shin. She had hit him, but she knew it had not been with the intended sufficient force. His head came back around and he was smiling, looking like he was enjoying himself except for a split lip. Her leg dropped to the ground, almost of its own accord.

Before she had fully recovered from his previous assault, he punched her in the jaw. "Only if you win the fight. Let me return the pleasure."

Barely able to stand, Dana spit out the blood from a tooth he knocked loose. He viciously jabbed the top of her foot with his cane.

Dana danced back a few steps to get away from his wicked weapon.

"I'm really enjoying this," he said as he twirled his cane around. "This is fun. I never knew a cane could make such a good weapon."

"Not for long. I intend to win." Dana, never taking her eyes off Drago, reached for her pistol again and Drago smacked her hand with the cane. The pain made her see stars. She was sure he had broken her thumb. The gun dropped to the ground.

"Now you're cheating. I thought we were doing this mano-a-mano."

Using his cane as a ram rod, Drago ran toward Dana. The cane pushed her off balance as she was squatting to pick up her pistol. They struggled, rolling around on the grass. Dana's leg hit something hard that did not feel exactly like a rock or her pistol. On the next roll, her back was on it and she realized it was Drago's cane. When she got the chance, she tossed it away. She did not want Drago to get ahold of it again.

A few more punches were exchanged before Dana finally got the better of him and stood up. He was red faced and seemed a bit out of breath as he lay on his back. Quickly she scanned the area, looking for her pistol.

"Looking for this?" Drago asked with a laugh.

Fearfully, Dana slowly turned her head toward Drago. She thought he was worn out and done for, but there he was standing, pointing her weapon at her. *Great!* She said to herself, *You just made a first class rookie mistake and it's going to cost you your life.* Out loud, speaking with a courage she did not feel, "You don't want to shoot a police officer. It will go harder for you when they do catch you. You know that, don't you."

"Maybe, maybe not. You put up a good fight," After taking in a deep breath, he added, "for a girl. I'm going to give you a break. Let's go." He used the pistol to show the direction he wanted Dana to head.

Dana started walking, slowly, trying to buy time. "What do you want?"

"I'm going to let you live. How's that? Give me your handcuffs, and no tricks. I've got the gun." He waved the pistol in her face. "Keys, too, please. Remember, I'm being polite."

"I suppose you expect me to thank you." Surprised, but not trusting him, Dana continued. "Where are we headed?" She stretched her arm out holding the handcuffs and keys for him to take.

"*We* are not going anywhere." He put the cuffs in his pants pocket. "Put your hands on top of your head. You should've called for back-up."

Dana's heart stopped when she heard the word *we* emphasized the way he did. So much for thinking she was getting out of this alive. Desperate to keep him talking until she could come up with a plan to escape, Dana stopped and twisted around, "I did call for back-up. They should be here any second."

"You can't fool this old man. Now get moving. Your back-up has had plenty of time to get here, so I don't believe they're coming. Either you lied about calling or they didn't get the message. Move!" Drago gruffly ordered. "Or I will shoot you," he added in a silly tone, "whether you're a girl or an officer."

Heavy hearted, Dana turned back around with her head drooping. She had taken only one step forward when she spied the tip of Drago's wooden cane sticking out from under a bush. It was barely noticeable. She prayed Drago did not notice it. By the time she took two more steps, she was sure it was his cane. All she needed to do was trip and she would have a weapon.

Dana waited until they had walked right beside the cane before she went into her act. She coughed and bent over, grabbing her stomach at the same time. It did hurt. That part was not an act. She dropped to her knees with a little moan.

"Don't go play acting on me. It won't work. Get up!"

Now on all fours, Dana gagged. "I'm not acting. You hit me really hard." She kept her tone hostile and agitated to distract him, "For all I know, I'm bleeding inside." She gagged and spit out a bit of bloody mucus. "Give me a minute." Her right hand inched its way toward the cane as she coughed and gagged again. When she felt the rubber tip, Dana slid her hand a little further up the wood to get a better grip. In one fluid motion she sprang up swinging the cane in an upward arc at his right hand to knock the gun out of his grasp.

It did not work. She did not have the element of surprise she had hoped for. The crook of the cane snagged on a branch which slowed her swing considerably. He fired three shots in the time it took her to jerk the cane free and finish swinging. Two hit the cane near the crook end and one grazed her hand, burning like fire. The bullets splintered the cane apart.

Dana was surprised and relieved that he did not shoot her, but that was all that she had time to think. He raised the pistol and the butt connected with her jaw. Her jaw felt like it had splintered the same as the cane. Her face exploded in pain and she collapsed onto the ground.

Drago, still a little short of breath, leaned over Dana putting the cold steel of the pistol against her slender throat. "You don't live long in this business if you're not a good shot. Now I'm pissed. That was my favorite cane and you threw away my favorite pocket knife. I liked you. You put up a good fight, especially for a woman. If I hadn't already given you my word to let you live, I'd shoot you and be done with it." He swung the pistol away and backed away himself. "Stand up."

Slowly. Care to tell me your name? We've had such a good time, we should be on a first name basis by now."

Dana got to her knees. She felt she owed Drago some pain in kind. He was probably going to kill her anyway. She did not understand why he could not do it while she was lying down on the cool grass. Since she was low already and did not have much strength left after that blow, Dana decided to play dirty. For what she was planning to do, it was only fair she tell him her name. "I'm Lieutenant Dana Morgan."

He had backed up a few steps, but that was easy distance for her to make up. Feigning weakness, she tried to stand then collapsed and crawled a little bit forward. That put her about the right distance. Getting up on one knee, Dana took a deep breath and punched him in his testicles.

He bellowed in pain and fell to his knees. Fueled by rage, he swung upwards and punched her in her already bruised jaw.

Dizzy and feeling faint, Dana tried hard not to pass out. Her vision kept fading in and out. Finally, Dana gasped and fainted.

When Dana awoke, she was being dragged by one arm across the grassy clearing. The tight metal handcuff dug into her wrist as he tugged and jerked on it. Dana winced but would not give him the satisfaction of crying out loud. The soft grassy earth ended and Drago stopped, but he did not let go.

"Don't get any smart ideas. This gun's aimed at your head."

Dana did not try to twist around to see if he was lying or not. She could hear the wheezing in his voice and knew he had stopped to catch his breath. That was okay with her. It gave her wrist a break, too.

Drago resumed the tug and pull, but he had switched to using her hand instead of the handcuff. She was thankful for that one small favor. Yet now he was dragging her over sharp stones, broken glass bits, and rocks that made her butt feel like cheese across a grater. Dana spit blood out of her mouth. "What are your plans?"

"I told you I was going to let you live. Don't make me regret it. Shut up."

He stopped at the house ruins, still keeping a tight grip on Dana's arm. When she tried to wiggle out of his grasp, he lightly rapped her across her sore jaw. The pain was excruciating even though it was not a hard hit. Her world spun and blurred. Dana let out a loud moan through her split lip and stopped moving. Tears spilled from her eyes even against her efforts not to let that happen. She did not want to cry in front of Drago.

Drago fastened the other end of the handcuff to a metal pipe that was sticking up out of the ground and curved into the remains of a block wall. Dana jerked hard, but all she did was cause her wrist to bleed and hurt.

With the pistol pointed at her, Drago ordered, "Put your left hand on your head."

Dana hesitated. Maybe it would be better to be shot dead now than to die a slow death chained to this wall.

Drago cocked the hammer. "Now."

Dana obeyed, knowing as long as she was alive there was a chance she could find a way to escape or be rescued.

Drago did not release the hammer which meant, at the slightest twitch, she was going to end up with a bullet in her, somewhere. Roughly, Drago jerked off her shoulder walkie-talkie and stuffed it in his pocket. He searched through her pockets and kept the thirty dollars he found. Lastly, he squeezed a breast none too gently then laughed, "Nice handful." Dana did not move or speak, but her glaring look spoke volumes.

He found her personal cell phone in one of her pockets. "Good. I'll trade you." He pulled his out then slipped hers in his pocket. "This is a throwaway. There's only a few minutes left on it." He tossed it in a nearby bush well out of her reach.

"Thanks. Not much point in giving me the phone. They'll track you with mine."

"I didn't want to make it too easy for you, and I'm counting on them tracking your phone."

Dana had no idea what Drago had planned, but she almost wished she had kept her mouth shut.

"Thanks, you've been a big help." Drago said with an ironic laugh. "I've got to go pack and get moving. Maybe you'll get lucky and be found soon. I'll see you around someday."

"I'll come visit you in prison!" Dana yelled after him as he disappeared into the woods.

Megan set her doll on the step beside her and was getting tired of waiting. "Mary Alice, do you think Miss Dana will get mad if I go get a drink of water? We'd still be close to the trailer. It's just on the other side. I'm thirsty." She picked up her doll. "Let's go. We'll be real quick."

Megan got her drink and returned to the step. She had no idea how long she had been waiting and she was getting hungry again. "I'm cold. Let's hug to keep warm."

Just then her mother's car pulled into the dirt parking area in the front yard. Megan jumped up and ran to greet her. "Mommy!" She flew into her waiting arms. "I missed you so much!"

"I missed you, too, Sweetheart." Sheri carried Megan to the steps and set her down. "I'm sorry I had to work over. I bet you're starving."

"I am. I was getting really, really hungry."

As Megan went up the steps Sheri finally noticed that she was not wearing her jeans and she was muddy. "What happened to you?"

Megan waited for her mother to open the door. "I fell in the mud when it started to rain." She excitedly described the fierce storm, "There was thunder and w-lightning all over the pw-place. Mary Alice and me were really, really scared." Megan took a breath and calmed down as she continued so she could pronounce her words better, "I remembered my lunch bag. Wasn't I good?"

"Yes, Dear, that was good." Sheri was getting supper ready and only half listening. She was thankful that Tom was snoring on the couch. "How does hot dogs and cheesy macaroni sound?"

"Yum," Megan rubbed her tummy for added effect. She continued her story, "I took a nap while it stormed and when I woke up, it was all stopped. I went back outside. I couldn't find my tea set anywhere. I think those mean boys took it. I told Tom and he said to tell the pow-police so I did."

"He did, huh?" Sheri highly doubted that, but let Megan continue with her imaginative tale.

"The pow-police lady came and looked around. She said she found a clue and went into the woods. I was waiting for her to come back when you came home."

"I guess she's gone because she wasn't there when I pulled in. You're getting good at correcting yourself. I'm proud of you." Sheri was thinking there would have been a police cruiser visible in front. She never thought about one that might be out of sight.

"Thanks! I'm trying hard. I don't want anyone to call me names at the new school because I can't talk right." Megan accepted her mother's word that the police officer was gone. She hoped that the officer found the man who stole her tea set so she could get it back tomorrow. Megan wondered why the lady officer did not bring it back today.

Dana dozed and woke as the sun was setting. Fearing Drago might still be nearby, Dana listened a minute to the sounds around her before opening her eyes just a slit. She did not see anyone in her limited field of vision.

"Bastard!" Dana cussed Drago under her breath after she fully opened her eyes. It did not help the pain, but it did make her spirits feel better. She had hated the feel of him touching her breast, but she knew she had to lie still. If she had moved to get away from him or had tried to take the pistol away, he might have shot her, whether by accident or on purpose would not have made any difference. If he had only wounded her, he might have decided to shoot her again to finish the job. She was thankful he wanted to inflict only superficial wounds.

Dana did not have to wonder which was better–to be shot and killed outright or lie here to die a slow agonizing death. She would take the quick death any day. Some favor he was giving her. She shifted her weight, trying to get comfortable and inhaled sharply. The rough gravel dug into her bruised body with the slightest movement.

As she tried to sit up, Dana groaned in excruciating pain. Everywhere hurt, especially her stomach. It had been a few years since her last fist fight when she had taken a stomach punch. She had forgotten how bad it could hurt.

Feeling a thin trickle of warm blood oozing from her right arm wound, Dana pulled a bandana from her uniform pants pocket. Using her teeth and left hand, she managed to wrap the bandana around the oozing gash. Dana guessed it must be deeper than she thought since it was still bleeding. Her forearm ached where a large bruise was forming from the cane striking it. She could move her arm and wiggle her fingers, but they still tingled and felt somewhat numb and cold. She blew on the graze on her right hand to cool the burning.

Awkwardly, Dana ripped open her pant leg to inspect that wound. It was about four or five inches long and was already forming a scab. "Thanks, Drago. Now I have a match to the one your buddy gave me a few weeks ago on my left thigh. I guess I'm lucky that you had only a pocketknife. Yet you could have done more damage than you did. Why did you make only teasing cuts?" Dana sighed, "Too bad you're not here to answer me."

She needed to pee. Dana got to her knees, slid the handcuffs up the pipe, past the bend and closer to the wall. She stood, as much as she could, and, using her left arm, pulled her pants down. It became a major production because then she had to squat and pull her pants away to urinate. She tried to do it far enough away from where she was going to be calling home and prayed the urine ran alongside the wall and not down her way. The thought to fly away home popped into her head. Dana gave a little chuckle and thought to herself, *It sure would be wonderful if I could fly out of here. Where was Superman when you needed him?*

Dana pulled up her pants and fumbled with the button again. After the third try Dana gave up and left the button undone. She hated trying to do things left-handed. Trying to vent some of her frustration Dana jerked on the handcuffs. That did nothing but cause more pain.

"Hello! Can anybody hear me?" Dana yelled to the empty woods. "Help!"

Friday Morning

All Megan could talk about that morning was when the police lady would come with her tea set. Sheri, busy getting herself ready for work, Megan's lunch packed and breakfast ready, only half listened to Megan's chatter.

"Don't forget I need something to put my water in," Megan reminded her mother. She kept her voice low even though Tom was asleep in the big bed and probably could not hear them.

Sheri searched through the cabinets. "I don't have another pitcher. How about this big mug? It has a handle." She held it up for Megan to see.

"But I can't pour from that," Megan whined.

"You don't have to pour. Just fill it up with water and drink straight from it."

"How will Mary Alice get her water?"

Frustrated, Sheri wanted to scream, but she knew that was not fair to Megan. Suddenly, she remembered the small ladle they got at the ice cream store for tasting samples. Sheri scrambled through the drawer until she found it. "How about serving hers with a ladle?"

"Oh, Mommy, that's a super idea!" Megan snatched the small white ladle from her mother's fingers and held it in front of her doll. "Isn't this g-weat?"

"Great. Remember the 'R' sound. Let me wash them off and pack them in your lunch bag. Hurry up and finish getting ready. I have to leave in five minutes."

"I'm ready. Bye, Mommy. I love you." She gave her mother a hug and dashed outside.

Megan's day started out with her usual routine. During the summer every day was the same for her, but today she was hoping Miss Dana would come by with her tea set.

Sheri came outside a few minutes later to give Megan her lunch bag and go to work. She gave Megan another hug, "Remember what we talked about. If Tom touches you down between your legs or hits you, you let me know. I love you and have a good day."

"I love you, too, Mommy," Megan said as she jumped into her mother's arms for another goodbye hug.

As she was getting into the car, Sheri called to Megan, "I'm not working over tonight. I plan to pick up a few groceries, so I shouldn't be too late."

"We'll be okay." Megan ran to the road and waved until her mother turned right on the main street and she could not see the car anymore.

"Mary Alice, I don't want to use the slide today. I know, let's go see if the pow-police car is there. Mommy said it was gone yesterday, but I don't think she knew where to look."

Megan held her doll by one hand, letting her dangle, as she excitedly raced around the big old willow tree. She had gotten half way around when she saw the cruiser. "She's here!" Megan exclaimed. "Oh, I hope she's got my tea set."

Megan went to the police car and, shading her eyes with her hand, stared into the window. There was nobody sleeping inside. "It's so clean inside, not messy like our car. Why did she go into the woods, Mary Alice?" Megan stared at the woods.

"Mary Alice, we can't go that way. Look at all those tangled weeds. We'd get all scratched up. Let's go around and follow the way she went in, okay?" Megan walked back around to her yard.

She held onto her doll securely, as always when seeking comfort and security, while she stood at the edge of the yard facing the woods where she stopped. She stared into the dimness, hesitant to venture any further. Thinking of all the television shows she watched, Megan had a thought, "Mary Alice, what if the bad man hurt the Miss Dana and she needs help?"

Megan stared at the dark woods a moment longer. She had never been in the woods, but they terrified her all the same. She hollered, "Hello!" Not a sound came back. A few butterflies fluttered nearby. Megan liked butterflies and felt safe when they were around.

Timidly, Megan ventured three small steps forward. She counted her steps carefully. The sun was still making it bright enough she did not feel afraid and took ten more steps, normal size this time. Birds were twittering and flying around. A few more butterflies flitted from bush to bush.

"Mary Alice, this isn't as scary as I thought it would be." Bravely she counted ten more steps.

Loudly then softly, she counted her steps as she moved deeper into the woods, sometimes adding them to music. Shafts of sunlight brightened her way. "You know, Mary Alice, it's cooler in here than in the yard. We could sit in here and watch the butterflies some days. Wouldn't that be better?" She held Mary Alice so she could see her face and waited for a response before moving on. The path curved a little to the left then swung back to the right, but Megan continued still carefully counting her steps.

She was beginning to think the woods were beautiful with all the colorful flowers, birds and butterflies. Megan heard a tinkling sound. "Mary Alice, did you hear that? Was that fairy bells? We need to be real quiet so they won't hear us. We don't want to scare them away."

Megan squatted and listened a minute. There was only silence. She tiptoed through the brush and stopped when she heard the tinkling again. Whispering, she said to her doll, "I think we're getting closer. Be real quiet."

Megan forgot about counting her steps, she had been so intent on listening for the fairy bells. She had gone two more steps when she suddenly remembered. Megan stopped and looked around. Tears welled in her eyes and her lower lip pouted out. She was surrounded by tall bushes and felt very small and afraid.

She looked behind her and saw the path she had come in on and thought she should go back out. A bright yellow and black butterfly was flying up that path towards her. It flitted past her and beyond. Megan then saw where the path was.

Megan followed the butterfly. Before she had gone too much farther Megan heard a cough and froze. Wide-eyed she looked at her doll and pulled it close to her, whispering softly, "What do we do? Do fairies cough? Is that the Miss Dana?"

Next she heard a soft moan. "That sounded like someone was hurt. Mommy does that when she has a bad headache. Maybe the police lady has a headache."

Tentatively Megan walked in the direction of the sound. She did not have to go much farther before she stumbled upon the clearing and saw Police Officer Dana Morgan lying on the ground with her eyes closed and one arm chained to a pole.

Slowly, on tiptoe, she advanced toward Dana. There was blood on the officer's face, arm, uniform shirt and leg. To Megan's young eyes, it was so much blood and she did not know what to do. Barely above a whisper she asked, "Miss Dana, are you dead?"

Exhausted from trying to stay awake all night, Dana, who had been sleeping, could hear a soft voice off in the distance asking her if she was dead. She wanted to tell them no, but she could not feel the rest of her body so she was not sure. Dana, hoping it was not a dream, struggled to open her heavy eyelids.

She blinked, thinking she was hallucinating. There was Megan standing over her. Dana had to smile. Dear sweet little Megan. "No, Honey, I'm not dead, but that mean man sure tried." She coughed and continued, "Can you get me some help?"

"Yes, ma'am." Megan answered without any hesitation. "You're stinky." She pinched her nose for emphasis.

Again she had to smile, in spite of the pain the split lip caused. Dana had hoped the drizzly rain last night had washed away the worst of it. "I had to pee in the dirt, but didn't have anything to wipe with. I think some of it traveled this way."

Megan giggled and did a little wiggle, "I do that sometimes under the trailer."

"The bad man threw a cell phone in those bushes over there," Dana raised her left hand and pointed. "Would you see if you can find it?"

"Okay." Megan ran to the tangled mass of bushes and stood looking into them. Dana worried that Megan did not know how to look for the phone. Then Megan dropped down to her knees and looked on the ground underneath. "I see it!" she happily exclaimed.

Relief washed over Dana. For the first time since she ran into Harry Drago she felt like she might live through this. Megan set her doll on the grass ordering her to stay put before she crawled under the bush until all Dana could see were Megan's thin little legs.

A moment later, Megan backed out of the bush and proudly held up the small silver cell phone. She ran back to Dana and handed it to her. Dana tried several different numbers, holding it at different angles, but could not get any dial tone.

"I guess we're too close to those towers to get the phone to work. Could you go back to your trailer and call 9-1-1?"

"We don't have a phone. My mommy has a cell phone, but she keeps it with her and she's at work."

Dana groaned, some with frustration and some with pain. "Do you think you could take my phone and walk out of the woods to call 9-1-1? Do you know your address to tell them?" Dana prayed there were enough minutes left for Megan to get help.

"Yes, ma'am." Megan turned to leave but stopped when Dana called to her.

"Come back when you get done, okay?"

"Okay."

Carefully Megan counted her steps back out of the woods. "Whew, Mary Alice, there are so many steps. I got to count to one hundred four times and add eight-two more–this many." She held up two fingers for Mary Alice to see. "Oops! I forgot I lost count when we were chasing the butterflies. Do you remember?" She looked at Mary Alice for an answer. "That's okay. I don't think it was very many." Megan kept walking as she talked. "We'll find our way out." With the great wisdom of her meager five years, Megan concluded it did not matter and whispered to her doll, "I think the fairies made a path for us. They don't want us to get lost."

She found her way, walked to the middle of her yard and got a signal. Just as she pressed the number nine button, Tom opened the door and jumped down the steps. Megan quickly dropped the phone into her dress pocket. He put a bag in the trash container and walked toward her.

"Where have you been hiding?" He demanded gruffly, standing close to her which made her feel small and afraid.

"Nowhere. I was just pwaying in the tree." With her head down, she pointed toward the huge broken willow branch. She did not correct her speech around Tom.

Tom looked at the tree then back at the cowering Megan and seemed satisfied. He had looked around quickly before and had not thought to check there. He did not think she would have run off, but he had decided to look again after he went to the bathroom and got rid of some of the beer cans. He did not want Sheri to know he was still drinking as much as always.

Suddenly he grabbed her arm and smacked her behind. "You stay in this here yard, you hear me!"

Megan whimpered, "Yes, Sir."

Tom stormed off back into the trailer. Terrified, Megan ran to her hiding place under the trailer. She let a few tears slide down her cheeks, but she did not take time to really cry. Megan waited a few minutes, making sure Tom did not return.

Megan dialed 9-1-1, but got no service. Silently she moved out from under the trailer and ran to the willow tree. She ducked under the broken branch and looked back toward the trailer. She did not see Tom watching out any of the windows for her.

"Do you think it's safe to try again, Mary Alice? I'll put you here, where you can watch. You tell me if you see Tom. I'm going to dial again," she whispered to her doll.

A female voice asked her what was the nature of her emergency. Still shaken from her encounter with Tom and not wanting him to hear her, Megan held the phone in front of her and spoke barely above a whisper, "The police lady's hurt. Miss Dana needs help." Megan snapped the phone shut and put it in her pocket.

The 9-1-1 operator tried to get more information, but was talking to dead air. All the operator had heard was '…lady's hurt.' When she called back the phone vibrated silently in Megan's pocket and she did not feel it. The operator chalked it up to a crank call, put it on the police report, and promptly ignored it.

Megan looked at the house trailer, ran to the spot where Dana had entered the woods, and stopped. She stood still, thinking and deciding. Tom had told her to stay in the yard, but the police lady had told her to come back after she made the call.

Megan squeezed her doll while she decided what to do. "Mary Alice, I think it's more important to obey the police w-lady, don't you? Tom won't miss us. He'll drink his beers and go to sleep." She paused while Mary Alice talked to her. "Right. Let's go."

Police Precinct

"Call her again!" the captain bellowed. "I'll have her badge for this!" He threw down a report that someone had the audacity to hand him during his tirade. "I'll have a piece of her hide, too."

29

Nicholas Coburn, Nick to his family and friends, waited patiently for Captain Ed Wells to calm down, which apparently was not going to happen anytime soon. They had already been trying for over fifty minutes to reach Dana Morgan, his new partner, and had been totally unsuccessful. She was not answering either her home or cell phones, her walkie-talkie, or the car radio.

When Dana was only ten minutes late, Captain Wells explained with an apologetic laugh, "She's a little upset about changing shifts and losing her weekend. She's probably throwing a little temper tantrum and will walk in any minute. She's a good officer. You'll see when you meet her."

At twenty minutes, he had dispatch call her. Then it became every five minutes. The Captain's bellowing belied his genuine concern. He claimed Dana was dedicated and would not pull a silly, childish stunt like this.

"Go see Alice. She'll give you a copy of Dana's phone numbers and her home address. Check her last route. By the way, welcome to the force," he said as he answered the phone.

Nick found Alice and got copies of Dana's information. As Alice handed the copies to Nick she said, "I hope Dana's all right. She's a good cop. Even if she had a flat tire or car trouble, she would have called. Something's wrong for her not to show. Oh, here's a county map."

"Thanks. I appreciate the help. Do you know Dana's route?"

"Brenda can help you with that. Let me show you her desk." Alice stood and wove her way around the maze of crowded desks. They stopped at one that had pink fuzzy dice hanging from the corner of the divider wall.

"Brenda, this is Officer Nick Coburn. He needs Dana's route."

Busy chewing on a large wad of bubblegum and typing on her keyboard, Brenda did not bother to look up. A pink hair band tried to tame the mass of black curly hair that framed her oval face and matched the shade of lipstick she was wearing. Nick waited patiently as she hit the final few keystrokes with a flare and the printer spit out three sheets of paper with the route information. Brenda grabbed the papers out of the tray and turned to hand them to Nick.

Her mouth dropped open, exposing the large wad of pink bubble gum she had been so vigorously chewing. "Wow!" She said to the six foot two tall man waiting for the papers she held. His looks were the kind she always read about in her romance novels, but never thought existed on any real live male—wavy, dark brown hair, a chiseled jaw, stunning deep blue eyes, and a dimple in his left cheek that only peeked out when he smiled. Definitely he had a smile. Wow! He had everything she liked—an athletic build, firm and muscular, but without the weightlifter heft look. His shoulders were the kind any woman wanted to curl up in, especially her.

Nick took the paper from her hand which seemed to pull her mouth shut. "You're gorgeous." The words were out before she had time to think about being embarrassed.

He smiled his killer smile again. "Thank you." He was thanking her for the map, but Brenda did not know if it was for the compliment or for the map, and really did not care. Forget about the husband and two kids at home. She was in love with that smile.

Nick was glad there was another door only a few steps away so he could make a fast getaway. He could hear the women's voices as he walked down the hall. *Who was that? Isn't he gorgeous? Isn't he handsome? George Clooney can't hold a candle to him. What's his name? Where's he working? He can sleep in my bed anytime. Does anyone know if he's married? He's working here? Can he be my partner? Who is his partner? Will he be back?*

Nick thought he was just average looking. His nose, eyes and ears were all in the right places. He still had all of his hair. He was a little surprised he made it to Brenda's desk before *The Reaction*, as he liked to call it, set in. Sometimes it was a help in his job and sometimes it was a hindrance. Maybe he should have been a movie star. The money would have been better. Nah, he decided, the adrenaline highs just would not have been the same.

CHAPTER 5

Drago had decided to get out of the area and needed new clothes, in particular new shoes. He had planned to leave yesterday after his encounter with Dana, but he sorely needed to rest after his little fight and had spent a restless night in his tent, worrying when he would hear sirens coming for him. He still felt tired this morning after a sleepless night, but he dared not waste any more time staying in one spot.

After surreptitiously checking on Dana this morning to make sure she was still there, Drago headed to Megan's trailer. Dana looked like she was sleeping, but he did not take a chance by going through the clearing. Instead, he struggled his way through the rougher parts of the woods, trying to go as quietly as his injured leg would let him. If she heard him, she might think it was wildlife of one sort or another.

Drago looked around the yard for Megan and could not see her anywhere. He had a story all prepared for her about why he needed to go into her trailer. He walked past the swing set and imagined seeing his new daughter giggling as he pushed her in the swing. He had not been there much for his other kids, but he wanted to change that with this one. He hoped she was as cute as Megan. It was risky staying around so long, but he had little choice. His gang was dwindling fast. They were either in hiding, dead, or in jail, so he had little help. He was used to having a governor or two plus any number of politicians to call on, besides three dozen gang members. He had been unable to find his first ex-wife and his second ex-wife had gone to North Carolina over two weeks ago. Now all he had were two young punks, a few reliable friends, and a handful of contacts.

Drago decided Tom looked close to his size and it would be easy to steal from him since he was usually drunk. Once he got a new pair of shoes he was going to head to the bus station. The last word he got was his second wife was in Charleston, but he did not have an address. His contact was supposed to call on Dana's phone to let him know what it was.

He had his disguise all ready. Long sleeves were too obvious in the summer months, but his doctor friend had given him a long arm splint to wear to hide his tattoo. He was letting his beard grow which was a salt and pepper blend. An added touch, a new cane so he could walk hunched over to make him look shorter and older. Now, thanks to the fight with Dana, he had facial bruises, so it looked like he had been in an accident or taken a fall. A simple faded baseball cap shielded his face, providing shadows and obscurity.

It took Drago a little effort to pull the door open. The jerk had shut the door all the way so little Megan would never have been able to open it when she wanted to go inside. Drago got to know Tom well while secretly watching Megan. Drago stepped on the first step without problem. Using his bad leg he stepped on the second block which wobbled significantly under his weight causing him to lose his balance. Drago cussed under his breath and grabbed the screen door to keep from falling. Now he was mad as well as in pain. He stood still a few minutes until the pain subsided.

Taking a deep breath, Drago, with his pistol at the ready, took the last step using his good leg and entered the trailer. He had no idea if Tom would be asleep or in a drunken stupor at this time of day, but he had his .380 pistol with him just in case. He also had no idea if Tom kept any kind of weapons or not.

Tom was sitting on the couch snoring with the television blaring. He was thankful since that noise would cover any sound he might make and Tom was probably drunk enough to sleep through the rest of the day. Drago let him sleep for now.

Drago took a minute to look in Megan's room. It was done in pinks and white with fairies and butterflies on the walls and bed covers. He wondered what his little girl's room looked like. He wished he knew her name. He would have liked to have named her Sarah Frances after his grandmother.

Drago looked for a pair of men's shoes–civilian shoes that would not lead the law to him like his convict boots did. After a thorough search, he could not find any. It surprised him that this guy had only the pair that were on his feet. Well, there was one way to take care of that Drago easily decided.

During his search, he found a twenty dollar bill hidden in a sock which he put in his pocket. He took three pairs of socks and a hooded sweatshirt that he slipped on in spite of it being a warm day. In the bathroom, he grabbed a razor, extra blades and dental floss. There was a cute fairy nightlight plugged into the wall outlet. He snatched that, planning to give it to his daughter. "Sorry, Megan, I'll leave you a few bucks later to buy a new one," Drago said to the empty room.

Everything Drago stole he stuffed into his pants pockets or the hand pocket on the front of the hooded sweatshirt. When he was satisfied that there was nothing more worth taking, he walked toward the living room. Tom was still snoring.

"I hate to waste a bullet if your shoes don't fit, but you're a waste anyway. This is for picking on Megan," Drago informed the sleeping Tom. He was only about ten feet away when he raised his pistol and fired. A small red dot appeared on Tom's forehead above his left eye. His head fell backward and his mouth slacked open. Blood splattered on the couch and floral wall paper. Tom never knew he had been shot.

Drago pulled off Tom's shoes as well as his own prison issue boots. After putting on the used sneakers, Drago picked up his boots. "Tom, your shoes are almost new and they fit decent enough. Now no one will be able to track me. Thanks." Drago laughed and slapped Tom's shoulder, "You're a real pal to give me the shoes off your feet."

He had just dropped his boots behind the sofa so they would not be readily noticed when his borrowed cell phone rang. Drago checked the number first before answering it. It surprised him how many times the police precinct had called looking for Officer Dana. He was almost tempted to answer and play games with them, but keeping them guessing was more fun for right now. This call was from his contact. "Tell me good news." The answer was not what he wanted to hear. Drago jammed the phone back into his pocket and stormed out the door.

Megan counted her steps carefully back to the police officer. She found her lying with her eyes closed just like she had been before. "Miss Dana, are you okay?"

Dana opened her eyes and smiled, "Yes, thank you. I was resting. Did you call 9-1-1?"

"I did."

"Did you give them your address?"

"No, I forgot." Tears started to run down Megan's cheeks. She had wanted to help the kind officer and she had messed up.

"Please, don't cry. It's okay. Help will come. They'll find me eventually." To herself Dana worried that the help would be too late. "Do you think you could get Tom to help?"

Megan's eyes widened, "No! He said he would shoot any police he saw. I don't think he really would help. He spanked me."

"Why?"

"I dunno. He said he couldn't find me. I lied. I told him I was in the tree. He told me to stay in the yard, but you told me to come back." She hugged her doll tightly and did her little hip wiggle, "I figured you were more important."

"Well, you are supposed to listen to your parents, but I'm glad you came back." Dana groaned.

"Tom isn't my dad. Do you hurt real bad?"

"Yes, I'd like help here fast. I'm thirsty, too."

"What happened to your hand?"

"The bad man shot it. I had to tear my uniform pants to wrap around it to keep the bugs off."

"Does it hurt?"

"A little. It burns more than hurts. Covering it makes it feel better."

"I can call again. I can get you water in a bottle," Megan eagerly offered.

"Let me see the phone, please."

Megan gave her the phone. Dana tried again, but could not get any bars no matter which way she turned it.

"Do you mind going all the way back? Could you bring a towel?" Dana hoped to wash her face a bit.

"Okay," Megan nodded her head.

"When you call, tell them Officer Dana Morgan needs help right away and give them your address. Then bring me the water and towel. What time does your mother get home?"

Megan looked up into the sky, thinking hard. "Sometimes five-thirty and sometimes seven-thirty." Then she put her right hand out in a stop motion, "No, wait, I forgot! Today she's coming at five-thirty after stopping at the store."

"After you bring me that stuff, you can go back and wait for you mother. She would help me, right?"

"Oh, yes, Mommy's wonderful. She takes care of people. That's her job. She takes care of old people. I don't think you're that old, but she'd help, I'm sure."

Dana chuckled, "That's good. When she gets home, will you bring her here if the ambulance hasn't come?"

"Okay." Megan got up to leave.

"Megan, Honey, I don't suppose you have a gun."

"Yes, Mommy has one and Tom has one, but I'm not allowed to touch them. I don't know where Tom hides his. I know where Mommy keeps hers."

"I know, but that very bad man might still be loose in these woods, and I would feel safer if I had a gun to protect myself."

"I don't know if I can get it without Tom finding out."

"That's okay. Help should be on the way." Dana doubted that any was coming from the first call. It had been long enough that she should have heard some sirens instead of silence. She hoped Megan had better luck with the second call.

Nick's Search

After the wild goose chase one of his fellow officers sent him on earlier, Nick found Dana's apartment building without much trouble. The first time he was told that Dana had moved and George jotted down her new address with directions. When Nick arrived, he discovered it was a local brothel. One of the girls filmed the entire episode with a video camera and another snapped pictures of three of the girls as they 'attacked' Nick and tore off his shirt.

His mother had taught him to treat a woman like a lady. He happily played along as he asked questions about Dana. It did not take him long to realize they knew absolutely nothing and wanted to have less talk. He had hoped to find Dana hiding amongst the girls.

He managed to escape after losing only his shirt, undershirt and one shoe. They graciously returned his clothes as he reached the front door. He expected to see his photo on the bulletin board at the Precinct within the hour; instead, the video was on YouTube. Not the part, however, where they returned his clothes before he left the building. They made it look like he left butt naked.

Any other time he would have joined in on the fun and had a great time. However, by now he was worried about Dana and he did not want to clown around anymore. If he thought that Dana was simply hiding and not in any danger, he could have relaxed and had some fun while they played their game of *Find the Lost Lieutenant*.

The next time he wanted to go to Dana's home, he used the address that Alice gave him. Finding someone to talk to in the middle of the afternoon was always hard. Most people worked, but this neighborhood looked like the women stayed home and had others work for them. Was he on another wild goose chase? What kind of salary did Dana make?

This area screamed money. Nick doubted if any of the homes went for less than a cool million. He checked to make sure he was on the right street. He was, so he kept going, looking for the right number. The price range looked like it was declining as he drove.

Down three blocks it became a decent neighborhood with a picturesque tree lined street that had four apartment complexes on one side with a small business district consisting of a row of shops—a florist, two drug stores, a dental office, and a deli. Some very pricey homes lined the other side of the street.

Dana lived in the second apartment building, The Northgate Manor House. It looked more like a colonial home. Nick drove his car through a tall, black wrought iron gate between two red brick columns, down a short curvy drive to the side parking lot. There was a small sign attached to the building which indicated apartment 2-A was up one flight of stairs. Nick looked at the steep, narrow, black metal steps and wondered how they got any furniture into the apartments. The third floor apartment had its own metal steps that jutted out over a small garden.

Taking the steps two at a time, Nick was out of breath when he reached the landing. He took a deep breath and knocked on Dana's door. No one answered. He put his ear to the dark blue metal door and listened. There was silence on the other side. He did not hear a television, radio, or hushed voices.

He knocked again, a little harder this time. The response was the same. He looked around. There was no way to go from this apartment to the third floor. He had to go all the way back down and walk up two flights on a separate set of stairs. *Who designed this mess?*

Nick grumbled to himself the whole way up both flights about how, most likely after all his effort, no one would be home. He liked to run everyday to keep in shape, but he hated to do more than one flight of stairs. He took a deep breath and knocked. He thought he heard movement, but no one answered the door. He knocked again.

This time a gravelly voice hollered, "Hold on! I can only get there as fast as I can."

Expecting a barrel of a man, Nick tensed slightly and had his vision focused at about his eye level. He heard the soft shush of a chain lock being released then the more solid click of a dead bolt being turned. When the door opened and the space he was staring at was empty, he quickly dropped his eyes downward and blinked in surprise when a stooped elderly woman supported by a flowery print metal cane was standing there. Nick was taken aback on two counts. That a woman belonged to that deep voice and that she could manage those stairs.

"You climb those steps?" He asked in surprise before he even said hello.

She cocked her head and replied as if she were talking to a complete dimwit, "No, I use the elevator in the lobby like normal folk."

Nick never considered that there was a main lobby. He thought it was a converted colonial mansion. Some detective he was. Now he was almost too embarrassed to ask his other questions.

Trying to cover his embarrassment, he flipped open his badge and in an official tone stated, "I'm Officer Nicholas Coburn. I'm looking for Officer Dana Morgan. Have you seen her?"

"Who?"

A second of panic gripped Nick that he had climbed all those stairs for nothing. Had he gotten the wrong house again? "Officer Dana Morgan. The woman who lives in the apartment below you."

"Oh, Dana. No, I haven't seen her for a few days. I just got home this morning from my sister's in Myrtle Beach. Lucy lives downstairs in apartment 1-A, she can tell you." The woman looked at her watch. "She'll be home in about fifteen to twenty minutes depending on traffic. Good day." She shut the door forcing Nick to take a step back so it would not break his nose.

Nick stared at the closed door while he decided what to do until Lucy got home. There was definitely no point in staying here. He checked the two dumpsters tucked neatly in the back under some overhanging trees before driving to the deli across the street. He bought a soda and a picked up a food magazine to read while he waited. He found an empty booth, but after five minutes, he felt antsy. He was never very good at waiting. One thing that worried him was if this was not normal behavior for Dana, what had happened? Was she in trouble? Was it a silly stunt? Did she need help? What kind of trouble was she in?

His gut was telling him she was in trouble, but his mind was having doubts. *None of her other coworkers seem the least bit concerned. What do I really know about her? That little bit of information in her bio could be all made up. But not all of it, right? The parts about her heroism, knowing French and having a degree had to be real.* Nick remembered the phone conversation he had with her captain roughly two months ago. Afterwards, Nick felt the bio info probably did not do her justice. Nick did not think he had been gone ten minutes when he decided to go back.

Just as he was ready to turn into the driveway he saw a slender blond woman shake a rug out and hang it over the railing. He was relieved to know that Dana was there after all!

Nick flew into a parking spot and raced up the stairs. He had to catch her before she got away. Nick charged through the open patio door. He had no idea what Dana looked like, but the petite blond woman in front of him must be her. They had forgotten to send her picture with her portfolio, and finally faxed an old scratchy black and white photo. She was not supposed to be a blond. Even in black and white, it looked like her hair was dark. Had she dyed it?

The woman was holding a small throw pillow. Certainly not a dangerous weapon, but something to throw him off balance when she threw it in his face and screamed. Before he had a chance to do anything but catch the pillow, the barefoot blond kicked him in his crotch. Breathless from his race up the stairs, he fell to the floor gasping for air and groaning in torturous pain. The blond fled out another door.

Nick could hear her bare feet running on a hard wood floor then steps again. He heard frantic knocking followed by a familiar gravelly voice and knew where she had gone. He managed to get to his knees and rested his head on the sofa as he gasped in a few more breaths before trying to stand. Nick thought how lucky he was there was not a steady girl in his life right now. He was afraid he might be permanently damaged after that wallop.

Nick controlled his breathing as the pain slowly subsided. Just as he finally made it to his feet the blond girl returned. "Mrs. Bailey upstairs told me you're a detective looking for Dana. Am I under arrest?"

Still a little out of breath Nick managed to utter in a slightly higher pitch than normal for him, "Probably. The Captain's pissed off and I have just added my name to the list."

"Whose going to take care of my little girl if I go to jail? I didn't know you were a cop. It's not my fault."

"Little girl?" questioned Nick. Something was not right. There was nothing in Dana's profile about her having a child. "Who are you? Aren't you Dana Morgan?"

"No, I'm Jean Alaño. I clean her house and the woman's upstairs."

"Oh," was all he could think to say and plopped into the nearest chair to think. He had hoped his search was over. Jean was average looking even though he did not particularly like blonds.

Jean rattled on, "Lucy should be back now. I can call her." She started toward the phone then stopped and turned around, "I am really sorry about kickin' you in the," she hesitated, "I mean, ahh." She blushed and pointed a finger to the front of his pants. As fast as she could say it without having it be one word, she spit out, "I'm sorry I kicked you there." She spun around and walked quickly to the phone.

She came back before Nick had finished sorting out his thoughts. He had glanced around the apartment. It was spacious and open. He liked that the tiny kitchen and large living room were separated by only a counter. It was a place he could feel comfortable in. All the kitchen appliances were black or chrome except for a bold fire engine red coffee maker. That surprised him, but he did not know why.

The place was neat and tidy. If there had been a struggle, all signs of it were gone. That was something that Nick was going to have to find out.

"Lucy's home now. I can show you her apartment. Do you need a drink or something for pain? Some ice? Dana won't mind if I give you something out of her medicine cabinet. Dana's sympatico."

A headache was beginning to form around his temples. "A glass of water and some Advil would be great. Tell me, when was the last time you saw Dana?"

Jean answered over her shoulder as she walked down the hallway to the bathroom. "I don't really see her. I have my own key. I come clean her apartment once a week, usually on Friday." She talked louder while she was in the bathroom. "She leaves a check for me every other week. I saw her about two or three weeks ago when she had to come home to change."

Jean returned and set the bottle of Advil on the kitchen counter. She got him a cold bottle of water from the refrigerator then took everything to him.

Nick swallowed the two pills while Jean explained why Dana had come home in the middle of the afternoon. "That was exciting. Dana helped catch a guy that robbed a convenience store. He had a hidden knife and cut Dana's left thigh." Jean showed Nick on her own shapely thigh about where the cut was located. "She had to have over twenty stitches and they cut off her pant leg in the ER. She came home, changed and went back to finish her shift!" Her face was beaming with pride as if Dana were her own family member.

"You know the best part? That thug was one of Dragon Man's men. Dana's a big hero."

Nick was pleased to hear that his new partner was not a whiner or slacker. He had had his doubts at first, but now was beginning to like Dana more and more.

He glanced around the immaculate apartment. "How much cleaning did you do before I got here?"

"None, really. I think Dana hired me just to be helpful."

"Why's that?"

"I didn't finish high school and can't get a decent job. I work part time as a waitress at Dugan's Restaurant over on Waller Street and clean for Dana and Lucy. I get some assistance for my little girl.

"Dana's apartment is always clean, like you see it now. I dust, vacuum and sweep because she pays me to. Sometimes I do errands for her like picking up her dry cleaning or getting groceries if she leaves a list."

Nick nodded. "Do you mind if I take a look around?"

"Is something wrong?"

"Dana's missing."

Jean slowly sank down onto the sofa. "Oh, no. I hope Dragon Man didn't get her."

"Who's Dragon Man?"

"Harry Drago. Him and his gang's been bad news around here for years. They finally got him in prison, and I'm not sure how long he's been in, but there was a fight and he got a broken leg.

He escaped, ah, I guess, about a month ago, the day he went to the doctor to get the cast off his leg."

"Do you know if Dana helped capture Dragon Man?"

"No, sorry. I don't. The news made it sound like most of police were looking for him."

Nick nodded, finally understanding some of the nervousness he sensed in the police station earlier. He did not think it had all been over one female officer being late for work. "Nothing's missing, out of place, odd to you?"

"No, not that I've noticed." She lowered her voice and asked conspiratorially, "Should I be looking for clues or doing anything different?"

Nick smiled, "No. You're fine. Keep doing everything the same way you have been, but if you do hear from Dana, let me know." He handed her his card. "Use the cell number. I don't have an office down here. Excuse me. I'm going to look around just in case."

Nick glanced around the living room again. It was simply, but tastefully furnished. A hardwood floor with a large soft blue area rug ringed by a plain beige, overstuffed but extremely comfortable looking sofa, a straight backed chair and a dark blue recliner. Several small tables were strategically placed to be of benefit to those sitting in the chairs or sofa. A large entertainment center covered half the wall. It looked like a new model and expensive.

He checked the living room door and window locks first. Nothing looked amiss with any of them. Nick took a quick look in the bathroom off the kitchen. It was small, just a sink and toilet. He crossed the living room and headed down the hall. The first room on his left was a small office. There was a locked four drawer filing cabinet in one corner, a mildly cluttered desk with a flat screen computer, a swivel chair and a straight back chair for a guest. That was all that could fit in the tiny space. Nick hit the space bar on the computer, hoping it might wake up to something he could use, but the screen that came up asked for a password. He did not bother trying different passwords. Later that might be necessary, he reasoned.

Nick looked behind the pictures on the walls, searching for a wall safe. Nothing. The closet had two narrow slatted doors. He opened them and a bright light came on automatically. He was surprised to see shelves with board games and picture puzzles. Scrabble. Monopoly. Chess. Checkers. All the puzzles were one thousand pieces that he could tell. He wondered how good a checkers player she was. Checkers was his favorite.

Nick turned and noticed that there were no pictures on one wall. *Odd. Was something stolen? Could she not find anything she liked for there, or was there a particular reason for not having something covering that space?* He looked closer at the paint. It did not look like anything had been removed recently.

He sat in the desk chair, facing the wall. Not very entertaining to stare at a plain off-white wall. Nick looked at her computer equipment. Her desk was a large glass top with a printer combo fax machine. On the floor underneath, were a tangle of wires and several other black boxes he assumed were more computer accessories. Nick moved his feet around and suddenly the wall in front of him lit up.

A pleasant female voice along with the words began–*Your conference call is scheduled for this Sunday at ten a.m. Your password will be required at that time.* The words remained, but the background changed to a mountain view. An older woman's smiling face showed briefly then everything faded away.

Nick, thoroughly surprised, sat there staring at the now blank wall for a few minutes. He looked on the floor to see what he had bumped with his shoe, but could not figure it out and did not want to try again, half afraid he might damage something in the process. His computer skills covered only the very basics.

Now there was a new worry niggling Nick's brain. Maybe Dana was a bad cop. This neighborhood looked high rent. Her entertainment and computer were not normal expenses for a single cop's budget. Did she have a second job? Was she on the take? Nick wanted to believe these were all simply gifts from her mother. Was there more to Dana than he realized?

Nick wanted to get finished and get out. He heard the vacuum running in the living room as he walked to the first bedroom. It was large and had its own bathroom. He checked the medicine cabinet. It had the usual supplies he would have expected. A bottle of generic Ibuprofen and one of acetaminophen. No prescription pills at all unless she kept them somewhere else. The room was decorated in lavender and soft earth tones. There was a sliding glass door that led to a small balcony. The lock did not look like it had been tampered with.

He checked through her night table and dresser. He was not sure what he was looking for, but he was not finding anything out of the ordinary. Although it seemed Dana preferred cotton panties, she did have some tantalizingly skimpy silky ones that he would love to see her in with the matching bras, of course. He felt no guilt looking through her personal things even though he knew he probably should.

He looked in the large closet. First on the left, a row of neatly pressed uniforms which he quickly moved past. The basic blouses, skirts and dresses were next. He liked her fashion sense. She had a few suits, about six dresses and at least two dozen blouses. There were a few slacks hanging in the closet, but most of her slacks had been in her dresser along with the sweaters, lingerie and socks. A flash of red caught Nick's eye. He moved the other clothes out of the way and whistled. She had a few skimpy dresses that looked like they barely covered the essentials. He let out with a soft wolf whistle.

Now he really wondered what kind of partner he was getting. Not that he wouldn't mind seeing her in one of those outfits.

So far he had not discovered a hidden safe or any evidence of her involvement in any nefarious schemes. Nor any indication of foul play.

Nick stood in the middle of the bedroom, absently staring around, wondering what he might have missed. The bio they had sent seemed complete even if it was only two pages. Nick felt like he knew Dana fairly well already except for her face and, out of the nine candidates, thought she fit the role best. One of the other candidates looked ten years older even though she was truthfully only two years older. No one would have believed they were newly engaged. Another one was only five foot and he did not feel comfortable with someone that short. The others were all various shades of blond, but three of them lacked the necessary skill in the French language.

Two other agents had been hiding the fact that they were pregnant. One was four months and the other was almost seven months! Because they were first time mothers their pregnancies did not readily show. They wore looser clothing and simply looked like they had gained a few pounds.

That left Dana Morgan in South Carolina and Nancy Porter in Ohio. Nancy was a stunning black woman. She was five foot ten and had done some modeling so she carried her height well. Nick liked her and thought they made a good looking couple. They started working together to get to know one another. Then she was involved in an auto accident that nearly took her life. She lost her left foot, broke four ribs, her left thigh and her right arm.

Nick went to see her in the hospital. Her beautiful face was barely recognizable. She had a tracheostomy to help her breathe. Nick kissed her forehead and told her he was breaking off their engagement. She smiled, her eyes laughing at him since her mouth could not and gave him a thumbs up. The nurse switching the bag of IV fluids glared at him then looked puzzled when she saw the thumbs up. After the nurse left Nick sat in a chair beside her bed and explained to Nancy as he held her one good hand, he found another agent in South Carolina that knew French. He talked until his time was up. Nick then called Sergeant Wells and arranged to come to South Carolina.

Dana was his last hope for his plan to work. He missed seeing in her dossier that she was in the same sorority as Adaire Fontaine the first time he read it or he would have picked Dana first and saved himself a ton of headaches, especially with a couple of the blonds.

Nick had a hard time forming any kind of relationship with blonds because of a childhood playmate. She had been a year older than he, taller and heavier. Her name was Angel, but she had been a devil as far as he was concerned.

Dana, Darling, I know your mother married a very wealthy shipping magnate after her divorce. Would she have set you up in a luxury apartment? Are you hiding something? You're not on the take, I hope.

It did not take Nick long to look around. Jean stopped vacuuming when he came in. She unplugged it and went into another room. The second bedroom was noticeably larger than the other, but he had to blink when he saw the color scheme. It was done in various shades of pink with touches of white even in its bathroom. The closet was empty. Nick could not stand being in that room for more than the few seconds it took to check that it was empty. *What was Dana thinking?*

Nothing was out of place. If she had planned to disappear, Dana had packed really, really light. When he looked in the bathroom he noticed her toothbrush was still there.

No, this was not planned, Nick decided. Doubts cropped up. She would not have bought a new toothbrush and a closetful of new clothes just to throw a fit. That made no sense.

Nick scrunched his hand over his face. Nothing was amiss that he could tell. Maybe that was a good thing. Maybe Dana had taken off on her own. Even though he did not know her, Nick did not feel that was right. The picture he had put together of Dana was that she was a dedicated cop, a good person and someone that cared. He did not want to believe otherwise. If there had been any flaw in Dana's character, she would not have been included on the list for this special assignment. If Dana had not taken off on her own, what happened to her?

When he came back out Jean was on the phone talking in a low voice. She blushed when she saw Nick. "I gotta go," she said to whoever she was talking to and quickly hung up. She stood up, "Everything okay?"

"As far as I can tell. How do I get to Lucy's apartment?"

"Oh, let me show you." Jean opened the door and Nick followed her into the building hallway. They turned left and went down a flight of stairs which brought them to a bright sunlit foyer. They walked passed a small elevator with mahogany doors trimmed in highly polished brass before stopping at a door marked 1-A.

Jean knocked. "Lucy, it's us."

The door cautiously opened, revealing one eye, expertly made up, that scanned them before opening the door the rest of the way.

"Come in." Lucy stood partially behind the door as they walked through. "Make yourself at home." She eyed Nick up and down. More pointedly, she hissed to Jean while keeping her eyes on Nick, "Jean, don't you have some cleaning to finish? I don't want you to be late picking up your little girl."

Jean looked at her watch. "Si." She looked at Nick. "It was nice meeting you and I'm sorry about you know what." She apologized again, giving a quick wave with a finger in the direction of his crotch. "I hope you find Dana and that she's all right."

Lucy glared at Jean to hurry up and get out then turned toward Nick, smiling sweetly, her whole demeanor changed. "Have a seat. I'll get us some coffee. Won't take but a minute. I always keep a fresh pot ready." Lucy, emphatically swaying her hips in her tight fitting white shorts, disappeared into the kitchen. Nick, busy looking around the apartment, missed her little show. True to her word, she returned a moment later carrying a tray with two cups of coffee, cream, sugar, and a plate with four huge chocolate chip cookies.

"I hear Dana's missing. I should have known something was wrong when she didn't come home last night."

Nick was delighted to see the coffee. "Thank you. I could use a cup of coffee about now." He sat on the cream colored, supple leather sofa never thinking that it might not be a safe place.

Lucy, in her very low cut square neck top, set the tray down giving Nick a clear view of her breasts. Normally Nick would have appreciated the effort however blatant. Today was just not a good day for that. Lucy was a lovely blond cougar and had a shapely figure, but, again, he was not turned on by blonds. Thanks to his blond childhood playmate who had bullied him. He just could not get over it and probably never would.

Nick made his coffee and took a sip. "This is good."

Lucy sat down beside him—right next to him, thigh to thigh. The heat from her shapely thigh penetrated through the lightweight thickness of his jeans. Nick tried to inch into the corner of the sofa, but he had nowhere to go, short of sitting on the arm of the sofa.

"Thank you. I get it from Mike and Walt's over on Beacon Avenue. The cookies are from there too." She chuckled and gave a little wave of her hand, "I'm hopeless when it comes to baking. There, now, you know my secret."

Nick was tempted to try a cookie. *What was the matter with him? He should have eaten at the deli. He never took any food offered by witnesses.* Chocolate chip was his favorite. They looked so good. Hoping they were not drugged, he took a huge bite. He chewed quickly and washed it down with a swallow of coffee. "I don't have much time. When was the last time you saw Dana?" The cookie was delicious. He took another big bite while Lucy thought.

She lightly touched the tip of her tongue to her bright red lips, "Let me think." Lucy tapped her full lower lip with a matching red polished nail, "Tuesday." She sipped her coffee then slowly licked her upper lip with the tip of her tongue.

Without a word, Lucy's hand stretched toward his face. He felt as much fear as if he was facing a fully loaded cocked pistol. As her hand approached his face, Nick backed away as far as he could get, which was only a few inches. Lucy used her thumb to lightly brush a cookie crumb from the corner of his mouth. He gave a half-chuckle when he realized that was all she was trying to do.

Lucy, upset that her efforts to entice him were failing miserably, noticed that in spite of his obvious reluctance, his lips twitched to touch her thumb. Maybe with a little more perseverance she could win him over, but for now she would back off. With a little half-smile and posing coyly, she asked, "Skittish, aren't we?"

Nick coughed, "Ah, personal space, you know." Lucy was on the prowl and, surprising himself, he was beginning to lose his resistance. He had the urge to kiss her thumb and draw it into his mouth as though they were lovers. Maybe the cookie or coffee was drugged after all. Nick knew he needed to ask his few questions and get out quickly. Taking in a ragged breath, Nick asked, "How'd you know she didn't come home last night?"

"We were supposed to watch a video together last night. Every third Thursday we have movie night with a few friends. Dana did not come. If she can't make it, she calls and she didn't call. I called her and left a message, but haven't heard back."

"Maybe she came home later by herself?"

"I stay awake until two in the morning most nights. I would have heard her use the elevator or the metal stairs outside."

"It's not like her to stay out with another guy?"

"Dana? No!" Lucy leisurely stretched which caused her skimpy top to ride up, giving Nick another generous view of her upper female anatomy.

"Does she have a boyfriend or lover?" Nick asked quickly, unable to take his eyes off her generous cleavage. He had to admit, she kept herself in shape despite her age, whatever it might be. His breathing was becoming a little faster, Nick noticed. This blond just might be his undoing.

"You must be new around here." Lucy leaned over and ran a single highly polished fingernail through Nick's hair, "Or, are you just trying to be coy and find out for yourself if Dana's available?" Lucy changed tactics and rubbed her hand up and down Nick's thigh, going right up to his crotch. "Some men like experienced women. I'm available."

Her brazen announcement surprised him. Nick gulped. Her nearness was beginning to unnerve him as well as give him an exceptionally close view of the tops of her nipples above the skimpy, pastel blue, lacy bra she was wearing. He could feel the unwanted heat in his cheeks and groin. His jeans were snug enough that Lucy would easily notice her success if he could not keep things under control.

With a faint smile, Lucy sat back. She took a sip of coffee, enjoying Nick's obvious discomfiture. She seemed satisfied that she had finally broken through his armor and expected he was ready to give in. Her eyes began to smolder with desire, but Nick could have sworn he saw a glint of mischief in her blue eyes to go with her smug smile. He bet she would be fun to have sex with, if he were interested in older women.

Lucy rested her hand lightly on his thigh as she continued, "Dana barely dates." Her hand slid up closer to his groin. "I've tried to fix her up a few times." A little closer.

Nick quickly glanced down at her hand then back to Lucy's eyes with the slightest pause at her breasts on the way. It was not fair. A man can only take so much.

"She's a homebody. As you know, she's quite lovely. Dana could have any man she wanted." As she talked her hand very slowly moved teasingly upward.

"I wouldn't know. I haven't met her yet." To himself, he wondered how far he was going to let her go and why he was letting her get away with any of it. *'Because you're fascinated and maybe you think you can use this in your criminal psychology thesis. Hey, Stupid, stop before you take her to bed. Okay?'*

Finally, Lucy's hand had reached the crease in his leg and merely had to do a single side step to create a major catastrophe. It did not seem to matter that Nick was not interested. A certain part of his anatomy was responding in ways that he did not want or care to have noticed. Nick took her hand, picked it up, and set it down on her own leg without a word. "I could consider that assaulting an officer and have you arrested."

Lucy's lower lip pouted delicately, but she ignored him as if he had not spoken and leaned in against him which gave him a very good view of her breasts when he turned his head toward her. In her best Southern drawl, she said, "Sweetie, when Dana gives you the cold shoulder like she gives all the men, you come on back and I'll take care of you." She kissed him lightly on the lips and sat back up. "You know where to find me."

He gulped again. Lucy stood up then bent down, pretending to reach for a napkin on the coffee table, deliberately giving Nick one more show. It seemed that every time she moved he could feel his jeans tighten uncomfortably.

"Coffee's good. Thanks for your hospitality. I've got to run." He was glad to know that the kick he had gotten earlier had not destroyed his manhood since it was now misbehaving on its own. He had never had an interest in older women before and saw no reason to start now, but none had ever affected him like Lucy.

Hurriedly, Lucy followed him. As he reached the door, she deliberately stumbled, falling into his surprised arms. An even bigger surprise followed when she kissed him full on the lips, but the biggest surprise was him realizing he was kissing her back.

Nick let go of her and stared at her for a second before he literally ran out the front door to his parked car. He pressed the unlock button on the keychain when he was ten feet away so he could jump right in. He did not want any delays getting out of there. He revved the engine and raced into traffic accompanied by squealing tires and several blaring horns.

Nick headed back toward the station but decided to stop for a bite to eat first. While he was eating, he reviewed the little bit of info he had on Dana. He had almost forgotten he wanted to drive around her patrol area before he went back to the station empty handed. In addition that would give him time to get himself back together.

Dana had a poorer section of town which surprised Nick that she traveled this without a partner. He was glad he was in his own car and not a police cruiser. He had a six-year old blue Chevy

Nova that hid a powerful engine which did not come standard. Its injected 396 cubic inch engine had saved his life on more than one occasion.

Nick traveled down most of the streets on the map getting a feel for the neighborhood. He was not sure there was any point in going to a place called Towers End, but he was curious to see it. It looked like a fairly deserted area, but Dana might have been aware of drug or gang activity in that area.

He turned down a short, rutted dirt road between an abandoned storefront and another vacant building. Nick did not think it would have been possible, but the road got worse the further he went. He passed between two old house trailers and came to a crossroads of sorts. The road straight ahead just faded away into an overgrown field. The one to the right looked like it could be a driveway for an abandoned house trailer.

Nick looked left and decided that part of the road obviously ended at the half-dead willow tree. The part that was still standing was green, but one of its huge branches was lying across the road and dying rapidly in the summer heat. It was hard to tell on the blurred copy of the map, but the tree itself blocked the road from this end. It did look like you could come in from another way, but he did not know that it would make any difference. There was nothing here.

Nick had just turned the car around when a movement caught his eye. Had it been an animal? His car was backed into the overgrown field, so he felt he had some protection from that direction. Out of habit, he glanced in the rearview mirror anyway. It would be easy for a miscreant to hide in the tall mass of overgrown grass and weeds. Nothing stirred in that direction.

He turned off his engine and radio so he could hear better. He listened and heard nothing, no dogs barking or cats meowing. Both house trailers looked abandoned. He thought the whole area looked long dead, but now he worried he may have let his guard down too long. The more he looked, the more he considered that maybe his first impression had been wrong. There was a folded lawn chair leaning against the trailer to his left that looked fairly new.

Nick pulled his pistol out from the small of his back and laid it on the seat beside him, clicking the safety off in the process. Then he leaned forward and rested his arms on the steering wheel. Slowly he studied the yard across the road where he thought he had seen the movement.

The yard had a rusted play set that was in bad shape and did not look like it had been used in years. The only new touch was the vase of orange, yellow, and white plastic flowers in the center of the concrete table. Not too far from the trailer was a large pile of odd size rocks, a couple were boulder size. Nick wondered what plans the owner had for those. Further back behind the trailer was a small shed with its roof half collapsed in and its door was held shut with a piece of rusted twisted wire. A section of aluminum siding was propped up along the front end of the trailer, acting as a skirt, but was it enough to hide a dog, cat or even a human, Nick decided. The movement had been so quick, he was sure it had to have been something fast and small, a bird flying off maybe. Besides, who was desperate enough to live in this area?

A gentle, warm breeze blew. A sheet of torn newspaper blew up with it.

Nick let out his breath. That blow to his privates must have done more damage to his mind than he thought possible. He was seeing running legs when it was only newspaper. Next, he decided he was going to be seeing ghosts or UFOs.

Suddenly his radio came to life. All available officers were to report to the warehouse district on Watering Street. Nick punched it into his GPS and found it was in another county. He got on his phone and called dispatch. Between the static and dead air he got enough to understand that Dana's phone was made active.

Nick gunned the engine. He did not like this area. It gave him the creeps. He did not care about the jostling the car or his body took going over the ruts, but he did care that his male pride was getting a beating. Dana traveled this as part of her regular beat and probably handled it better than he did.

CHAPTER 6

By the time Nick arrived at the scene, there were a dozen police cruisers, four fire trucks and three ambulances, yet it was as quiet as a funeral service. The bomb squad was working on defusing a bomb in a car that was parked in an abandoned warehouse building. Everyone was waiting patiently, but nervously, in the parking lot across the street.

Not quite everyone. Alone, Captain Wells, red faced and obviously mad, paced and fumed. "The idea of him claiming my daughter was a bad cop. I'll kill him personally!"

Nick heard him repeat the same thing over and over as he warily approached. "Is now a bad time?"

"I'll say! The nerve of that guy. Drago left a note." He paused long enough to look around for a certain officer. "Hey, Fisher! Bring that note!"

Fisher quickly did as ordered and promptly left after handing the note to the captain. He slapped it in Nick's hand as if to emphasize his obvious displeasure and disgust. Nick angled it so he could read it without the sun's glare reflecting off the plastic evidence envelope.

This takes care of the last of my old enemies. Now I get to see my youngest daughter and spend time with my family. I'm retiring out of the country, but I'm not telling whose taking my place. I put the bad cop in the trunk with the bomb. She deserved to watch the time count down. You'll find all the evidence at the bus terminal, locker #136. By the way, Dana Morgan put up a good fight. You should be proud of her. Drago

Whew! Nick could understand Captain Wells frustration, a fellow officer was in trouble. "I see your problem." He felt a touch of pride himself. His new partner was a good fighter.

"That note was attached to the left door. The right hand door was partly open, and they didn't find any trip wires, so they went in and got out the four guys that were tied up and gagged. Drago and his men had beat them up and wounded two of them rather badly." Captain Wells looked back at the building before adding, "They've been taken to the hospital already. None of them were seriously wounded. They'll all live."

"She's still alive in that trunk!" His frustration was evident in his tone. He looked at Nick with such a helpless expression that Nick wished he had an answer. "While one team was freeing the men, they could hear the woman in the trunk crying and screaming. It sounded like she was gagged. We've been waiting for ten minutes now for them to figure out how to diffuse the car bomb."

"I'm sure they'll get it soon."

He walked away from the men mumbling, "My Baby, my Baby."

Nick could not make out what the captain was muttering and dismissed it as unimportant since he was walking away. He had other things to worry about, primarily who he could find to help him on his case in Pittsburgh if Dana did not survive. He was running through the blond candidates he had dismissed before when the bomb squad came running out, yelling and screaming, "Take cover!" They were running as fast as they could in their heavy suits, but they could not clear enough distance by the time the bomb exploded. All three of them were blown four to five feet into the air, landing on the hard tarmac, and getting the wind knocked out of them for their valiant effort. Nearby car alarms sounded and glass windows shattered.

After being given the go-ahead, the firefighters ran in to put out the fire, but it was too late to save anyone in the trunk of that car. Body parts, not all easily recognizable at first glance, covered the walls, floor, and remains of the fluorescent lights that hung down from the high ceiling.

The chief pounded the hood of the car they were hiding behind with his fist then buried his face in his hands. Nick could not understand why he was so upset. Nick felt bad because he had wanted to work with Dana and now would not get that chance. Nick put a hand on Captain Wells' shoulder. "Are you okay?"

Before he answered, another officer came by, muttered his condolences, "Sorry about Dana," and kept on walking.

Staring across the street at the building, Captain Wells softly answered, "Thanks." He started walking toward the building.

As he passed by them, fellow officers each quietly offered their condolences. The captain shrugged them off and bulldozed through others that tried to stop him from going to the warehouse. Tears streamed down his cheeks as he steadily walked, eyes facing forward, aimed for the door to the warehouse.

Several officers tried to keep the captain out of the building, but he was not to be deterred. After threatening to fire anyone who tried to stop him, some of whom did not work for the police department or even his county, they relented and let him inside.

It was nearly his undoing. Once inside the building, he dropped to his knees and bellowed in rage. Everyone stopped what they were doing and turned to look at Captain Wells. Finally Captain Bryan Lorring, who was really in charge since this happened in his county, approached and kneeled on one knee beside him.

Captain Lorring spoke softly and slowly, knowing his news needed time to sink in. "Ed, good news. It wasn't Dana inside. The ID in the glove compartment and in her purse, both of which surprisingly stayed intact, say it was Officer Marilyn King. I've had my eye on her for a few weeks now, but I guess Drago put it together faster than I did. I've already sent someone to the bus depot to get the evidence he says is in the locker."

Captain Wells looked at him rather dumbfounded for a moment then broke out with a huge grin. He wiped his cheeks with the backs of his hands as he stood up. "Thanks. That's the best news I've had in two days. I'm sorry that you lost an officer." He vigorously shook hands with his long time friend and fellow officer.

Towers End

Carefully, Megan counted her steps back out of the woods again. She counted slowly and out loud. As soon as she reached her yard she ran over to the willow tree because the phone worked there the last time. She pressed 9-1-1 again. The operator answered, but this time it was a male voice. Men still scared Megan.

Half afraid, she barely squeaked out all the information needed. The operator was trying to write down what he heard. He guessed a young child was calling for a parent in trouble. The connection was terrible and full of static.

All he got were the words *Anna, help, end, blood* and *Megan.* He was a fairly new operator, having been there only three months, and the word 'blood' panicked him somewhat, mainly because of the fact it was such a young child calling. As his voice became louder trying to overcome the static, and more urgent trying to elicit the needed information from the reticent Megan, her voice became softer. She rapidly spit out everything and hung up.

He checked the number and called back. He got a recording informing him that number was no longer in service and notified the police of the call.

The operator's loud, agitated voice had scared Megan a little, but this was an important mission, and she struggled to overcome her fear. Megan had been relieved that she had talked normally and did not talk baby talk. She was sure she had told him everything that the police woman had said to say. Satisfied, she hung up and dropped the phone into her dress pocket. Megan was sure they would come this time and she had a lot to do. Megan never realized she talked too softly at times.

That part completed, Megan went inside the trailer to finish the rest of her mission. She was glad to see Tom sleeping. He was not snoring, but the television was loud enough she knew that it would help cover any noise she made. Megan went to her room and put her twin size fairy blanket on the floor. "The fairies will protect us, Mary Alice." Megan heaved a big sigh. "I'm a big girl. I can do this by myself." She threw her bed pillow onto the blanket.

Cautiously she peeked around the corner of the door to make sure Tom had not moved. He was still sitting with his head thrown back and his eyes closed. Megan tiptoed into her mother's bedroom and shut the door. She did not want Tom to see her in case he woke up.

Last summer she had gotten into her mother's bedside table and found the gun. Her mother had panicked and gotten mad at her and spanked her. Megan did not want another spanking. Later, her mother had explained that she kept it there to protect her from bad men. She had instructed Megan never to touch it again and made Megan promise she never would, but Miss Dana needed it to keep the bad man away. Megan rationalized with her best five-year-old logic that since her mommy said that's what the gun was for, it would be okay to borrow it and give it to the police lady.

When she pulled open the drawer it squeaked loudly. Megan stayed very still, but was ready to dart under the bed if she needed to hide. She waited, holding her breath. When she did not hear Tom's pounding feet coming after her or hear his loud yelling, calling her names for waking him, Megan gasped in a breath. On tiptoe, she went to the bedroom door and slowly pulled it open a few inches to peek out. Tom was still sitting on the couch. "He must be really sound asleep. I don't think he's moved at all." Megan told her doll. Quietly, Megan closed the door and went back to work.

She reached to the back of the drawer and took out the large, heavy blue and white box. It had the big letters Tampax on the outside. Megan could say the letters, but did not know what they spelled. Her Mommy told her that Tom would never touch that box because of that word. Megan thought it was odd that a silly word could scare Tom. Megan thought that the next time Tom was mean to her maybe she would yell that word at him and see if it scared him.

She looked inside to make sure the gun and box of bullets were all there. She did not know how many bullets it would take to kill a bad man, but she wanted to have enough. Curious, Megan took out a bullet. It glistened and shined. She loved the gold color. Suddenly there was a noise.

Quickly, Megan darted under the bed sliding her treasure under with her. She waited. No pounding footsteps came her way. Relieved, Megan inhaled and accidently breathed in some dust. She coughed and dropped the bullet. She put her hand over her mouth to stop the coughing, but it did not help. She started coughing and sneezing so much that her eyes watered and she could not see. Megan slid out from under the bed.

She wiped her face off on the bed covers and looked under the bed for the bullet, but could not see it. It was too dark and her eyes were still watery. She peeked out the bedroom door and saw that Tom was still sleeping, so she did not know what she heard and decided it was safe to go back to work. Carefully, Megan tucked the top of the box closed and closed the drawer again, but she could not get it to shut all the way.

Next, Megan got two towels and one washcloth. She could reach only the ones on the lower shelf, so she hoped the police lady did not care about the color. She piled those on top of her fairy blanket and dragged everything to the kitchen.

She opened the refrigerator and took out all six bottles of water. Megan deliberated for a minute and took two cans of soda, too. She made two peanut butter and jelly sandwiches for them and put them in her lunch bag along with two packs of cookies. She pulled out the vegetable bin and found two apples which she put in the lunch bag.

Megan worked as quietly as she could and often glanced toward Tom who never moved. "He must really be tired," she whispered to Mary Alice. She went to the tall narrow cabinet beside the refrigerator that had the canned goods. She took two lunch packs of applesauce and four of the fruit cups.

She put the lunch bag on top and tried to make a bundle that she could carry back into the woods. It was too heavy and much too big for her small hands. Megan wanted to cry. She needed help. Maybe Tom would help this time.

Timidly, Megan approached Tom, afraid he would open his eyes and yell 'Boo!'. He liked to scare her that way sometimes. She took a deep breath. She had to be a big girl to help the police lady. Bravely, she stood in front of him, but his name came out timidly, "Tom."

He did not move or open his eyes. She thought he must not have heard her and called louder, "Tom!". Still he did not open his eyes to look at her or yell like he always did. Megan lightly patted his knee and quickly jumped back. His leg did not fly out to kick her. Normally, whenever he was touched, he jerked awake and raised his hand as if to hit her.

Megan whispered to Mary Alice. "See that little red spot on his forehead and there's blood coming out his ear. He must have a bad earache or headache, or maybe both. Remember when Mommy got a bad headache and had to take something and lie down until it went away? I got that splinter in my hand and couldn't wake her to take care of it. Maybe Tom took some of that same strong medicine.

"I have an idea!" Megan exclaimed loudly, immediately clamping a hand over her mouth and running to hide under the table, her safety zone. Tightly holding onto her doll, she anxiously waited for Tom's angry approach. All remained quiet.

Again she whispered to her doll. "I don't think he's going to wake up. Let's go. I remembered we have a suitcase with little wheels. I can put everything in that and drag it back to Miss Dana." Megan went back to her mother's room and looked under the bed. She had to crawl under a little ways to reach the handle and drag it out.

Megan fit everything inside the case, although her blanket stuck out around the zippered edge. She wadded it up smaller and managed to zip it part of the way around. Megan felt like she had been gone a long time and needed to get back quickly. She did not hear any sirens yet and did not know how long it should take for them to come. Then she worried that maybe they had come already and taken Miss Dana away.

Megan did not worry about how much noise she made now since Tom was not going to wake up. She set Mary Alice down while she worked. The suitcase had a strap handle so she let the suitcase slide down the steps while she held on. Once she got the case to the bottom Megan went back and got her doll.

She had just reached the end of the house trailer when she heard the sound of a car coming. The engine had almost the same rumbling sound as those mean boys that liked to drive by and throw garbage at her.

Megan raced with her precious cargo to her hiding place under the trailer. She dropped her doll and had to go back for it. She grabbed her doll by one arm and the rest of her went flying in the breeze. Megan could see out over the piece of tin sheeting, but knew no one could see her. She watched the blue car stop at the corner. It was the same color as the one those mean boys drove, but there was a strange man behind the wheel. He looked a lot older than those boys.

The man looked around. Megan stayed hidden, afraid to ask him for help because of the rumbling sound of his car. She wondered why he was taking so long to leave. A paper flitted up in the air and the car roared off.

Dana licked her dry lips, wishing she heard sirens coming her way. She heard sirens several times, but they always faded off into the distance. Drago was getting his way after all. He may have said he would not kill her, but that did not mean he would not leave her to die on her on. Why hadn't she thought to ask Megan to bring back a paperclip or bobby pin so she could pick the lock on the handcuffs? She had hoped she might live through this, but her five year old angel was just not enough help.

Dana dozed off and on in spite of fighting hard to stay awake. She had no idea how long Megan had been gone. It could have been five minutes or two hours, wishing she had thought to look at her watch when Megan left. Then she thought what good would that do but make the time drag by more slowly.

Looking around for something she could pick the lock with Dana wondered how much longer she could survive, certainly not another night. She was hungry, but dehydration was the primary problem. Thankfully it had stopped raining, but now the myriad of bugs were a nuisance. She moved a few stones and pieces of debris, but had no luck finding any kind of wire to pick the lock. Bored, Dana soon found herself dozing again.

Softly, a voice called her name. Dana, enjoying a pleasant dream, reluctantly opened her eyes and was relieved to see Megan standing there. Dana smiled, "Hi. Did you get through on the phone?"

Proudly, with a big smile, Megan answered, "I did. I gave them everything like you told me. They'll be here soon."

Dana's heart sank. Something was wrong. She was sure Megan had been gone long enough for an ambulance or another officer to have gotten here. They did not get the info like Megan thought. Maybe they were just having a hard time finding her in the woods. Maybe they were simply too deep in the woods to hear the sirens.

"It's all dirt and stones here where you're at. I'm going to put my bw-blanket on the grass right here so it'll stay cleaner." Megan busied herself with unpacking. First she got a bottle of water and handed it to Dana. "Mommy likes this brand because the bottles are easy for me to open."

Dana took the bottle, but could not manage to open it. She put it between her thighs, but the bottle would not stay still while she twisted the cap with her left hand. When she placed it between her knees Dana discovered another painful bruise where Drago's cane had whacked her. She pulled her pant leg up and saw a nasty looking bluish purple area on the inside of her left knee with a narrow laceration transecting it. It hurt too bad to apply enough pressure to hold the bottle in place to open it. No matter how she tried to hold it with her hands to twist it open, her right thumb was too painful and swollen to help.

After all her attempts had failed, Dana finally had to interrupt Megan's work, "I had to fight the bad man and I think he broke my thumb. Can you help me?"

"Okay." Megan stopped her careful unloading of the suitcase and walked over to Dana. She easily twisted open the bottle cap and handed it back to Dana.

Dana choked a little in her eagerness to get those first few swallows down. The cool water tasted like heaven to her.

Megan had started toward the suitcase, but turned around and came back to Dana. She gently patted her back and rubbed it. "Careful. My mommy says she does this for her patients that choke on their drinks. Is it helping?"

"Yes, thank you," Dana smiled. "Do you plan to be a nurse when you grow up?"

"Maybe." She stopped rubbing Dana's back and stood still for a moment before crossing her arms and doing a little hip wiggle. In a soft whisper she said, "I thought I might be a real doctor."

Dana made a contemplative face, putting a finger to her chin. "I think you would make a fine doctor."

Megan's face broke into a huge smile. "Thanks!" She skipped away to finish unpacking the suitcase. "I brung a pillow for you." Megan got it out and kneeled beside Dana.

"Thank you. I can use that to rest on the pipe when I don't want to lie down. Please, I've told you to call me Dana. We're friends. It looks like you brought a lot. Did you bring the towel?"

"I got two towels and a washcloth."

"Good girl." Dana licked her lips. They were still dry and chapped. She gulped down half the bottle of water before stopping. She knew she should go sparingly with the water, but she was so thirsty, it was hard to resist.

Megan liked the police lady's smile. She got out both towels and asked, "I hope you don't care about the color." She held them for Dana to pick which one she wanted.

"They're both pretty." Dana pretended to pick which one she wanted. It really did not matter to her.

Megan's head jerked up, "I hear sirens!" Dana did not hear any, but trusted Megan's younger ears.

"I knew they would come this time." Megan jumped up and down. The sound faded as did her bright smile and excitement. "I guess they weren't coming here."

Dana used the little that was left of the water in the bottle to wet one corner of the towel. Both towels were thin and worn. With the cool water, she gently dabbed at the bruises around her eyes and wiped her split lip. With the dry end, she blotted her face dry. Even without the benefit of a mirror, she could tell her left eye was swollen because some of her vision was blocked. The water was a big help. She felt some of her strength returning. Hunger she could deal with.

Dana commented, "I'm afraid I'm a mess."

"Don't be afraid. I brung my fairy bw-blanket. The fairies will protect us."

Dana had to smile. Megan was so sweet and loved being helpful. Maybe she would survive after all.

"What else did you bring?"

"I made us each a peanut butter and jelly sandwich in case you were hungry. I got applesauce and fruit cups."

Dana was so happy to hear that she could have jumped for joy. "I'm starving. Are you ready to eat?"

"I remembered the gun, too."

"Could I see it?" As much as she wanted to eat, Dana wanted to see the pistol more.

"We need to eat first." Megan handed out sandwiches, making sure Mary Alice got her small corner. Dana never realized a peanut butter and jelly sandwich could taste so good. She tried to take her time, not wanting to upset her stomach by eating too fast.

"Thank you. That was a good sandwich." The peanut butter was a thick glob in the middle and the jelly ran over the edges, but to Dana's starving stomach it was a gourmet meal.

"I learned how to make them when I was four years old." Megan held up four fingers so Dana could count them. I can make a good peanut butter sandwich, too, but I like peanut butter and jelly best.

Dana laughed. "I don't think I learned until I was six."

Once their meager meal was finished, Megan reached into the suitcase and pulled out a Tampax box, carrying it like it was heavy which confused Dana. Her heart sank because she needed a weapon not a tampon. Maybe because of all the blood Megan thought she was on her period. *What does a five year old know about periods?* Dana mused. *I didn't learn until I was eleven.*

Megan sat on the ground beside her and opened the box. Much to Dana's surprise and delight, inside was a small black pistol and a box of cartridges. Dana picked up the pistol and sighed with relief. She was happy to have a means of defense at last.

She checked the pistol. It was not loaded. She opened the box of cartridges and readily noted that only one bullet was missing. "There's one missing. Do you know anything about it?"

"No." Megan's rapid fire answer was a sure indication of guilty knowledge.

"Megan, Sweetie, you're not in any trouble, I'm just curious. It's odd that only one is gone."

Megan put the tip of her finger in her mouth and lowered her head, holding onto Mary Alice for reassurance. "I was just looking at it and I dropped it. I tried to find it. Honest, I did, but it

48

was dark under the bed and I couldn't see it, but you still have enough to kill the bad man, don't you, or do I need to go back and look for it?" Megan finally stopped to take a breath.

"Why were you under the bed?"

"I thought Tom was coming so I hid me and everything under the bed."

"He didn't catch you?"

"No."

"Good." Dana was right handed, but had taught herself to shoot left handed as well. She got a feel for the light weight of the small caliber pistol. It took a bit of effort, but she was finally able to get it loaded.

"I'll help," Megan offered, setting her doll down.

"No, Dear. This is dangerous and I don't want you get hurt. Why don't you sit on the grass and play for a few minutes until I get done?"

Dana made sure the safety was on and slipped the weapon into her pants pocket. "We'll be really safe now. Between your fairies and the gun nothing can get us. Tom didn't give you any trouble, did he?"

"No, I tried to ask him for help, but he was sw-sleeping real hard. He didn't wake up. I think he had a bad headache. My mommy got a bad headache once and had to take some medicine that made her sleep. She didn't get a red spot like Tom did. He's got a red circle right here," Megan pointed to her forehead. "I saw some blood in his ear, too."

Dana groaned more from dread than pain. She would bet that Drago had been to their trailer and killed Tom during some time that Megan was in the woods with her. Megan would be safer with her than going back to the house trailer to wait for her mother. She wished she had some way to warn Megan's mother.

"Are you hurting again?" Megan asked with her honest five-year-old concern.

Not wanting to alarm Megan, Dana opted for a partial, but honest lie, since she was having some pain, "I am." She wished she had some ice for her thumb. The constant dull, throbbing pain was very distracting.

Megan picked up her doll and held her tightly, doing her little hip wiggle. "I should have brung you some pain pills. I'm sorry."

"No, that's all right, sweetie, I need to stay awake so I couldn't have taken them anyway."

Megan's face brightened. "I'm still hungry. Can I eat my cookies?"

"Sure," That sandwich had taken the edge off her hunger, but some cookies would be great. Who knew when they would get to eat again. Dana was not going to let Megan leave her side. "but do you have enough to share?"

"I do. I brung a pack for you, too."

"Thank you. The correct word is brought. What else do you have to drink?"

"I have water and one soda for each of us."

"I'd like a soda for a change. How much water do you have?"

"A six pack."

"That's good." To herself Dana thought they might need to conserve since she had no idea when they would be rescued.

They sat in silence for a few minutes while they nibbled on their cookies.

Megan was happy to stay here. "It's nicer here than I thought it would be. Tom always watched movies that made the woods look so dark and mean. People did bad things in them and sometimes they," she leaned in closer to Dana and whispered, "died."

"I loved to hike in the woods back in my hometown. They were green and cool like these, but they had tall hills that were fun to climb. We had a few injuries, but no one died."

"Did you see any fairies or butterflies?"

"Lots of butterflies, but I never saw a single fairy. I understand they're very hard to find."

Megan giggled. "They are, but some people must have seen them or they wouldn't know how to draw them in the picture books."

"Ah, very true. Maybe we'll get lucky and see some. I noticed you have a little trouble with your L's and R's."

"I'm getting better. I have a special teacher that helps me. I start the big school next year and Mommy says I need to talk right or the other kids will pick on me."

"Some might. When I was younger, my front teeth were kind of big and had a large gap between them. I used to whistle when I talked, especially when I said something that started with an *S*. I got picked on a lot."

"Is that why you became a police lady?"

"What do you mean?"

"So you could shoot those mean kids that picked on you."

Dana laughed, "No, Sweetie, I wanted to be a police officer because my daddy and granddaddy were police officers. Can you keep a secret?

"Yes, me and Mary Alice are good at keeping secrets."

"I want to be an FBI agent."

"Is that better than a police w-lady?"

"Ooh, that's a tough call. I guess it depends on who you ask. Both jobs are important. An FBI agent gets to travel more and that's what I want. That's why I had my teeth fixed so I could talk and look right."

"Let me see."

Dana bared her front teeth.

"I don't see nothing wrong. You have white straight teeth."

"Thank you. I spent tons of money to have them fixed."

"Oh." Megan finished her cookies and half the can of soda. "I'm gonna go play." Megan danced around in the grassy area, humming and pretending she was with her fairy friends. When she tired of that, she sat on her blanket for a while and talked to Mary Alice.

"I'm gonna go potty," Megan announced.

"Stay close by. I don't know where that bad man is. If he's smart, he's long gone."

Megan found a tree to hide behind to take care of her urinating. She walked back to Dana, holding her doll by one arm. "I'm getting tired. I need to go back to my house to take a nap."

Dana did not like that idea at all. She was positive Tom had been shot and did not think it was safe for Megan to be in the trailer. Drago was known for using explosives and may have planted a bomb in the trailer. She did not like the fact that she could not contact Megan's mother. Then she remembered the phone.

"Can I see the phone?"

"Sure." Megan pulled it out of her pocket and handed it to her.

Dana checked. Not only could she not get any bars, it was out of minutes. They had made their last call for help.

"Sweetheart, that's a long walk. Why don't you lie down with me? We can use those towels you brought for covers and lie on the blanket. I have a wristwatch so I can watch the time. When it's almost time for your mother to get home, I'll wake you up. How about that?" Dana suggested.

Megan rubbed her eyes and yawned, "Okay, I'm too tired to walk all the way back. It was a long way."

Megan got the other towel out of her suitcase and carried it back to Dana. It covered mostly her shoulders, enough to take care of the evening chill. Being July, Dana knew it would not get too cold; she prayed it was not due to rain.

Dana slid the handcuffs down the pole so she could lie down. "Megan, come lie on my right side. That will help us keep each other warm." Dana's primary reason for that was to have her left arm free in case she needed to defend them. She slid the towel over to cover Megan.

Megan curled up in the crook of the police officer's right arm. "You're sweet like my mommy. I've had a busy day and am really, really tired. I can't wait to tell my Mommy everything." Her voice faded as she finished her sentence and she fell soundly asleep.

Dana fought hard to stay awake. If a rescue team came, she needed to be awake to respond to their calling for them. These woods were a big place. She watched Megan's steady, slow breathing for a few minutes and realized quickly that was a big mistake as her eyelids fluttered closed. She tried humming, concentrating on the report she had to write, where Drago was headed and what his next move might be. When her eyelids clamped shut again she tried doing math problems in her head, but the numbers faded before she could think of the answer. Her brain was too tired to concentrate. In the distance, she saw a helicopter flying and wondered if it was looking for her. It never came in their direction. She fought to keep her eyelids open. Everything she tried was to no avail. Dana fell asleep almost as fast as Megan did.

CHAPTER 7

Nick dreaded going back to the precinct without Dana or even a clue of her whereabouts. He considered himself a good detective as evidenced by his excellent record with the FBI for the past six years. Now he could not even find his own partner who probably desperately needed him.

After parking, Nick sat in his car thinking of what he may have missed. He had not called her parents. Her mother lived in Oregon with her second husband. Would she have gone that far? How pissed was she? Was it simply a temper tantrum?

Absently he stared out the front windshield. Everyone was going about their daily routine again. All the excitement was over. No one cared about his predicament or Dana's dilemma. Where was she? He pounded the dashboard in frustration. Was this a big elaborate joke on the supposed new rookie? If it was, he wasn't laughing.

Finally Nick got out of his car. How slowly could he drag his feet? Should he check all the local brothels? Maybe the zoo? He did not know anything about this town. It was not that big. Where would Dana hide? Would she be holed up in a bar? Was she simply hiding, venting off some steam with a few brews, or was she in deep trouble desperately needing his help?

Nick's gut was telling him Dana was in trouble. Bad trouble. The profile info he had told him that Dana was not the kind of cop to pull any kind of a silly stunt. She might have shown up late and given him the cold shoulder all day, maybe even for a week, but she would have done her duty.

Her neighbors and coworkers thought highly of her, too. When his gut was talking, Nick had learned to listen. It had saved his life a few times. He was the fourth generation in his family to be in law enforcement, although he did not stay on the police force as his great grandfather on down to his father had done. His grandfather and father both told him stories of how listening to their gut had saved their life. Dana was in trouble. He was sure of it. He hated that he was helpless to do anything for her.

While his mind still raced, Nick held the door for an elderly man coming out. He was doing everything he could to delay talking to the captain. This did not bode well for him. Maybe this was a test to see how good a detective he truly was. Deciding to try one last thing, he stopped at dispatch. "Any news? Anything? I'll take any oddity."

"No news about Dana. We did get three crank 9-1-1 calls, and, apart from two minor traffic accidents, a convenience store robbery, and a domestic dispute, there's been nothing else. It's been a relatively quiet day. We're all getting worried about Dana." She handed him the printout with the past two day's calls.

Nick sat in a nearby vacant chair and reviewed what he had. Jasmine had already given him yesterday's calls and the 9-1-1 report as well. There was Dana's call at the end of her shift. There were a number of gaps, but it looked like she was simply checking out. *How chatty was she normally when she checked out?*

Today's crank call list had one that piqued his interest. With the numerous static-filled gaps it was hard to hear according to the report filed, but it had two names, Anna and Megan. The operator noted that it was a very young child calling. EMS and the 9-1-1 operator both had tried to call back, but no one answered the phone either time. It was not a phone they could trace. It was put on the police report and forgotten. The name Anna was close to Dana, but did not necessarily mean anything. He had no idea who Megan was. Nick did not go any further with that call.

Nick was beginning to feel less and less like a detective. He slouched in the chair, put his head back and closed his eyes. In his street clothes, he looked more like a guy waiting to be booked than a fellow officer. The only difference was the badge clipped to his belt and the pistol tucked in the waistband at his back.

Think, Nick, think. What happened to your six years of experience? Being in an unknown area should not have this effect on you. Maybe that blow to your balls did more to rattle your brain than you thought.

What's next? Call her parents. See if she did go to Oregon. Try not to worry her parents if she isn't there. Next. Talk to her coworkers. Next. Check her bank account. Oops, already did that. Next. Check the airport, taxi, train and bus stations. Next… It was blank after that 'next'. There was not another 'next'.

None of that seemed right. Dana would not have left town over this. He did not know Dana other than from her profile. He knew that what was on paper did not always match the real life person. Yet somehow he knew that Dana was a dedicated police officer. Nick's brain knew that.

What have you got, Nick? You've got no evidence of anything being wrong. There was no sign of a struggle in her apartment. So far there's been no ransom demand nor her body turning up anywhere. So why is my gut telling me that Dana is in trouble? Is my gut wrong? Could it be that it's failing me after all these years? Maybe it's nothing more than indigestion or constipation this time.

Nick got up, taking the list of calls with him. He passed a waste can and considered throwing the report in, but did not. He guessed it made him feel like he had something instead of being completely empty handed.

It was six-thirty. Dana was a little over four hours past due for her shift. How long had she been in trouble? Four hours? Eight hours? Twenty-four hours? If it had been that long, how much longer could she hold on?

Nick decided he would pass on his bad news, see if anyone else had had any luck, and get a bite to eat before patrolling her route again. He did not feel so much tired as defeated. Maybe he should take a nap before heading out again. Maybe he would have better luck after resting, or downing a few beers.

As Nick walked into the captain's office with his head down and mumbling to himself, 'Your gut's telling you there's trouble and you know you won't rest until you find her.'

Before Nick bothered to raise his head, Captain Ed Wells looked up from his paperwork and loudly questioned, "Well?"

Nick took in a deep breath and started listing his failures. "Her downstairs neighbor said she didn't come home last night. I haven't called her parents yet. There's no sign of her around town. She hasn't been at the Y in one week or the library for two months. Her body wasn't in the trash bin outside her apartment building. There's not been any unusual activity with her bank account and no ATM withdrawals in the past three days."

Captain Wells stood, put his hands behind his back and stared out the window while Nick talked. When the captain turned around, he was wearing a frown. Not the response Nick hoped for. He really wanted this all to be a joke on him. He thought the captain would laugh and Dana would pop out of a hidden door, crying *Gotcha!*

They stared at each other in silence for an agonizing few seconds before the captain finally spoke, "There's no need to call her parents. I already did. Her mother hasn't talked to her since last week. She's catching the next flight out. I couldn't convince her there was nothing to worry about at this point. She informed me that if Dana didn't show up for work, it was not by her choice, and I'd better have the entire force out looking for her. I didn't tell them I had only the new guy looking."

"Wait a minute. Did I hear right? I'm the only one looking for Officer Morgan?"

Captain Wells stretched his aching back, "I didn't have much choice. I'm down three officers. Johnson is out with a broken leg and Gardner is on Family Leave. His father passed away yesterday and he's in Florida. Williams started her maternity leave this morning. She's due in two weeks. I let her work as long as I could. I couldn't have her driving around and go into labor" He sat on the corner of his desk. "The rest are out on patrol, but they're keeping their eyes out for Dana. Sergeant Douglas drove around part of Dana's route and checked in with some of her contacts until five when he went off-duty. Officer Marks went around another part of her route and checked with a few contacts that he was familiar with. They both came up empty handed. He's still out there, but he's having a busy evening with fender benders. He's had four back to back. Do you think he's jinxed?" The Captain added with a little chuckle.

Nick gave a little smile and shrugged his shoulders. Any other time, he might have come back with a comical one-liner, just not today.

The Captain's smile faded quickly, too. He stared at his shoes briefly before continuing. "I really thought Dana was just a little pissed about the schedule change and would show up late. She's a good officer and knows her duty. This is not like her at all. I planned to tell her about her promotion to sergeant today. I haven't told her anything about your assignment or why you're really here like we agreed according to our phone conversation. Dana's got brains. She deserves a chance to better herself. This is a good move for her even though I'll miss her."

"She'd be stupid not to take the offer, in my opinion. No insult intended against you, Sir. Whether she wants to work with me on this temporary assignment is entirely up to her."

"Wait until you find out how great she is," Captain Wells smiled proudly.

Nick said with a smile, "Too bad we can't assign her to look for herself."

"I thought we had something when her phone went active. Now I have to suspect that Drago had a hand in her disappearance. Her detective skills helped capture him even though…" The captain's phone rang. While he talked on the phone, Nick looked over the 9-1-1 call sheets again looking for anything he might have missed the first time. Nothing new caught his eye. He felt like he was chasing windmills. The call was brief and the captain hung up as a thought occurred to Nick.

"Her car!" Nick exclaimed. "It just dawned on me! I never looked for her car!"

Captain Wells waved his hand. "No need to bother. It's been in the shop for the past four days. She's been using her cruiser until it's fixed. Don't bother to ask about that either. It's not rigged with the latest and greatest. We can't hit a button and tell where the cruiser's at." He heaved a huge sigh, "Wish I could. We've upgraded two of them. Next year hers was slated to be done. I've put in for a grant. If I get that, I might be able to go all out and have six vehicles completely decked out."

"What did you plan to tell me about Dana's detective skills? She helped capture this Dragon Man?"

"She wasn't in on the actual capture," Captain heaved in deep breath as though readying to tell a lengthy story. "Everyone was looking for Drago. She did some deductive reasoning which had to have some female logic in it because it made little sense to some of us guys." Another deep breath passed through his barrel chest. "I figured if she wanted to make a fool of herself, I could stand a little embarrassment. I let her call the guys in Richmond County with her idea. They caught him that day." He beamed again with renewed pride. "I couldn't have been prouder. Now get out. Go back to work."

Just then a frantic woman came flying in the front door yelling, "My daughter's missing! I need help! My little girl's gone!"

The captain threw down the papers he had just picked up and exclaimed, "Great! Just what I needed. I have an officer missing and now I have an Amber Alert. What's next?"

He picked up a clipboard that held the duty roster, quickly scanned it and bellowed, "Tianna!"

A disembodied female voice answered back, "Restroom, Sir. She'll be back in a few minutes."

Captain Wells pulled open a file drawer and quickly flipped through the folders. He snatched out a form and handed it to Nick. "Here. Go over to the empty office across the hall and start this form. When Tianna gets back she can take over, but you'll probably have it done before then. She has IBS or something," he paused then waved his hand in dismissal of a notion, "anyway, her bathroom breaks are ten to twenty minutes."

"What is it?"

"A missing child report." Nick looked at the form and left the office. It was not hard to find the distraught mother. She was still pacing, anxiously waiting for someone to help her.

"Hello, I'm Officer Coburn. Come with me." He guided her gently with his right hand at the middle of her back and his left hand, still holding the pale yellow form, swinging toward the office door.

"Where are we going?"

"We have a form to fill out to start the Amber Alert," Nick answered simply.

"Fill out a form? My daughter's missing! We have to go find her!"

"We will. Are you sure she's missing and not just at a friend's house?"

"There are no neighbors for her to go to. We live in Towers End. She's only five."

"I see. Okay. Have a seat." Nick pointed to a chair as he walked around to the other side of the desk and sat down. He took a pen out of the pencil cup and asked, "Child's name?"

"Megan Smith."

"Address."

"Number 1224 Towers End Road."

Megan…end. The words clicked in Nick's mind. Sheri rambled on with the rest of the address, but Nick suddenly stopped writing and slapped the pen down on the paper. He jumped up and held up his hand, "Wait a minute." He ran out of the office.

Sheri screamed at him, "Come back! Where are you going? What could be more important than finding my daughter?"

"That's what I'm doing." Nick ran into the captain's office. He was on the phone but put his hand over the receiver. "Do you have the info for the Amber Alert already?"

"We may not need it? Where are those papers I left on your desk?"

"Probably right where you left them. I think I set that folder on top of them."

Nick picked up the folder and there were his papers. He snatched them up and ran back to the other office.

He laid out the two sheets side by side that had the two 9-1-1 calls he was most interested in. "You live at Towers End?" He circled the word 'end' on the one sheet.

"That's right," Sheri answered somewhat confused by his excited agitation.

"Your daughter's name is Megan?"

"Yes," her answer was slow and the single syllable word was questioning, drawn out.

Nick circled that word on the second call. *What if Dana had stopped there for some reason and was hurt? What if Megan was the child that called? What if Anna was supposed to be Dana instead? Why did it take this long to report the little girl missing? Where was Dana all this time? Was this woman a criminal or a victim?*

Nick was not going to waste any more time. His instinct was telling him that Dana and Megan were together, now, at Towers End. It made sense. As much as he hated the thought of having to return to that creepy place, he knew he had no choice.

"What's your name?"

"Sheri, Sheri Smith," she answered still puzzled.

Nick ran around the desk and grabbed her hand, "Let's go. I think your daughter is still there, probably in the woods with my partner."

Sheri pulled her hand away. "Megan would never go into the woods. She's deathly afraid of them."

Ignoring Sheri, Nick called from the doorway, "Chief, I need a cruiser."

"I need that paperwork so I can get that Amber Alert out. What are you doing?"

"I know where both the little girl and Dana are. Dana's gotta be hurt or she'd be calling instead of a little girl. Can I have a cruiser so I can go fast with lights and siren? I'll even ask with a pretty please."

"Tell dispatch it's okay, but you'd better be right!"

Nick used his long legs to their full advantage to get to dispatch quickly. Sheri had no choice but to follow, practically running to keep up. Nick was given the keys to a cruiser. "I need you to ride with me."

"Okay," Sheri was caught up in Nick's excitement. She did not think he could be right but was willing to trust his judgment.

Nick found the cruiser easily. Before pulling out, he asked Sheri, "Is there another way in to where you live? I went by there earlier today and everything looked like it was a dead end. I should have seen Dana's police cruiser."

"I haven't seen one unless its on the other side of the willow tree. It's a huge tree and one of its branches broke during a recent storm. It covers most of the road."

"Then that's the way I want to go in—on the other side of that tree." Nick had to think a minute. "I went down Curry Road and ended up at what I thought was a dead end with two abandoned house trailers. I saw that willow tree."

A blush of embarrassment reddened Sheri's cheeks. She softly answered, "That willow tree is in my yard. Truthfully, it's Tom's place. I'm planning to move out soon."

Nick glanced at her as he turned the ignition on and felt like he should apologize but could not think of any appropriate words. His mother had raised him to always be polite, especially to a woman. Yet he found he was often chewing on his size thirteen shoe. "I'm sorry," meager as it was, finally popped out.

"That's okay, I know it's bad. You're not hurting my sensibilities. If you get on the Bowman Highway, we'll make better time. Take the Highland Pottery Mill Exit. That mill's been closed over ten years now, but they've never changed the exit name."

Nick headed out of the parking lot as she talked. He rode with the lights flashing but did take the liberty to go over the speed limit as much and as often as he could. He gave a short burst when he felt sirens were called for. They rode in silence, keeping the radio on for company.

Everyone was out tonight it seemed to Nick. He gave a blare of the siren at a truck that was reluctant to get out of the way. Before long traffic became too congested for him to speed through without the siren. Nick glanced over at Sheri who had her eyes closed. He guessed she was praying.

Suddenly her soft voice surprised him. "It takes about fifteen minutes to reach the exit. Once we get off the exit, go to the stop sign and make a left. We'll go two more blocks then left, ah, I'm not sure how many blocks it is, four or five maybe. There's an old white frame church on the left with a dark mahogany door. I always look for that. We make a right across from that church. That takes us down to Tom's trailer. It's about two miles down the road."

He felt like he had wasted enough time already. Sheri might have some answers. "Have you noticed anyone or anything unusual around your trailer, anything missing lately?"

Sheri took a moment to think. "No," she started slowly, "unless you think that escaped con might have had something to do with my daughter's missing tea set. Surely he had more valuable things to steal than a child's toy."

"What did the tea set look like?"

"It was simply scraps put together—a cracked coffee carafe, a small plastic plate and the metal lid from a coffee thermos. I'm not sure if the plate is missing."

"The coffee carafe and metal lid sound perfect for a guy hiding out in the woods. He may not have had his own or needed to replace his." He flipped the turn signal on and changed lanes. "It makes me wonder if Drago hadn't been staying in the woods since his escape." He flipped the turn signal on and changed lanes. "Tell me what happened when you came home today. Start with what time you got home."

"I got home at six. I stopped at the store to pick up a few things. Megan wasn't playing in the front yard like she usually is. Sometimes she'll take a nap so I checked in the trailer, but she wasn't in her bed." Sheri started to cry. "Her blanket was missing, too. I stay with a guy, his name is Tom Jenkins. I tried to ask him where Megan was, but he was stoned again and didn't answer." She put her hand to her forehead, "I don't know why I trusted him to watch her. He's drunk most of the time. I called and called for Megan, but she didn't answer me. I looked in all her usual hiding places and couldn't find her. When I couldn't get my cell phone to work, I drove to the police station. Mr. Murphy has a land line phone, but he's been in the hospital for the past week. Maybe I shouldn't have left. Was I wrong?"

"No, it was better to get help first. Who's Mr. Murphy?"

"He lives in the trailer across the road. He was in the hospital for a week and they transferred him to a nursing home three days for therapy."

"Oh," Nick took in a deep breath. "I don't know if I should tell you this or not, but I was down your way earlier, looking for Officer Dana Morgan. I didn't see your daughter in the yard then, but I thought the area was deserted."

Sheri looked at him with her mouth gaping open, not certain how to process that new bit of information. Suddenly she punched his shoulder then buried her face in her hands in a fresh torrent of tears.

Nick let her cry for a minute. He could not imagine the anguish she was feeling. She had no husband to help with the burden and he was a stranger. An official, to boot, and to some, officials were not the kind to be confided in.

Finally he offered, "There are some woods next to your trailer, she could be lost in there."

"Megan's afraid of the woods. She wouldn't go in them. I just know it." Sheri raised her head and wiped her tears. "Megan's never left the yard before. Tom is sometimes a little rough." She took in a breath. "He's mean to both of us. Not that he's ever hit Megan!" she defended him as any good abused girlfriend does. "I made Megan promise to tell me if he ever did. Anyway, we're moving out in September. I've had to save some money for my share of the deposit on a house with one of my coworkers."

Sheri looked at Nick, "Do you think Tom hurt Megan and she ran away?"

"I don't know. It's possible."

Sheri turned her face toward the window and bit her lower lip, letting the tears fall silently.

Nick was sorry he had said anything. He had not meant to say what he did, but it was out before he could stop it. He caught a glimpse of her reflection in the window and saw she was biting her lower lip. Also, he did not believe that Tom had never hit Megan before. Tom probably slapped her a little, threw things at her, and said mean things to her. He had seen it all before, too many times. Any bruises Tom might have caused were explained away as the results of playing. Nick knew the type all too well. Tom most likely threatened Megan that if she told anyone, he would hurt her mother. Megan kept quiet to protect her mother.

At the last minute, Sheri saw the church. Loudly she said, "Turn right here!"

Nick swerved sharply right, causing the cruiser to bump wildly over the curb. Nick continued speeding over the black top, but was forced to slow down when it turned to rough gravel. He turned off the siren, but left on the flashing lights.

"We've hit the two mile mark," Nick said, worried that they had left civilization behind. The last house had been shortly past the turn. All he had seen since then were open fields and wooded areas.

"I'm sorry. I guess it's farther than I realized."

Suddenly Nick caught the reflections of taillights ahead. He hoped, yet almost dreaded, that it would be Dana's cruiser.

A pack of wild dogs ran across the road in front of them. That was not good. He did not want to think what a pack of dogs could do to a human body. His heart raced knowing he needed to find Dana fast. *Am I going to find only scattered remains?*

The gravel faded into a deeply rutted dirt road. Nick did not want to slow down any more than they had to. He swerved around deeper ruts only to bounce jarringly in and out of smaller ones. As they cautiously approached the parked vehicle, it was easy to see it was not an abandoned car. It was a police cruiser.

He pulled up behind the cruiser and parked. Nick grabbed a flashlight and before getting out, turned to Sheri, "Stay here!" he ordered more sharply than he intended.

It would not get dark until almost nine. That gave him roughly two hours. Cautiously he walked around the cruiser. It was locked and looked fine. No blood or bullet holes. He blew out a breath of relief and went back to Sheri.

"I should warn you. This is my first day on the job here. If my gut's wrong, I'm going to be greatly embarrassed besides leaving my partner still in trouble somewhere. We're going to take a walk."

Nick opened the trunk and gave Sheri a flashlight and a flak jacket. "Let me help you with the jacket. I can't imagine you've ever worn one before. Since I don't know what to expect at least you'll have some protection. I have reason to believe my fellow officer is in danger which means your daughter could also be in danger. Stay close to me. I think you're safer with me than out here alone."

Wild briar bushes had control of this territory. Nick looked along the edge of the woods for some sort of path, but there was nothing even a rabbit could get through easily. Finally he spotted some footprints by the remains of an old stone wall.

"It doesn't look like anyone has gone this way in a long time, but I don't want to waste time searching around unless you know something." He looked hopefully at Sheri.

She shook her head no. "I haven't gone into those woods since I've lived here. Sorry. Megan was afraid of them and there never was any reason to."

Nick moved quietly and quickly, amazing Sheri that he could walk silently on the clutter of leaves, pine needles and twigs. She felt like she was making enough noise for an entire army, snapping every twig she stepped on. Nick started calling, "Dana, Megan," when they entered the woods. Sheri added her voice calling, "Megan!"

The first obstacle they came across was easy–a shallow dry gully to jump over. The next was another briar patch. It stretched far and wide. Nick used his knife to cut, or his long black, heavy-duty plastic flashlight to beat a path to walk through.

Unbeknownst to Nick and Sheri, Dana and Megan were unable to hear their calls. Nick and Sheri cleared the briar patch and continued to head toward where the wild dogs had entered the woods. The going was slow due to having to climb over fallen trees and numerous snakelike vines growing along the ground that liked to trip their feet.

Nick picked up signs of someone being in the area, but he was not sure who. He hoped it was Dana. He followed the signs which, in truth, took them closer to the electrical towers and farther from Dana and Megan. They came out into a large clearing. Nick saw a tent and ordered Sheri to stay hidden behind the trees.

There was no cover for him to use. He walked along the edge of woods, studying the area and watching for movement. He heard and saw nothing for a full three minutes. It was possible Dana and Megan were being kept prisoner in the tent and unable to answer their phone calls.

Nick crawled on his belly to the nearest tower. He stood, using the tower for cover. Still no movement from in or around the tent. He ran to the next corner post and stopped to watch. Either the guard was sloppy lazy, dead or there was no guard. Maybe his worst fear had come true and there was no need for a guard.

Taking a big chance, Nick ran the last fifty feet out in the open to the tent.

It was empty–at least of any people. There was a small heater, a coffee maker with a cracked carafe, and thermos cup lid. A mess of extension wires were lying around which Nick could not make sense of. There was a fold-up cot and bedding along one wall and a small refrigerator. It had been left unplugged and smelled rank when Nick opened it. He was able to identify the remains of the cheese, bologna and milk by their containers. All the comforts of home, if you were an escaped convict.

Nick went back to Sheri. "Dana and Megan aren't there. I think I found where Drago was hiding out."

Sheri gasped, putting her hand to her mouth. "He was staying this close to us!" She ran into the tent. "I need to make sure Megan wasn't here."

He chased after her. "You can't touch anything. Look for anything that might belong to Megan."

After scanning around the inside of the tent, Sheri disobeyed Nick and rummaged through a cardboard box of clothes. She held up a pair of men's large white briefs. "I doubt these are Dana's," Sheri mumbled to herself, "and I don't think she would be interested in the man that fit into them," she finished with a hint of laughter. Then she saw a black coffee maker with a white carafe sitting on the hot plate. Curious, she looked closer. Without touching it she could see a crack. It was in the same place as Megan's, near the handle. What were the odds of that? Sheri looked around for the metal thermos lid. She saw one lying on its side on the canvas floor of the tent. Her face paled. It looked like the one Megan played with. The thermos cup had the same dent. Silent tears started to fall. Sheri went outside to tell Nick.

Nick was trying to use his phone to call in about his find, but it would not work. He had no idea if Drago was coming back or not. It looked like he had abandoned this spot. "Let's head back. We'll try a different path."

"I found a carafe and thermos lid that I think were Megan's."

"How can you be sure about those? They're fairly common items."

"The carafe is white and has a crack in the same place and the metal cup is dented the same as hers."

Nick nodded, "And hers is missing. We'll leave everything as is." He quickly scanned the area. There was no lake or pond that Drago could have dumped two bodies into. The field of electrical towers offered no hiding places. In front of them was a sparsely wooded area on a gently sloping hill.

"What about my daughter?" Sheri asked so softly Nick almost did not hear her and he was standing next to her.

He grabbed her upper arms. "Look at me!"

Slowly Sheri raised her tear stained face and looked Nick in the eye.

"We have to hope for the best. I don't believe Drago would hurt your daughter if he has her. I think she's with a missing police officer. Okay? Do you believe me?"

Sheri did not answer at first. She kept staring a Nick's unwavering blue eyes that seemed to hold the truth for her. Finally she replied, "Yes, thank you." She wiped her eyes with the back of her hand.

Regretting his decision to bring Ms. Smith with him, Nick abruptly changed topics. "We need to get moving. Maybe we'll have better luck trying in that direction," Nick pointed toward the hill. "It's a little higher elevation. We'll see more and hopefully get some bars on the phone." *These woods are bigger than I realized. I'd like more help to search them. We might not find them before dark.*

His ears perked up and his body tensed when he heard the echo of a pistol retort followed by a dog's sharp bark. His adrenaline kicked in, ready to run, but which way? He was having trouble figuring the direction the shot came from. This little valley put an odd twist on sound. Taking a chance he raced up the hill. If nothing else, he would be able to see better from higher up and, if Dana fired again, he was already running.

Both girls had been sleeping when the pack of wild dogs came sniffing around. A small light brown one took Megan's lunch bag in his powerful jaws and ripped it open seeking the source of the smell.

A dark brown one sniffed around the area, more interested in the blood around Dana. His cold nose touching her arm startled her awake.

Dana was glad she had taken the precaution to put Megan on her right side just in case needed to do any shooting, keeping her left hand free. She held the still peacefully sleeping Megan securely in her right arm. Dana threw the towel she had used to wipe her wounds as far away as she could. The dog chased after it. Carefully she pulled the pistol from her waistband with her left hand. While the dark brown dog had his nose to the ground busily sniffing the bloody towel, Dana got a clean shot and he dropped.

While Dana was preoccupied with the dark brown dog, an old grizzled black one quietly came around behind them, waking Megan when he jerked her doll out of her arms and scratching her forearm in the process. Megan screamed and kept on screaming.

The black dog was busy shaking the doll when Dana turned her head around. "Shh, shh, Baby," she whispered to Megan, "lie real still. I'm gonna shoot the bad dog."

She hated firing over Megan, but she had no choice. Dana knew that once the dog was done toying with the doll, he would come after one of them.

Megan stopped screaming, but continued crying in soft little gulps. Then, squeezing her eyes tightly shut, Megan pressed her body tightly against Dana. Her left ear was snugly fitted against Dana's side. She pressed her hand over the right one so she would not hear the loud noise of the gun.

Dana took two deep steadying breaths. The pistol now felt heavy in her hand. Her vision blurred and she blinked rapidly, trying to clear her focus, but it did not clear. She dropped her arm and grunted. That cane must have done more damage to her muscles than she realized.

The dog dropped the doll and turned, facing them. He barked once then lowered his head and bared his teeth, making a low guttural growl.

Knowing she was out of time, Dana raised her arm, held her breath, and fired, at the precise same time a pain gripped her arm muscles jerking her aim off.

She hit the dog, but was sure she had not killed him. He yelped, moved off, and disappeared around some heavy brush. He was too well hidden by the underbrush for Dana to get another shot safely. She could only see a small dark area and did not know if it would be a kill shot or just enough to make him angry to want to attack again. Dana hoped he died, but she had no way of knowing. The spot did not move. The other three dogs took off frightened by all the noise, leaving their wounded and dead comrades behind.

Megan lay beside Dana crying softly. Her doll was gone and her arm hurt. Dana checked Megan's arm. There were three scratches, one that was going to need a few stitches. They were all oozing a small amount of blood. At least they had the dog to check for rabies. Dana was mad at herself. That had been an easy shot and she blew it.

"Don't look at it and it won't hurt so much," Dana whispered to Megan. She held Megan tightly and prayed for help to arrive soon. She was exhausted and now she would have to fight sleep because those dogs had a reason to come back. They had smelled blood.

Breathless, Nick and Sheri reached the woods at the top of the hill before he heard the second shot. He veered slightly to his left and kept their pace as fast as they could manage. Nick was hesitant to call their names, not knowing who was doing the shooting. When he heard no more shots, and just before they started down the other side of the hill, Nick dared to call, "Dana, Megan."

Sheri added her own cries, "Megan! Megan!"

With Megan crying softly in her ear and her own pain, Dana was not sure she was hearing right. Was someone calling them? "Here! Over here!" Dana answered, waving her left arm.

Megan stopped sobbing long enough to ask, "What?"

"I think I hear the calvary coming."

"What's calvary?" Megan hesitantly got out the word.

"Help, Sweetie, wonderful help."

After listening for a moment, Megan smiled, "I hear Mommy!" She ran to the center of the clearing where she started yelling to add her own small voice, "Mommy! Here we are!"

"Megan, stay with me in case those dogs come back," Dana called with quiet urgency. She would have no way to save Megan if a dog attacked her in that clearing. Help was too far away, and Dana had no idea if she would be able to get a clean shot at the dog without hurting Megan.

Obediently, Megan raced back toward Dana and stood on the other side of the pole, yelling as loud as she could.

Nick stopped in his tracks. "Listen! I hear them!" He started to move forward again, frustrated by their slow pace but relieved to know they were on the right track. He called back, "Keep yelling! We're trying to find you." He changed directions again, heading more right.

"Megan! It's Mommy, I'm coming, Sweetie," Sheri cried loudly.

"I'm worried why my partner can't walk out of these woods," Nick commented to Sheri. To Dana, Nick yelled, "I think we're close. Were you shooting at some wild dogs?"

"Yes, but we're okay."

"Yell as loud as you can so we can find you."

Relieved, Dana smiled at Megan and winked. "Are you up to that?"

Megan grinned, nodded enthusiastically, and did her best rooster crow twice. Then she started simply yelling "Mommy!"

Nick and Sheri followed the sound of their voices. Now that they were close, it seemed that their progress had slowed. They had to climb around a grouping of boulders. Sheri was afraid, but managed with Nick's encouragement. The hill was steeper on this side. It was hard not to look down at the long, rough fall she would have if she slipped. It was frustrating to have her daughter so close and yet she still felt like they were miles apart.

After the boulders they found a foot path that suddenly dead-ended. Nick and Sheri could hear their voices clearly, but still could not see them. They looked at the steep hillside they needed to go down to reach Dana and Megan. Nick started and Sheri eagerly followed. Both were wearing sneakers, not really appropriate gear for steep hillsides. They used the trees to act as brakes to keep them from sliding too fast down the hill.

Nick reached the back side of the burned house first and signed for Sheri, who was holding onto a tree about ten feet behind him, to remain quiet. Sheri decided to come down the rest of the way. Dana and Megan, hoarse from yelling, had stopped momentarily.

Nick pulled his pistol out and walked down the short slope along the side of the burned down house. He saw no one. The silence was broken when Sheri slipped on the loose gravel and slid, exclaiming, "Oh!", in surprise. She fell into Nick who had no choice but to try to keep his balance and run ahead of her, with her sliding on his heels.

Hearing all the noise, Dana stretched to peer around the collapsed wall and watched in surprise as the Nick and Sheri shot out from the other side of the dilapidated building. Megan screamed, "Mommy!" and raced to her mother. Sheri collapsed to her knees to hold her daughter and cry with her.

With his pistol at the ready, Nick quickly surveyed the scene. Dana was sitting up, handcuffed to a pole. Her face was bruised, bloodied and swollen. A bloodied handkerchief covered a wound on her arm, and there was more blood on her legs. Before he raced to her side, he quickly assessed the scene for their safety. There was one dead dog. The area was littered with food wrappers, water bottles and soda cans.

Nick rushed to Dana's side and dropped to his knees. "If your face weren't so beat up, I'd say you two had been having a picnic and cite you for littering."

"Thanks. I suppose I should have done a better job of policing the area. We did have a picnic of sorts and we had a very pleasant time," Dana replied sarcastically, annoyed by her rescuer. She was worried about Drago, in pain, and tired from being awake for nearly thirty-six hours. She definitely did not need a jerk with a quirky sense of humor no matter how good looking he was. "Those dogs made a mess of our little pile of trash, I'll have you know."

"It's a good thing you don't have a mirror." He added with a smile, ignoring her sarcasm. Her face was a variety of colors—red, blue, and purple. The split lip and swollen eye added a grotesque touch. Nick was enchanted by her soft green eyes. He loved her reddish brown hair with strands of gold that the late afternoon sun highlighted making it glow with slender licks of golden flame. Something inside him softened. All those years of wondering how to tell when you met the right woman, now he knew. He fished in his pockets for his handcuff keys.

"Will you please take these cuffs off." Dana's tone was demanding and surly in spite of the word please.

He smiled, "If you promise to go out with me."

"I'll think about it." Her little smile was replaced by a groan when she moved. Her earlobes were the only things on her body that did not hurt.

After fishing in his pockets for the keys and coming up empty handed, Nick felt on the left side belt loop. He unclipped them and quickly released Dana. "I guess I'll have to settle for that answer."

"Do you know who did this to you and is he still around?" Before Dana had a chance to answer Nick stood up to use his phone to call for help. There was some static, but he talked slowly and loudly, pausing after every three words to make sure the whole message got through correctly. "Officer down, urgent, EMS and animal control, Code Three, Towers End, repeat, in the woods by the electrical towers at Towers End, Code Three, officer down. Please, repeat."

The dispatch operator repeated everything back correctly much to Nick's relief. Nick asked her to transfer him to Captain Wells. "Sir, I want to let you know I found Officer Morgan and the little girl."

He had to put the phone away from his ear to keep his ear drum from bursting from the captain's loud exclamation, "Good work, boy!"

"Welcome to the force. I take it you're my new partner?" Dana's voice was soft, but Nick could not miss the obvious annoyance in her tone. She was still sitting and gently rubbing above and below the bruises on her wrist. "Harry Drago, an escaped con did this. He's long gone, I'm sure."

"Nick Coburn, at your service. Let me check your wounds." He held her right hand as he tenderly palpated the injured area. He noticed her wincing in pain in spite of his careful touch. "I don't feel anything out of place. I see your pant leg is sort of missing. You two had a good fight."

He untied her makeshift dressing. "The laceration's crusted over except on the inner thigh area. You're still oozing a little bit at this end." He pointed without touching her. "I didn't think to bring my first-aid kit in with me, but the medics should be here soon."

"I can walk out. I'm not hurt that bad." Dana tried to stand and grabbed her stomach, groaning at the same time.

"I guess that takes care of that. I take it you took a punch to your abdomen. Let me see it."

Dana raised her shirt but only to the bottom of her bra. She did not need a mirror when she heard Nick's whistle. "That bad?"

Nick raised his eyebrows at the sight he saw. Most of her abdomen was black and blue with touches of purple. "It matches your eye, so you're color coordinated if that's any consolation."

"Thanks. I'm glad to know that."

"Where else are you hurt?"

"He sliced my arm, too." Dana jutted her shoulder forward, making the bandana more noticeable.

"Yeah, I noticed that already." Nick removed the bandana so he could check the wound. "That looks good. It'll need a few stitches, too."

"Drago used a knife and his wooden cane to fight with. He finally knocked me out and took my service pistol."

"Might as well lie still and rest. The ambulance should be here any minute. Take the last of the water. There isn't much left in this bottle."

"I've never cared for lukewarm water before. Now, it tastes heavenly," Dana said with a crooked smile.

"I bet. Now lie down."

She did as ordered, surprising him by resting her head in his lap. Nick could not imagine what was wrong with him. His mother always told him when the right girl came along he would know it, but he never expected it to be like this. He felt like he had been punched in the gut the first time he saw her soft green eyes.

He did not like being this close without being able to hold her in his arms, but he was somewhat mollified with her head in his lap. He brushed a strand of hair from her eyes. Did Dana feel anything for him? Most women had some gleam in their eye that he could see. Dana had nothing. *You're not being fair*, he reprimanded himself, *she's been through a lot the past two days. Don't be stupid and push her.*

Without thinking, Nick leaned over and kissed her forehead. "A kiss to make you feel better," he whispered. His mother had always done that to him when he was a young boy and it had always made him feel better.

After Nick did it he was ready to stammer an apology, but Dana did not stir or open her eyes. He felt a measure of relief. Either Dana had fallen asleep or she considered it simply brotherly reassurance. With any luck, maybe it did make her feel better.

Suddenly, with her eyes closed, Dana asked, "How's Megan doing now?"

He looked toward mother and daughter. "She looks happy now that she has her mother."

"Check her arm. One of the dogs scratched her with his tooth or paw. It all happened so fast; I'm not sure exactly. I shot it, but it wasn't a clean shot. He crawled under some brush by that dead tree over there." She pointed in the direction she meant. "Did the black dog finally die?"

"I didn't see a black dog when I got here. The brown one's dead. I'll check on Megan and look for the dog. I'll be right back." Reluctantly, he gently moved Dana, replacing his lap with Megan's pillow, so he could get up.

Nick hurried over to the mother and daughter. They were still sitting on the ground holding each other, silent tears were coursing down their cheeks as they talked.

Nick spoke softly to Sheri. "I need to check Megan's arm."

Sheri looked up at Nick. "Her arm?" She grabbed Megan's arms, one in each hand and turned them over. When she saw the three slash marks Sheri gasped. A thick crust of dried blood on each of them made it look worse than it was.

"It don't hurt much now, Mommy," Megan whimpered.

"We'll let EMS take a look at it when they get here. She probably should go to the ER." Nick looked over Megan's head and mouthed the word 'rabies' to Sheri. She nodded understanding. "I need to get back to Officer Dana. Would you two mind standing out on the road to show EMS how to find us? Can you find your way back out?"

"I can Mommy! There's a path over there. I counted my steps from the Miss Dana to the edge of the woods."

Nick gave a wry smile, "It sounds like we came in the hard way."

"I think you're right. Megan, I just realized how well you're talking."

"That's 'cause I'm a big girl and I've been practicing," Megan smiled brightly. It took her a little effort to get the word 'practicing' out right.

Sheri gave her daughter a hug. "I'm so proud of you. Let's go. I'll follow you."

Nick used his flashlight to scan the area for the black dog. Warily, he walked around checking under several bushes in the area Dana had indicated and behind nearby trees. There was only one dead tree, but no dead dog. Figuring it had not died here, he hoped that the dog had wandered off to die elsewhere.

Nick returned to Dana's side. She looked like she was sleeping peacefully. He hated to disturb her, but he wanted to get his questions out of the way before the ambulance got there. He needed to know what happened.

"Dana, are you up to telling me what happened?"

"I might as well get it over with." She heaved a huge sigh and yawned, "I'm sorry, but I've been fighting sleep so I could guard Megan." After another yawn, she began, "Yesterday afternoon I stopped here because Megan was standing at the road's edge. She wanted to report that someone stole her tea set. I phoned in, but I wasn't sure if all the message was received. This area…"

Nick interrupted, "Save your breath. I know about the bad reception in this area, and, no, your message was only partly received so dispatch got it wrong. Go on."

"I only had a little while before my shift ended, but I figured I'd find it quickly. I was looking for her tea set when I saw a boot print by the rock pile belonging to an escaped con. I thought about Harry Drago. Have you heard about him?"

"Some, not the whole story."

"He's dangerous. So, keep alert. He might still be in the area. He told me he wasn't going back to jail until he saw his little girl. Anyway, I tried to phone in, but again, you know." Dana paused, coughed and licked her lips, carefully touching the scabbed area. Nick rummaged around and found another bottle of water to give her.

"I thought I would track him a little ways and see what I could find. The prints were hard to see with the recent rain storm, and I think he may have tried to wipe some of them away. Anyway, I was so focused on looking for more prints that I didn't get very far before he jumped me. We fought a little and, he cheated so he won. He took my radio, exchanged my cell phone for his throwaway phone and took my service pistol. Then he chained me to this pole."

She directed a glaring look at him. "Of course, I'm left lying here all night because somebody needed to work the evening shift, and I had to change shifts to accommodate him. If I had been on my regular shift, they would have been looking for me hours earlier. Wouldn't they?"

"All right! I feel guilty enough without you rubbing it in. One look at your face did me in. Would you feel better if you hit me?" Nick stuck his chin out, "Go ahead. Have a free one." He closed his eyes and grimaced. Dana probably would never understand how badly he felt. He agreed with her that this was partly his fault. He needed to work second shift and her shift was changed to suit him. They would have been looking for her this morning if she had been on her regular shift. "I'm sorry about the shift change, but I'm taking a college course in the morning. It took an act of Congress to get the approval for the video conferencing so I could come down here to meet you and still finish my course. If I did not complete it, the crotchety old professor was going to give me an incomplete and make me take it all over again. I have five weeks left plus finals."

"I see." Dana could understand that about professors, time and money. Enough said on that subject. "I intend to take you up on your offer, but not today. I'm going to do it when I have the strength for you to feel the punch."

"I'm looking forward to it. I just don't know how all the other women will feel if you mar this beautiful face." Nick winked. "I know it's not any consolation, but my classes don't resume until next week. You weren't supposed to change your shift until then." Nick put up his arm to protect his face from the blow, but he forgot that Dana would be swinging with her left arm since her right was injured. She connected with a mild blow, but it was enough to jar his teeth.

"That was for the schedule screw up. I still get a free one. I'm going to make sure that one counts."

Nick lightly rubbed his sore jaw. "I'm really looking forward to it after that punch. Maybe we need to renegotiate the deal. First, I need to make sure everything still works." Nick kissed her lightly on the lips. He raised his head far enough to see she was frowning. Slowly, without closing his eyes and losing eye contact until Dana closed hers, he lowered his head and kissed her again, still very lightly, so as not to hurt her lips. Happy and surprisingly satisfied, Nick grinned, "Okay, everything still works. Please, continue."

Flustered by the kisses and his smile, Dana lost her train of thought, and trying not to show it, covered with a cough, "Where was I? Oh, Megan came. She used his phone and called 9-1-1 for me. Apparently she didn't have any better luck than I did." Dana took in a breath, "I don't think she gave them the right info or spoke loud enough the first time." She wished Nick had not done that. She was not sure if she wanted another kiss or wanted to punch him again.

Nick offered, "You rest a minute. I'll fill in a little for you. Megan did get 9-1-1 twice. Her voice was weak and only partly received. No one knew what to do with either message. They wrote your name down as Anna instead of Dana and she did not give an address on the first call. Megan never answered when they called back."

"She kept the phone in her dress pocket so she may not have heard it ring."

"Why was Megan with you?"

Dana turned to look at Nick and her eyes widened in alarm. Up to that point the wild dog had been approaching silently. Just as his and Dana's eyes met, he bared his teeth and growled, a low guttural sound that sent chills through Dana's body.

From Dana's expression, Nick, still squatting, realized with dread that the wounded dog was back and out for revenge. In one fluid motion, Nick twisted around as he grabbed his pistol from his waistband, swinging his left arm up for protection.

All he saw was the hairy black belly of the beast. The dog's teeth bit deeply into Nick's arm before the bullet sank into the dog's heart. The dog fell heavily onto Nick knocking him over and spraying him with blood. Nick managed to throw most of his own weight along with the dog's off to the side to avoid falling on top of Dana.

Nick pushed the dog off himself and jumped up. The front of his shirt was soaked in blood. The deep bite in his left forearm dripped blood and hurt bad enough for him to let loose with a few expletives that were not meant for an angel's ears.

CHAPTER 8

Nick noticed the dog was still breathing, although raggedly, and fired again. He was not taking any chances that the dog would try another attack. A small cloud of dust swirled up with the dog's last and final exhalation.

"Damn mutt!" Nick cursed again. "First day on the job and look at the paperwork."

He turned back around muttering to himself, ignoring the many thin streams of blood coursing down his arm. "I think when this is all over I'm going to find a bar and have a few cold beers." He started hunting for a towel, gauze or something for his arm among the clutter of things on the blanket. Nick found a clean wash cloth which was not big enough. He moved a fold in the blanket and found another small towel spotted with dried blood and wrapped that around his arm, using his hand to apply pressure for a few minutes.

Dana softly replied, "Jessie's on Logan Road. Ask anyone for directions. I'll buy the first round. Some of the guys will probably buy you a round or two."

"No, thanks just the same," with a hint of laughter in his voice. They've sent me on one wild goose chase already, besides swapping out my uniforms for the wrong size. I'm sure you think they're a great bunch. Maybe finding you will give me a few brownie points. In the mean time, I think I'll keep my distance for a few more days," Nick chuckled.

"That's right. I was so glad to see you I hadn't thought about you being out of uniform."

"Let me check your wounds again. I knocked against you fairly hard," Nick quickly checked Dana's leg and arm. "I just want to make sure I didn't make them worse."

"I'm fine. You didn't bump me very hard at all. No harm done." She took in a breath to finish her sentence. Her skin tingled at his warm touch when he lifted up her shirt to look at her stomach. "Give the guys a chance. They're a good bunch."

"No new bleeding." He felt her pulse. "Pulse is good and strong. I'm no doctor, but I'd say you're in good shape."

Dana had closed her eyes again. He was sure Dana was as relieved as he was that she was found. He did not want to push her, not knowing how bad the damage was to her insides. "If I help you, do you think you could try standing again? I'd rather get us back to the house trailer where we're not so isolated."

"I agree. Nothing is hurting that bad now. Let me try again." Dana sat up slowly, with Nick supporting her all the way. "That worked. Now for the hard part." Dana smiled at him. He was cute, but she was not interested. *Right, like you're not already. Didn't you learn anything with your last partner? We fell in love and he was killed. Was it because we got careless? I'll never know, but I'm not going to repeat the same mistakes. Why did he have to kiss me? Why do I want another one? Why couldn't Nick have been an ugly, bald, fat forty year old? Did my father have anything to do with this? I won't fall for his plan.*

There was that smile again, lopsided as it was. At that moment Nick knew he was a goner. He did not understand how he could fall in love by simply looking into her soft green eyes and having her smile at him, just for him. Nick decided it was the drama of the moment and would wear off soon. Love at first sight was not something that really worked, was it?

It had always been easy for him to get dates, since turning sixteen and the dreaded acne had cleared up. He had lost count of the number of women that had literally thrown themselves at his feet, young and old. He laughed inwardly at the memory of those hectic weekends when he had two dates scheduled on Saturdays, one in the afternoon for a picnic or matinée and one in the evening for a movie or dance. He had never felt serious about a woman—until today.

None of the women he had known before had ever created such a stir of emotions like Dana did with one simple look. He stared at her face while she readied herself to stand wondering what it would be like to really kiss her, not that teasing kiss he had given her earlier, but a deep heartfelt kiss. He wanted desperately to make love to her.

Nick held ninety-nine percent of Dana's weight as she stood. He did not let go until her legs no longer wobbled beneath her slender, but very nicely shaped form.

"How's the pain?"

"Not bad. I think I can walk."

Nick supported her around the waist and she slipped her arm around his shoulder. Supporting her stomach with her right arm, they slowly hobbled out of the woods together.

"This would be easier if I could do a firefighter's carry or even drape you over my back."

"I don't think I could tolerate that much pressure on my stomach either way. Do you need a rest break?"

"No, you're not heavy. I'd rather keep moving." Nick was not going to let her know how badly his arm hurt.

"Me, too. It's going to be a long time before I can enjoy a picnic again. I'm afraid I'll always remember that spot and being handcuffed to that pipe," Dana said with a faint hint of laughter in her voice.

"Here I was thinking about how much fun it would be to come back next weekend with a bottle of wine and a picnic basket."

"Right. Ooh," Dana groaned.

"What's the matter?"

"Can we stop a moment?"

"Sure. There's a wider patch up by that tree where we can stretch our legs. Can you make it that far?"

Dana nodded and Nick slowed their pace the few feet to the tall maple tree. Nick sat on the ground with his legs outstretched to let Dana rest her head on his thighs. She heaved a heavy sigh then her eyes fluttered closed.

Nick cocked his head and listened. "I can hear Megan singing so we're near her trailer."

"You moved fast even with carrying me."

"I served in Iraq for ten months. We learned to move the wounded fast. It was either that or both of you were dead. You weigh nothing compared to some of the guys I hauled out. A man weighed anywhere from one twenty to two hundred pounds then you add whatever equipment was on him. That could be another thirty to seventy pounds. We tried not to leave anything behind for the enemy."

"How long did you serve?"

"Two years, eighteen months altogether. I was wounded and sent back to the states. The Army decided to give me an honorable discharge and here I am." Nick gulped. He had almost given himself away. He planned to tell her the whole truth, but now was not a good time.

Maybe not everything. He was not sure what he was feeling for Dana. He doubted it was love. He did not believe in love at first sight. Nick figured it was just the adrenaline high all heroes get after rescuing the heroine. He simply knew he felt a strong attraction to her soft green eyes and wanted to see her smile every day. That attraction was going to make his next assignment a lot harder.

"Good for us."

"I guess," he offered a vague reply since he had let his mind wander and it took him a second to recall what Dana's comment referred to. *Not good for an agent, Nick, old boy, get your act together. She's not the first attractive girl you've worked with,* he scolded himself. "Ready to go. We should be close," Nick gently encouraged.

Nick helped Dana sit, then after getting himself up, he helped her stand. They heard the wail of sirens as they started walking.

"By the sound of them," Nick said, "there's an army of vehicles coming. Hold on tight." Nick grabbed Dana tighter around the waist and lifted her completely off her feet. She expelled a soft grunt, but Nick kept moving. He practically ran the rest of the way with her.

This part of the path was easy and Nick made it seem like it was no effort for him to carry Dana those last fifty yards. She was only one hundred and twenty-six pounds. At five foot seven she carried her weight well.

They reached the end of the woods just as the first ambulance pulled in. Nick was surprised to see where he came out. It was near the pile of stones by one of the house trailers that he thought had been abandoned and there was the crossroad he thought had been a dead end. This dilapidated house trailer was apparently where Megan lived. *Surprise. My detective skills are really taking a blow,* he thought sorely.

Their sirens died the instant they arrived in the yard. There was one ambulance and two police cruisers. Surprising Nick, Captain Wells was the second police cruiser.

Nick stopped and helped Dana sit down on the ground. Her face looked unusually pale. "Dana, are you okay? I didn't hurt you, did I?" Nick asked with deep concern.

Dana opened her eyes and smiled at him. "Everything hurts now. I don't think you made it any worse."

Relieved, Nick stood up. It was only then he realized how terribly his left arm was hurting. He had used it to hold Dana's left arm across his shoulders as he supported her while walking out together. His injured muscles were revolting against the unwanted abuse.

The paramedics, loaded down with their gear, pushed around Nick to get to Dana. The EMS crew wasted no time reaching Dana to take care of her. "I got a pulse!" One of the medics yelled as another started an intravenous line in her left arm.

"No kidding?" Dana said sarcastically to the paramedic. "I'm so glad to hear that. Ouch! Is that necessary?" Dana asked when the IV needle punctured her skin.

"It's just you were so pale. I…ah, heck. Afraid so. We don't know what all is wrong with you. How's your breathing? Think you need a little oxygen?"

"No, I'm okay that way. That bully did a good job of beating me up. I think my worst injury is the punch to my stomach."

The medic lifted up her shirt and whistled. "I'll say. When did this happen?"

"Yesterday."

"Where have you been all this time?"

"Chained to a pole."

The medic nodded and clipped an oxygen saturation monitor onto her finger. "That explains the discoloration. Oxygen saturation looks good. We'll have you packed up in a few minutes."

Nick stood nearby Dana while the EMS crew worked. The Captain finally got out of his cruiser. Nick said to Dana, "The Captain's here." He gently pressed on the bloody towel covering his arm, trying to soak up more of the blood. He winced when he put too much pressure on it, noticing that it did not feel right. It was spongy, not simply like several fang scrapes. He decided to take the towel off and see what was going on.

Captain Wells stopped at the edge of the yard. He was normally tough and had seen enough blood during his years on the force, but when he saw all the blood covering Nick and his daughter, his face paled and his knees started to buckle. Captain Wells looked back at Nick. In spite of all the blood, Nick was standing and very much alive. Finally he looked down at Dana's face and heaved a silent sigh of thanks when he saw her green eyes looking at him and her sweet smile. He smiled at her as he ran to her side.

Captain Wells dropped to his knees beside his daughter. He tenderly placed a hand on her brow. "Hey, Baby, Daddy's here." Then followed with a light kiss to her forehead.

"Hey, glad you could make it to my little party," Dana said, then adding with as much mock defiance as she could muster, "I told you I wasn't going to work this weekend. Of course, I think my other plans have changed," she coughed. "Think I could have a sip of water?"

The Captain looked to the medic who answered. "Better hold off. We have no idea what kind of trauma your stomach sustained. We'll have you in the ER in fifteen minutes and they can give you some there if it's okay."

At that moment, Captain Wells looked up to thank Nick and saw the raw gash in Nick's arm. Almost afraid to ask, he barely sputtered out, "What happened?"

Before Nick could answer, Dana interrupted, "Chief, did you call Mom?"

"Yes, when you were late for work and we couldn't find you. She and her new husband are flying out. They were already in the air so I couldn't let them know we found you."

"Sorry to hear that. I'm in no shape for company. Dad, you do remember, Mom's been remarried five years now?"

Nick was panicking and did not pay attention to any more of their conversation. *Dana was the Captain's daughter? They didn't have the same last name. Was she married? Why wasn't that on the bio? Hastily he looked at her left hand for a ring. It was bare. Maybe she didn't wear a ring on the job. Could he be arrested for his nasty thoughts about the boss's daughter?*

Captain Wells, satisfied that his daughter was all right since she was still as bossy as ever, turned his attention back to Nick who was dabbing a blood soaked towel to his arm. "What happened to you?"

Nick swallowed hard and hoped the Captain could not see the blush in his cheeks under the blood splatter. "A wild dog attacked us. Dana had already shot two that came scrounging around just before we got here, but one was only wounded. That one came back a few minutes later. This," Nick pointed to his shirt and face, "is all from the dog as well as this." He removed the towel covering his arm.

Captain Wells winced at the large bite. "Some first day you're having."

"Tell me about it."

"Guys," Dana's voice got their attention easily. "Harry Drago has probably left the area, but keep on the alert, just in case."

The Captain looked surprised. "Harry Drago? Here? You found him? He did this?"

"Yes," Her answer was more a sigh than an actual word as the two medics jostled her stretcher into the back of the ambulance.

Nick spoke, "Dana told me what happened. I can explain it to you. Let her save her energy. You might want to thank Megan, the little missing five year old girl. She stayed with Dana trying to help her."

Nick spent a few more minutes explaining what he knew. After he finished, Captain Wells sagely nodded his head and said, "Okay, now I need to talk to my littlest hero. Where's that little girl?"

Megan and her mother, holding hands, were standing nearby watching the activity. Megan's arm had been cleaned and bandaged by one of the medics.

Megan watched the big man walking towards her and felt intimidated again. She squeezed her mother's pink uniform pants tightly and hid behind her. He had a pleasant voice even though it was deep, so she peeked out from behind her mother; however, she did not release her death grip on her mother's pants.

"Hello, my name is Captain Ed Wells and I'm the Chief of Police. I want to thank you for taking such good care of one my officers. You did a good job and I'm proud of you." He extended his hand to shake hers.

Megan relaxed her grip on her mother's pants a little when he told her he was the Chief of Police. That was an important title and the police protected people, but he was still a man and had a loud voice. Those two things still worried her. Megan did not know many good men. She had a very short list of three—her dead daddy, the bus driver and the crossing guard. This man's voice reminded her of the bus driver's voice. He told them jokes and laughed so Megan decided this man was okay too. She came out from behind her mother. "Thank you. I'm sorry I didn't do better." She hesitantly put her tiny hand in his comparatively large one.

They shook. "Don't think that for one minute, young lady. You did just fine. You did a wonderful job, from what I've been told. You're a hero and the mayor will probably give you an award certificate for this. I think that makes you the youngest hero ever to get one."

Excited, Megan smiled and looked up at her mother. "Is a cer…tif…cate good?"

Sheri smiled down at her, "Yes, Honey, that's good."

One of the medics approached Nick, "Sir, Dana said you have an injury. Let me take a look at your wound."

Nick stuck out his arm and, not wanting to look at it again, turned his head before the medic uncovered the wound. Curiosity got the best of him and he turned back to look. Nick saw the guy's eyes open wide before he quickly turned to get his supplies. He opened a pack of sterile gauze and picked up a bottle of sterile saline. He squirted the saline generously over Nick's forearm, washing the wound area. After patting it dry with more gauze pads, he used a pair of sterile tweezers to carefully lift the flap of skin and look beneath it with his high powered flashlight.

The guy winced. "That mutt tore your arm up really good. I've been doing this job for eight years and yours is the second worst bite I've ever seen. The first had his arm half torn off, clean to the bone."

"Thanks," Nick replied simply. His arm was starting to hurt worse now, but he had a job to do. Drago may not have been an FBI case before, but he was making it one now, even if it was for personal reasons. He wanted to get even for Dana's sake.

"You'll still have to go to the ER for the doc to see to this. It needs stitches. Are you injured anywhere else?" The medic indicated the front of Nick's shirt.

"No, most of this blood belongs to the wild dog I shot." Nick considered how much his pride was taking a beating. "I'll see to my arm after Dana's taken care of. There might be an escaped con or more wild dogs in the area and I need to keep watch."

The medic's eyes widened with alarm, "Are we safe now?"

"Probably. I don't think either of them will come around with this much activity going on. Those sirens most likely scared them away."

"That's good. We shouldn't be here if the scene's not secure." He wrapped the wound as he talked. "That's done. As pale as your face looks, I'd better take your blood pressure. Why don't you sit down on this stretcher while I get a cuff?"

He was back in a minute with the necessary equipment. "Your pressure's a little low. You're probably safe to drink some water now since I doubt you'll get to surgery right away. I don't recommend you drive. I realize you have a job to do, but your arm needs surgery. I'll call for another truck to take you to the hospital."

Suddenly a voice yelled, "Hey, Rick, get over here! We need your muscles."

"That's me. They must be ready to carry your partner out."

Nick had turned around ready to run until he realized that it was not his name they had called. He was relieved to see that Dana was finally ready to go.

Nick followed the medic over and touched Dana's arm as she passed by him. "Hang in there, Dana." He watched as they loaded her into the ambulance and slammed the door shut. He wanted to see her smile at him again. He wanted to know what it would be like to kiss her, to hold her, to love her.

"Hey, Nick!" Captain Wells called, snapping Nick out of his little reverie. "I've got Brown and Porter working the scene. You go get that arm looked at. I'm going to the hospital to be with my daughter."

"Sure thing." As much as Nick wanted to check things out here, it would be convenient to be at the hospital to see how Dana was doing. The siren started wailing as the ambulance pulled out.

Nick decided he would rather drive. Other than pain he felt fine, and he really did not want to come back to this area late at night without back-up to get his car. He was not sure it was safe for Sheri and Megan either. Even without knowing him, Tom did not strike Nick as the kind of guy to come to anyone's defense but his own.

Animal control had not shown up yet. So that meant there were at least three wild dogs still on the loose as well as a murderous felon. Hopefully, the dogs and escaped felon were all long gone. Maybe he should not be wishing that Drago was easily escaping. He simply did not feel like dealing with it now. Nick checked his watch, thankfully they had nearly an hour of daylight left.

Megan and her mother were on his heels. He had forgotten about them for a little while. He smiled when he heard Megan whisper to her mother.

"Mommy, I have to go potty."

"Go ahead. We'll go to the hospital when you get done."

"Okay." Megan took off.

"I can't believe the change in her," Sheri said to Nick with amazement evident in her voice.

"You have a lot to be proud of," Nick stated simply, wondering if he and Dana could have a little girl as great as Megan. *There you go again,* Nick fussed again, *Dana may not even like you, let alone want to have kids with you. She kissed you back. So, all girls kiss back. It's almost an automatic response.*

"I'd like a drink of water and use your bathroom before I go, if you don't mind."

Sheri hesitated before saying, "Of course." She added with a tinge of worry in her voice, "I'm surprised Tom hasn't come out with all this noise. I can't believe he could sleep through all this. Let me check on him first. Wait right here. Don't move!"

Nick did move closer to the trailer, but stopped at the front end. He wanted cover in case he needed it. Nick got the impression Sheri was a little bit afraid of Tom. Based on his FBI training, Nick figured Tom was probably more abusive than Sheri let on. He hated that he was putting her at risk for a beating.

It was barely a minute later that Sheri appeared in the doorway and paused. Her eyes were dazed and unfocused as she stumbled down the wobbly concrete block steps. Nick did not know what to make of it. He had not heard any fighting or screams, and she had not had enough time to take any drugs. He did not see any bullet holes nor was there any blood showing on her.

She reached the bottom. In slow motion she turned her head and looked at Nick. Her eyes were vacant, like nobody was home. Suddenly, her face drained of all color as her eyes rolled back, and she collapsed onto the ground. Nick ran but was one step too far away to catch her. It happened too fast.

Her head hit the corner of the last step. The dull crack was mortifying to hear. More blood began to color the dry ground.

Nick kneeled beside her and checked her head. There was a small gash with a bump forming, but it did not look too bad. Gently he called her name. "Sheri! Sheri!"

She opened her eyes, turned her head and threw up. Nick was really worried that she was worse off than he thought. After gagging a little more, Sheri finally sputtered, "He's dead."

"Don't move. I'm going to check inside the trailer. If you need anything, yell," Nick commanded as he pulled his pistol out of the back of his waistband and cautiously but quickly scanned the area around the trailer.

Nick kept his pistol in front of him as he entered the trailer. Nothing looked amiss. Nothing looked remotely like a crime scene at first. There was a short stack of three beer cans on the coffee table and an open bag of chips on the floor. The rest of the place was surprisingly neat.

The man sitting on the couch looked asleep until you looked closer. He was not breathing. Nick checked that there was no pulse either. The baseball cap was sitting low on his forehead. Using only the tip of his pistol, Nick pushed the hat up and saw a neat hole above his left eye. Then he noticed some blood splatter on the back of the couch and patterned wall paper.

As he was walking down the hall to check the rest of the trailer, Megan opened the bathroom door. Nick jumped back a step then reacted by pushing the door shut.

Megan hollered, "Hey!" as she fell with a thump to the floor.

Nick, upset that he had forgotten Megan was inside the trailer, quickly uncocked his gun and hid it in the back of his jeans waistband before going to her rescue. "Did I hurt you?"

"No. Why'd you do that?"

"I'm sorry. I thought you were the bad man that shot Tom."

"Tom got shot? Is he okay?"

"Go on outside. I'll be out in a minute."

"Can I…"Megan started to ask, but Nick snapped 'No' at her so fast she started to cry.

Nick got down to her level. "I'm sorry. Your mommy doesn't feel well. She needs you."

Megan, head drooping and gulping back her tears, did her little hip wiggle and wished she had Mary Alice to hold. "Okay." She squeezed past Nick and raced outside.

Nick finished checking the rest of the trailer. He doubted that Drago or whoever the shooter was would still be in the trailer, but he wanted to make certain. It did look like someone had rummaged through the closets and drawers. His flashlight caught a glint of metal under the edge of the night table. Nick reached down and picked up an unspent .038 round.

After clearing the trailer, he pulled out his cell phone to dial 9-1-1 but could not get any bars again. Unable to hold it any longer, he used the toilet before looking for a land line phone. He could not find a phone in the trailer so Nick went back outside.

Sheri was sitting on the ground, still dazed, and in shock. He sat beside her and held her hand, rubbing it lightly to bring back some warmth. Her hand trembled as he held it.

Tears silently flowed down her cheeks as Sheri stammered out. "I didn't know what to do. He didn't wake up. I took his hat off to hit him with it. I h-had to cover it b-back up." Sheri looked down at her hands. "Earlier when I was in the trailer, I didn't get that close. When he ignored me, I let it go. I was used to that. This time I wanted an answer. I…, I…," Sheri put her face in her hands and cried harder.

Nick wrapped his arm around her to give her some support. "Look at me. Sheri, you're going to be all right. Let's get you and Megan to the hospital. You took a good wallop to your head. You can't stay here tonight. We'll get the Social Worker at the hospital to find a place for you two if you don't have someone you can stay with."

"No, we can stay with my parents for a few days. It'll be crowded, but they won't mind. They love to spoil Megan." Sheri stood and wiped her eyes. "Megan, Honey, come here," Sheri called, looking toward the swing set, but it was empty. She was still too dazed to panic. "Megan, where are you?"

There was no answer to her calls.

Nick had walked off, trying his cell phone in various spots to get a dial tone to call in the murder, but was having no luck. He was by the broken willow tree before he could get enough bars to call it in. After hanging up he noticed the animal rescue truck.

"When did they arrive?"

"While you were in the trailer. I'm sorry I didn't think to tell you about it."

"I bet Megan followed them back into the woods." Nick asked, "Would you rather wait here or go with me?"

Sheri looked around the yard again and hesitantly answered, "I think you're right. Megan's always curious. I'd rather go with you. I don't want to be alone.

They had not gone very far down the path when they were met by two animal control officers coming out. Each one was carrying a small cage.

"Hey, I'm Officer Brownley, we found two dead dogs. One of the officers back there said you were bitten."

"That's right." Nick held up his injured arm.

He raised an eyebrow. "Big bite. Well, you know the procedure, I'm sure. We'll do our paperwork and you do yours. Keep in touch."

"Thanks, appreciate the sympathy."

The officer gave a little salute as they crowded past.

"Hey, wait a minute!" Nick called. "Did you see a little girl, about five years old?"

"Yeah, we were surprised to find she had followed us in. She's helping the other two officers finish up." They laughed.

Daylight was fading fast and that was going to be a big problem, Nick thought as he turned his flashlight on and continued back into the woods. Night was arriving faster than he'd like. He looked for Megan along the way just in case she was heading out.

The officers processing the scene were packing up their equipment as Nick approached them. "Hey, I'm glad I caught you. We have another crime scene."

"Yeah, right, like we're going to believe you after the tricks that were pulled on you," Brown snickered.

"Yeah, we already heard about your uniforms and the hookers," Porter added with a chuckle.

Tired and in pain, Nick could not believe these two goons. "Where's the little girl?"

"I'm here," Popping out from behind a tree, Megan chimed merrily. Then her lower lip pouted out, "They told me I couldn't have my doll because it was part of a crime and they had to keep it."

Sheri ran to her daughter. "Megan, I've been so worried about you. Why did you run off?"

"I wanted to see them catch the doggies."

"That wasn't a good thing to do. You could've gotten hurt."

"I was careful and real quiet." She added with a giggle, "They didn't even know I was following them until one of them said a bad word and I told they shouldn't say those kind of words. I think I scared them. You should have seen how big their eyes got." Giggling, she made a circle with her hands to show her mother how big she meant.

"The animal control unit was already at the clearing by the time they realized Megan was following them, so we thought it was better if she stayed with us. She refused to go out with the animal control guys and said she would go with us. We couldn't get any bars to call, but we were almost done. Sorry to worry you, Ma'am." Officer Brown tipped his hat, adding to his apology.

"I was serious when I said there was another crime scene."

Officer Porter and Brown looked at each other and replied simultaneously, "No." They started to head out the same way they came in which was through the rough and wild growth.

"It's easier if you go this way."

"You can't fool us." One of them threw over his shoulder as they started pushing through the tangle of vines.

Nick shrugged his shoulders and calmly said, "Okay, guys, have it your way." Nick disappeared down the easier path with Sheri and Megan.

The two officers continued to talk, expecting Nick to be a little ways behind them. When they got no answer to their question they stopped and looked back. No one was there. They gaped at each other before shrugging their shoulders and continuing their trek back out.

Before Nick and Sheri cleared the forest, the sound of an engine revving could be heard. Nick thought it sounded a lot like his, but knew his car, hopefully, was in the precinct parking lot, safe and still locked.

Megan panicked and grabbed her mother's hand. "Don't go out there now. Those mean boys are there."

Sheri looked at her daughter, "What are you talking about?"

They stopped to rest on a newly fallen tree, but Nick did not let them rest long. He decided to move on and see what had Megan so worked up. It took them over ten minutes to reach the yard, but the car was long gone. Megan and Sheri stayed behind a tree while he looked around.

He yelled back, "It's okay. They're gone." He wasn't sure about the okay part. They had thrown raw eggs on the cars and some sort of red stuff, either overripe tomatoes or ketchup. That was bad enough, but to make matters worse they slashed all the tires on all the vehicles parked there. He hoped and prayed that they might have missed the cars on the other side of the willow tree, but when he walked around the dying, broken branch, his hope faded instantly.

Sheri and Megan walked into the yard. Sheri started explaining what Megan told her about the teen boys when she suddenly stopped and stared at the mess. "They've never done that before. Megan told me they threw cabbage water on her one time and a few other times they've thrown garbage in the yard. The little dear would clean up the trash before I got home." She looked at the trailer and exclaimed, "They've even thrown eggs at the trailer! I don't understand why they're doing this."

"Some kids will do it to be mean or they think it's fun. The worst news is we need to get a ride. They slashed all the tires."

At that news, Sheri sat down on the concrete bench her hand gingerly cradling her head. Her face paled again. Nick heard her mutter, "I don't understand why." What Sheri had to deal with today was not something your average person knew how to handle. Heck, if it had been happening to him, he was not sure he would know how to handle it either.

Nick went to his cruiser to phone for help. He tried to put the key in the lock, but it would not go in. Thinking he had missed the keyhole in the dark, he tried again. Still missed. He walked back to the table where Sheri was sitting and picked up his flashlight. "I can't seem to hit the keyhole in the dark."

'Mutt and Jeff' had not exited the woods yet. Nick figured they would be another ten to fifteen minutes if they did not get lost in the dark.

Sheri and Megan were sitting at the little play table. Sheri started to shiver. Nick decided to go back into the trailer to find a jacket for her. Feeling chilled himself, he picked up a windbreaker for his use. It was still in the plastic store bag with the sale price tag attached. He did not know if Megan needed something or not, so he grabbed a pink sweater that was lying on her dresser just in case.

Nick handed Sheri her jacket and the sweater for Megan. "I hope you don't mind, but I borrowed a jacket." Sheri nodded. He slipped it on. "That EMT said he would send another truck, but I guess they came while we were in the woods and must have left. I'm going to try again to unlock my cruiser since I've got a flashlight now. I'll call for help and get us out of here."

Again, Sheri merely nodded.

Nick hurriedly walked to his cruiser, letting his long legs take their usual lengthy stride. He was eager to get out of this area. Too bad they had not left earlier. Nick clicked on the button and shined the light directly on the keyhole. Something did not look right. He tried to put the key in and it would not go. He got down on eye level and noticed it was filled with some sort of clear gel. He pressed his finger to it and it felt a little tacky. Superglue.

Great! He checked all the locks on both cruisers and Sheri's car. Each one was in the same condition.

Nick returned and plopped down at the table with the two girls. "They glued all the locks." He was really getting pissed at himself for being so helpless. In the city he could always get enough bars, grab a phone or walk two minutes for help.

Sheri did not need any more bad news. Her mouth gaped open as she looked at him blankly. He was not sure how much of the shock was from her injury, the awful prank, or the brutal murder. Most likely it was a combination of all three. He figured to lose your child twice, even briefly, in the same day would be especially hard to deal with. Now to have no home or lover, even if you didn't like him all that much, would be unimaginable. He could not begin to fathom the agony she was feeling. Nick was sorry she had to go through this alone. Suddenly, it dawned on him that maybe she did not have to. "Is there anyone I can call for you?"

"No, that's all right. I'll call my parents," Sheri said while looking at her shoes. She hugged herself tighter. "I have a boyfriend, David, but I don't feel our relationship is at the point where he should come to my rescue." She reached into her pants pocket and handed Nick her cell phone. "If your phone can't do it, maybe mine will."

"Thanks." He got up and paraded around again trying to get a signal.

Finally, by the willow tree, Nick got enough bars to make a call with his phone. He preferred using his phone so they could trace it if needed. Again the connection was garbled, but he talked loudly and enunciated clearly, "Need help at same crime scene. Towers End Road. New murder victim. Officer injured. Repeat officer injured."

Just as he hung up Nick heard a car engine and crashing brush sounds. He raced around the fallen limb, looking up and down the road for the source of the noise. Suddenly a police cruiser burst out of the woods about a hundred feet up the road. Nick yelled and waved, but the cruiser drove on, neither one of the two officers in the vehicle looked in the rearview mirror.

Nick thought they were being stupid for going out that way and it turns out they were the smart ones. He wished he had thought to drive through that tough brush.

When Nick had used the 'Officer Down' code he had felt almost ashamed that he was playing on his injury, but the pain was a lot worse, and his stomach felt queasy, since he had used his arm like a flag, trying to wave the cruiser down. His fingers were swollen, numb and tingling.

He sat on the concrete bench next to Sheri wishing he had a warmer coat. The evening air was not that chilly, but he could not get warm. Neither one of them had much warmth to share with the other.

"I finally got through. They should be here in a few minutes. The other cops were smarter than I gave them credit for. They drove into the woods, saving themselves from those brambles along the road. They just now drove away. I tried to get their attention, but had no luck."

Still with the distant look in her eyes, like she wasn't really there anymore, "I could drive," Sheri offered.

Nick studied her face. Her eyes were glazed over. He was not sure she heard any of what he had just said, but it did not really matter. There was nothing to drive and, even if there was, he was not letting her get behind the wheel. Sheri probably did not realize what state she was in. "I really don't believe you're in any shape to drive. We'll wait for help. With my arm as bad as it is, I'm not sure I could drive either. Besides, remember, all the cars are disabled."

Megan was sitting very quietly beside her mother with her head resting in her lap. She had been quiet for so long Nick thought she was asleep.

"Do you want me to get some things for you and Megan?

"No! I don't want anything more out of that place." Sheri snapped. Then more calmly she added, "I'm sorry. Yes, I suppose I do need a few things. I just can't go back in there."

"You don't have to. I'll get what ever you need. It's a crime scene, but I'll let them know we took a few personal items."

"I'm not worried about anything for me. I can pick up a few things at the drugstore and I keep a few clothes at my parents' home, but Megan will need her fairy nightlight. It's in the bathroom. She has an extra butterfly and fairy blanket on the shelf in the closet in her bedroom. She can't sleep unless she has that to protect her." She wiped a silently falling tear with the back of her hand. "I don't know what she'll do without Mary Alice tonight."

Just then they could hear sirens for the second time that day. A police cruiser came slowly down the dirt road Nick had driven the first time. Nick stood and waved with his good arm. He blew out his breath in relief as the cruiser pulled in. Only then did he begin to feel a bit of embarrassment coming on thinking of how he was going to explain this mess and was almost glad he was pretending to be a rookie officer.

"I'm Sergeant Rally, care to tell me what's going on?" He addressed Nick and did not look too happy.

"I'm Officer Nick Coburn."

Officer Rally interrupted Nick, "Oh, yes, I heard you were the new guy working with Dana Morgan. Pleased to meet you." Instead of offering his hand to shake, Rally stepped into Nick's personal space, using his burly build and bulldog face to intimidate. "You treat Dana real kindly, you hear me, or I'll make sure you pay, if you get my drift."

Nick stood his ground. He clipped out his words. "I intend to and I don't need your foul breath threats to make me do anything. Now, let me bring you up to speed." He wanted to add a few choice names, but decided that would waste time while they butted heads, so he bit his tongue and continued. "Officer Dana Morgan has been missing since yesterday and I found her injured in the woods earlier. She's already been transported out. I was helping Sheri Smith and her daughter, who's the real hero, when Ms. Smith found her boyfriend, a Tom Jenkins, murdered in the trailer."

"Did you shoot him?"

"No. I'm not sure who did. Ms. Smith lives here with the man that was shot."

Again, Sergeant Rally interrupted, "Did she shoot him?"

Frustrated, Nick rubbed his hand over his face. "No," he drew out that single syllable, indicating his impatience, "can I finish my account without your interruptions? I'll answer your questions when I get done. It could have been Harry Drago that did the shooting. Officer Morgan found his tracks and followed him into the woods where he attacked her. After I rescued Dana and Megan, Sheri went into the trailer, found her boyfriend shot to death, and hit her head when she fainted coming back down the steps. She needs to have her head checked. I think she's in shock. Now, any questions?"

"Where's the injured officer?"

"That would be me," Nick offered.

Already annoyed with being told to keep his mouth shut and wait his turn by a rookie, Sergeant Rally looked at Nick in disbelief. "We don't take kindly to the misuse of 'Officer down.' You talk like a Yankee and maybe that's okay where you come from, but here I will slap a fine on you and maybe a little jail time." Sergeant Rally's beefy hand grabbed Nick's injured arm as he finished his sentence, readying to put handcuffs on him.

The pain that roared through Nick's body was indescribable. He groaned loudly, yet gasped for air almost at the same time. Nick wanted to move away, but was frozen immobile, afraid to move and cause more pain, if that were possible. He felt dizzy and lightheaded as his knees buckled.

Suddenly his world went dark.

Sergeant Rally had planned to cuff Nick, but released his grip the moment Nick howled. Even in the fading light he could see the color drain totally from Nick's face. In the next second Nick was lying crumpled on the ground. The ambulance pulled in then.

"Hey guys, get over here quick!" Sergeant Rally yelled.

The EMS crew grabbed their gear and ran over. The gorgeous young blond medic asked, "What happened?"

"I don't know. I touched his arm and he passed out."

She cut away the jacket sleeve then the blood soaked bandage while her companion checked Nick's pressure in the other arm. When the wound was exposed all three of them gasped. "No wonder. That thing's gotta hurt something awful. It looks down to the bone. He gets a ride to the ER. I sure would like to know what happened."

"So would I," Sergeant Rally murmured, "so would I." He decided to talk to the woman who looked like she was high on something and see if she could tell him anything coherent.

Even before he opened his eyes the pain was back with a vengeance. Nick wondered if they could give him something to put him to sleep. He groaned as he tried to sit up, cradling his arm.

"Take it easy," A woman's voice firmly ordered, pushing him back down.

Nick turned suddenly at the sound of the soft lilting voice. With her long blond hair pulled back in a ponytail, she looked like a high school cheerleader. The sudden movement made his stomach turn, but he was more surprised by the youthful blond.

"Ooh," he moaned, "what happened? Who are you?"

"You passed out and I'm Joanne Boyd, an EMT."

"I know you're not supposed to ask a woman her age, but are you old enough to be working? You look like you're still in high school."

"Thank you, but I'm twenty-six and the mother of two lively little boys. How are you feeling now?"

"I think all right. A little dizzy and hurting a whole lot. How long was I out?"

"About five minutes. Let me check your pressure again."

"How's Sheri?"

"If that's the woman with you, she's fine. We're going to take her to the ER, too. Her head needs a couple of stitches. Sergeant Rally is talking to her now."

"I'm ready whenever you are. My arm's killing me. I'd like to get it fixed. Can you get Rally over here. I need to talk to him."

"Hey, Rally!" she called and waved him over.

Sergeant Rally was quick to apologize. "Listen Nick, I'm really sorry about your arm. I didn't know."

"That's okay. I know. I'm the new guy and a Yankee to boot. I got worse treatment in Georgia so don't worry about it. You need to know that Harry Drago was in the area and may still be, but I highly doubt it. There's a tent set up by the electrical towers which could be his hideout. When I checked the trailer, it was neat except for the bedroom. It looked like someone tore through it looking for something. Drago may have gone through the trailer after beating up Officer Dana Morgan. That crime scene is further in the woods. Officer Brown or Porter processed that scene and can fill me in on it. All the cruisers need to be towed. Some teenagers came by and vandalized them. They slashed the tires and glued the locks as well as gave them all an egg and tomato shampoo. I don't think the teens were in the trailer since they like to do more damage than the little I found. Sheri needs a few things out of the trailer. Would that be a problem? She plans to stay with her family for a few days."

"I suppose if one of the officers goes with her she could get a few things."

"She doesn't want to go back in there."

"Okay, Do you want to get her things?"

"That'll be all right with me. After I'm done, do you mind if I go to the ER and leave you to finish up with this mess?"

"Hell, no, get out of here. Wait, Ms. Smith isn't on any drugs, is she? She looks spaced out."

"No." Nick's tone was like he was talking to a child, annoyed but patient. Rally did not seem to notice. "She's in shock. She's an aide at a nursing home, but she found her boyfriend with half his head blown off; add to that a good whack to her head on a concrete step. How do you think you would handle it?"

"That makes sense. Thanks."

It did not take Nick long to gather the few items Sheri had asked for. He informed Officer Rally that the fairy nightlight was not in the bathroom and suggested he might want to check for prints around the outlet and the medicine cabinet. Rally may have brawn, but Nick did not know how much brain went with that or if he had Attention Deficit Disorder.

Nick watched them help Sheri and Megan into the ambulance as he walked toward them. Sergeant Rally checked out the trailer briefly then jumped up into the back of the ambulance to talk to Sheri. After that he came over toward Nick. "We didn't find any shoes on the victim. We checked the rest of the trailer then asked his girlfriend. She said he had only one pair of tennis shoes. They're a cheap off-brand because he liked the circle pattern on the bottom. Probably whoever shot him took his shoes."

"Figures." Nick said.

Joanne called, "We're ready when you are."

Nick gladly hopped into the back. Megan was buckled into a small jump seat. He sat since Sheri was lying on the stretcher. Her face remained a strange ashy color and she still did not seem totally aware of what was going on. He hoped someone would be around when that happened.

CHAPTER 9

Drago's New Hideout

"What do you mean you can't find her?" Drago asked angrily.

"Boss, I know she was there before when we told you," Sam answered nervously, watching Drago's fists clench and release repeatedly, knowing that at any moment they were going to find his face as their target. His face started to ache, remembering the last beating it took only two weeks ago.

They had been out on a robbery together. He was waiting with the engine running for Drago to come out of the convenience store when another car pulled in behind him and blocked him in. He had yelled at him to move his car, but the guy had ignored Sam and given him the finger as he walked into the store. Drago came out a mere fifteen seconds later and they were stuck. Drago ordered Sam to back up into the guy's car and push it out of the way. Sam did as told and they got away without getting caught, but he still got his face punched. He was happy Drago did not punch him as often as the guys in the other gang did.

"Are you absolutely sure she was there?"

"Yes, I saw her myself. Rico and I had gone like you asked to the address her lawyer gave you. We were careful like you told us. She did not see us. We had that old picture of her to look at. Her hair was different, but it was the same face."

"You saw my little girl?"

"Just a little bit. Rico took a picture."

"One picture?"

"That's all we could get. The police cruiser came by and we took off." Sam's nervousness was getting worse. Drago was calmer which should have been a good thing, but he had pulled out his gun and pointed it at him. Sam stood still, but inside he was quaking in his high tops. His mother had preached at him for years to go to church, but no, he wanted to be a tough guy and had joined different street gangs. All they ever did was give him the dirty jobs to do and beat him up. He had joined Drago's gang only a few months ago thinking he would be a big man now.

That last little street gang had a big reputation, but it was nothing compared to being with Drago. He knew Woofer, the gang leader, had not thought much of him and considered him a baby. Sam had seen a glint of fear in Woofer's eyes when he told him that he had signed up with the Dragon Man and would not be back. None of them were brave enough to face Drago and would not join the new gang Drago was forming.

His first week had been easy. Simple errands and a few easy robberies. His reward for all his hard work had been two casino girls on the same night and at the same time. Sam did not know if Drago knew he was still a virgin or not. He could never make it to first base with any of the girls in school and had dropped out in the ninth grade. He lost his virginity that night and then some. Sam smiled shyly remembering that first night. That reward made Drago a great guy in his book.

Rico Regales had joined them two weeks after Sam. Rico was a few years older, smarter and more experienced. More wily Drago feared, but his reputation seemed to keep both boys in line and he was satisfied so far. Drago knew how to plan a robbery and planned bigger robberies now that he had more help. Sam had never seen so much money before, but Drago would not let them spend it wildly. They got one wild night to celebrate, but he warned them it was an easy way to get caught. The money was put up and they knew better than to complain. He and Rico got a weekly allowance plus a bonus for their wild night. He loved having one or two thousand dollars to throw around in an evening. The girls let him feel all over them for the little bills he tucked in their garters and one or two would take him to bed.

Yet here he was at sixteen, facing the barrel of a gun, and at any second he could be dead. Not the way he had planned things to go. Now Sam wished he had listened to his mother. Thinking of his mother made him smile.

"Something funny?"

"Ah, no."

"You were smiling."

Sam waved his hands in front of him. "Not at you, boss." He gulped, "Just a last thought of my Mom, you know, before you shoot me."

Drago nodded. "I'll give you time to say a prayer before that happens. Now tell me, where is this picture now?"

"Rico's looking for it."

"Is that why I haven't seen you two punks for the past three days?"

"Sort of," Sam answered lamely. Thankful he did not feel the pain of a bullet hitting him and a little curious what it would feel like. Would Drago shoot him so he'd die quickly or make him suffer?

Drago cocked the pistol.

Sam gulped and felt the salty tears well up in his eyes. "You're not going to kill me, are you?"

"Thinking about it." Drago did not really want to. That would have meant a body to dispose of and he did not want the hassle. Besides, he knew Sam idolized him and he liked that. Most teens were rebellious, haughty and mouthy. Sam was still docile and moldable, without guile. Drago knew he could trust him. In this line of business it was hard to find anyone you could trust. Sam was not too bright, but he followed orders and knew how to make himself invisible.

"You need me."

"I do?" Drago did, at least right now, but he was not going to admit it to him. It was important to instill fear to keep the young recruit in line.

"Sure," Sam tried to act nonchalant, but his heart was racing. "You don't have anyone else but Rico and me to help you. We're both young, healthy, willing to learn, and…" he stammered, unable to quickly think of enough good reasons why they were both needed. Maybe he could think better without the pistol being pointed at him. "and Rico speaks Spanish."

"So I need him, not you."

"I know a little Spanish."

"Five words. Big deal. I know that much, maybe a few more."

"I could learn."

Drago did not reply. He tilted his head as though taking aim.

Tears started rolling down the young man's cheeks and he dropped to his knees, putting his hands together in prayer. "Please, I'm begging you, don't shoot me." The words rushed out. "I didn't do nothing wrong. Maybe we didn't get enough pictures, but we didn't want to get caught and, and," he stammered in his haste and a single tear rolled down his left cheek, "we would have if we had stayed any longer. It's like she heard the camera click, but she couldn't have. We were across the road behind some bushes, but just as Rico snapped the picture the woman looked right at us. We ducked and waited, thinking we'd try for another one. Then the cop car came by, driving real slow, like he was looking for something. We were done for if they got out and looked in the bushes. Rico dropped the camera and it wouldn't work after that. He left the picture lying on the front seat while we drove back and when we got here we couldn't find the picture. We looked in the car already and then drove back to Charlotte to take more. That's how we found out that she was gone." Spittle flew out of his mouth as he finished the rapid fire explanation.

Drago uncocked the pistol and laid it on the table. "Good answer. I would have preferred not so much theatrics. Get up. I liked you better when you were facing the gun, standing like a man. Tell me, what did the little girl look like?"

"I got a quick glimpse. She was really cute with blond hair and she giggled a lot. We could hear her all the way over where we were."

They were suddenly interrupted by someone entering the hideout. Quickly Drago snapped up the pistol again and pointed it at the door until he recognized that it was Rico.

"You almost got your head blown off, Idiot! You forgot to knock."

"Sorry, D-Man. I guess I was excited. I found the picture. It was stuck under the seat." He handed the Polaroid to Drago.

Drago's fingers twitched with excitement as he grasped the snapshot. He hoped it did not show enough that the two young men would notice. He did not want to appear weak in any way. He took in a deep breath as he turned it around to look at it.

He was disappointed. The photo was slightly out of focus and taken from too far away to see much detail. Even with the short hair cut he easily recognized his ex-wife's profile standing on an upper deck surrounded by a white wooden railing. She was looking down at her child, but all Drago could see where parts of an arm, leg and some blond hair between the spaces in the posts. The railing's white square posts blocked most of the view of the child.

"You're sure she's gone?"

Rico answered, "When we went back to get more pictures, there was a moving van pulling away. I checked in the windows. The whole place was empty. I even went over to the next door neighbor's house. Everything was gone out of their place, too."

"Do you have the name of the moving company?"

"Of course, I'm not stupid. I bought a picture phone so I could take better pictures. I got my friend to print this out on his computer. Don't worry. Dingo's safe. He won't rat on us. He'd join us if he had two legs." He handed Drago another snapshot. This one was in sharp focus. It showed the back end of the van with the company name, address and phone number.

"Smart kid." Drago's excitement died almost immediately, another disappointment. The identity change was glaringly obvious to him.

Rico smiled, proud of himself, and hoping it made up for his goof. He had expected to take a number of pictures, but the house sat alone just on the outside edge of the town with a marshy swamp behind the small fenced-in yard. The nearest neighbor on the left side, closest to town, was at least three vacant lots away. On the right side, there were acres of open fields and no cover. Directly across the road had been open ground except for that small stand of bushes that he and Sam used for cover. He should have stolen a phone that took pictures instead of buying his cousin's old Polaroid at her yard sale. He knew Drago was a dinosaur when it came to computers so he figured a ready-made picture was a good idea. If he had known the layout, he would have thought twice.

"Look again."

Rico stared at it for a minute then said, "I don't see nothing wrong. It says *Charleston Movers, Charleston, SC,* and the phone number."

"Look at the corner above the *C* in Charleston Movers.

Rico took one look and his heart sank. He had been thinking that Drago was old and needed somebody sharp like him to take over in a couple of years, maybe sooner. He figured he would learn how Drago planned his jobs and how to make bombs. Bombs excited him. He would bring in a few more guys to help. Guys that he knew he could trust, and they would have a gang to be feared again like the one he had heard stories about when he was a teen. Now he sees this careless mistake–a big mistake he made.

Rico had to admit to himself that Drago was still sharp. He had looked at that picture for only two seconds and noticed the problem right away. Rico had seen the truck in person and had stared at the picture for a long time on three separate occasions—when he first took it, after finding it in the car to make sure it still showed the sign and had not mysteriously morphed into a different picture, and now, before giving it to Drago. Yet he had managed to miss something so obvious. The mover's sign was a fake. That one corner hung down covering part of the *Ch*. All you could make out of the real word underneath was a blue arc. He had been so eager to get the picture, he had not noticed that one important little detail.

Annoyed at himself, he looked back at Drago with his mouth open ready to speak, until he saw the pistol pointing directly at him. He closed his mouth and gulped, hoping that was not his last act among the living. He almost wanted to laugh. What a silly thought to worry about in the last second of your life. Say a prayer to the God you never cared to know before this moment, or say goodbye to your family even though they could not hear it. Something useful.

Wanted for armed robbery in Alabama, Rico had shot and wounded two people before joining up with Drago. He was used to handling firearms, but not facing them up close. That was his most violent crime and it happened almost by accident, but it started his life of crime. He did not know how to get out of the mess so he kept digging himself deeper. Rico thought he would go out in a knife or gun fight, not standing speechless in front of an old man, gulping down his fear.

Drago's voice was even and low, but the annoyance in his tone was unmistakable. "You can't help it you're stupid. Sometimes it's in the genes, and I'm not talking about that penis in your pants, and sometimes it's in the raising. Now, get out!"

Rico did not need to be told twice. He bolted for the door. Sam just stood there gaping, dumbfounded, and anxious. He did not know if he should run or stay put. He remembered seeing the floppy sign but did not think anything of it at the time. He almost blurted out 'I saw that!', but managed to keep his mouth shut, somehow knowing that admission would earn him a bullet for sure. Sam waited. Would Drago give him a reprieve, too?

Drago pointed the pistol at him next. "You, too. I'll call you when you're needed. Go!"

Sam turned and fled.

Drago got himself a cold beer and sat in his recliner. He had come so close to seeing his little girl. He pounded his fist into the padded armrest to vent his anger and frustration. Maybe he should have shot those boys for being so incompetent. He probably scared them when he told them there were at least a dozen cops living in that area. That tidbit he got from a cousin who worked in that town. Did Lisa know that? Is that why she went there?

Regretting that he had not taken a chance and gone to see Lisa himself, he took a gulp of the cold beer and flipped on the police scanner. Maybe he would get drunk tonight and think about what to do tomorrow.

No. He needed to think up a plan tonight. Most of his usual contacts were avoiding him and the few that were left of his old gang were now with Max Carello who wanted nothing to do with him and certainly would not give him any assistance of any kind. He needed more help to find his ex-wife and could not hire a PI to do it. Sam and Rico were too wet behind the ears to be much help other than errand boys and for small time heists. You don't get resumes in this business, but he thought Rico was sharper that what he turned out to be.

He had no desire to start building a new gang, but was thinking he may have to. He could run it for three or four years with Rico as his right hand man then turn it over to him. What Rico did after that was Rico's problem. He was going to be with Lisa and his new daughter. Drago snorted. Impetuous Rico will probably be killed his first week, Drago thought, or else they'll run through the money faster than water through a sieve. Most likely, they'll get caught within the first three months after they're on their own.

Drago considered he might be unfair. *Rico's not that stupid. He made one careless mistake, but in this business, you don't last long making careless or stupid mistakes. They've robbed enough times with you that Rico will do all right. Sam probably not. He's still too trusting and naive.*

As far as they know, you now have enough money for a decent room with a TV, coffee maker, police scanner, and, don't forget, a real bed. You've stashed away plenty of money for your retirement. Of course, they don't know how much I'm worth. They think we're living fairly decent. If they only knew about the two and half million dollars I have stashed in the bank. He smiled thinking about the interest he was earning. The bank did not know they were paying him interest on money he had robbed from them eight years ago.

Sudden activity on the scanner caught his attention. He turned on the television to get more detail. The newscaster was already into the story...*aka Dragon Man. Officer Dana Morgan has been rescued and taken to East Side Hospital in stable condition. She was found by a fellow officer, rookie Nick Coburn.*

Also this afternoon, another officer, Sergeant Marilyn King, was killed by a car bomb. Escaped convict Harry Drago left a note at the scene, but further investigation is pending. Captain Ed Wells stated that efforts have been stepped up to capture the wanted felon.

Drago clapped his hands at the news. That gave him an idea. He needed a new gang and he needed someone with brains. The police had the man power and the brains, well, some of them did. They were having a hard time catching him, but he was deliberately making it difficult for them. He did not want to be captured. He had no desire to go back to prison. All he had to do was think of a plan.

He made a phone call to the hospital and found out what he wanted to know. That helped him formulate a plan that he could quickly put into play. He called his boys back to help out.

Hospital ER

After a long wait in the emergency waiting room, Megan now sat on the exam table silently watching the activity going on around her. A girl with short brown hair and glasses wearing a blue scrub suit bustled about putting bottles and small boxes on a small table that she wheeled around with her. Every now and then she looked at Megan and smiled.

Megan did not worry until she saw the syringes with their sharp needles. She knew what those were for. She cringed, scrunched her eyes tightly shut, and looked away. No smile or wink was going to help now.

"The doctor will be here in a few minutes to fix your arm. Does it hurt much?"

Daringly, Megan turned her head and opened her eyes. The cute nurse was empty handed. "Not a lot. Where's my mommy?"

Pointing, she said brightly, "She's in the exam room right next door. You've been so brave. Do you need me to get her now?"

"What are they doing?"

"They're fixing the boo-boo on her head. She needs a couple of stitches and they want to get an x-ray to make sure she didn't break her skull."

"Oh," Megan sighed and swung her feet.

"Do you know what the skull is?"

Megan pointed to her head.

"You're a really smart kid!"

"I am smart. I'm five years old," Megan declared, putting up all five fingers. "I'll be going to the big school this year."

"That old, huh." She pointed to her name badge, "My name is Carrie. I'm a nurse. Dr. Meredith Stanley will be taking care of your arm. I don't want to leave you alone. When she gets here, I'll go get your mother."

"Okay. I miss Mary Alice."

"Who's that? A friend?"

"No, she was my doll. The bad dog that scratched my arm ate my doll." Megan heaved a huge sigh and slowly shook her head, "Poor, sad Mary Alice, what a way to go."

Carrie laughed softly at Megan's theatrics. "I bet your mother will get you another one."

"She won't be the same."

"No, I'm sure it won't, but you'll learn to love her, too."

Dr. Stanley walked in and glanced at the chart. "Hello, Megan, isn't it? How are you? I understand you had a dog bite you."

"No, he scratched me."

"Well, that can be just as bad. Let me see your arm." She looked at Carrie. "Where are the parents?"

"Only the mother came with her. She's in exam room five. I didn't want to leave Megan alone. Now that you're here I'll go get her."

Megan quietly said, "My daddy died when I was real little."

"I'm sorry to hear that." She spoke as she cut the dressing off. "This doesn't look too bad. You're a lucky little girl."

"Everybody keeps telling me that," Megan heaved a huge sigh and slapped the back of her other hand on the paper of the exam table. "We use sheets on our beds."

"There's a sheet under that. That just saves us having to change the sheets so often if we don't need to."

"Oh," Megan replied, but she was busy poking her fingers along the paper sheet listening to the different sounds she could make.

Carrie came back in and announced, "Her mother's having a CT done now, so she'll be awhile."

"Well, I see you're all set up. Are all the consents signed by chance?"

"I'm sorry, I should have told you that." Carrie walked over to the counter and picked up a clipboard. She flipped through a couple of pages and showed Dr. Stanley the treatment consent forms. "Ms. Sheri Smith signed everything when she first got here. Although I will admit, she did not look in too good of shape to be signing anything."

"That's okay. This is minor surgery, no big deal. Let's get started." She faced Megan, "Sweetie, I need to give you a little shot to numb the area right here," the doctor gently touched where she meant, "after that little pinch you won't feel a thing. Carrie, the nurse, is going to hold your arm."

As she was drawing up the Novocaine, an orderly appeared suddenly in the doorway, grabbing hold of the door jam to stop his momentum. "Dr. Stanley, you're wanted in triage STAT," he spit out excitedly. He let go of the door jam and disappeared as suddenly as he had appeared.

Dr. Stanley and Carrie looked at each other. Dr. Stanley was the first to speak. "I wonder what that was all about. I'll be right back. If something disastrous has happened, go ahead and clean it again, butterfly it and redress it. Give her back to her mother with the usual wound care instructions and have her follow up with her pediatrician in one week." She wrote a prescription as she talked, "Give her mother this prescription for an antibiotic. It's only for three days just precautionary."

Even though she had no children of her own yet, Carrie was an aunt to four girls and three boys so she was comfortable around children. She and Megan chatted while she cleaned the wound. Carrie waited another ten minutes then went ahead and applied the butterflies and redressed the wound.

"Let me get the wound instruction sheets and we'll head over to the room your mother's in. She should be done with that CT by now." Carrie rifled through the file drawer. "Here it is. Let's go." Carrie stood in front of Megan and put her arms out, "Jump."

Megan jumped gleefully into her waiting arms.

"Now, let's go find your mommy."

"Good. I miss her. I'm thirsty, too."

"I don't see any reason why you can't have a drink. What would you like?"

"Apple juice," Megan stated emphatically without any hesitation. "That's my favorite drink."

"I think I can round one up for you." Carrie set Megan on a chair in exam room five. "I wonder where your mother is? She should be back. Wait right here. I'll get your juice and be right back. Remember, don't leave this spot. Promise?"

Megan put up her hand and crossed her heart, "Promise." She started swinging her legs.

Satisfied that Megan would stay in the room, Carrie hurried down the hall to get the juice. She looked in the refrigerator and saw none. She looked in the cabinet and grabbed one of the boxes, hoping Megan would not care that it was not cold. She hurried back to the room knowing she had been gone maybe two minutes.

The room was empty. Carrie's heart sank before the panic set in. She had never lost a patient before, let alone a child. That was not exactly true, but she never really counted that guy that was high on whatever it was. It had been crazy that night in the ER. His arms and legs had been fastened to the bed by leather restraints when she had to dash across the hall to start CPR on another patient. No one but Houdini could get out of four-point leather restraints. Ten minutes later security found him dancing naked on the roof of one of the doctor's brand new SUV in the side parking lot. Every time one of the security officers got close they got hit with a short stream of urine. The man decided to urinate on the hood of the SUV while singing off-key praises to his moon god. When his bladder was empty, security was finally able to get him down and back inside. Carrie had heard he was a big hit on YouTube.

Quickly, Carrie looked up and down the hall. No little girl in sight. Small children were naturally curious. Had Megan gone into another exam room to see something? There were ten exam rooms to search plus the utility rooms, two offices, cast room, minor procedure room…oh, Carrie thought, she could not look everywhere herself. She turned around to head for the front desk to call security to report a missing child. She did not care about the embarrassment or the good natured ribbing she would get, as much as for the child's safety. Suddenly it dawned on her, maybe they were both discharged and she was worrying for nothing. She was probably safely with her mother.

Before she had taken two steps a small voice chimed, "Here I am! I had to go potty." Carrie turned and, to her great relief, there was little Megan.

"I was wondering where you were."

"Another nurse showed me where to go. I promised I'd come right back."

"I'm glad you did. Here's your juice." She handed Megan the boxed juice with the attached straw. "Can you do the straw?"

The elevator doors opened and Carrie looked up. She watched a stretcher come down the hall their way. By the time she looked back, Megan already had the straw unwrapped and, with her intense five-year-old concentration, was trying to poke it through the small foil opening.

The orderly stopped by Carrie. "I have a Sheri Smith. What room?"

"Exam room five." Carrie pointed and started walking in that direction.

"Mommy! Mommy!" Megan jumped up and down, shouting excitedly.

"Shh," Carrie gently admonished as she picked her up so she could see her mother better. "I'll put you on a chair next to her once we get her in the room. Okay?"

"Megan, Sweetie, I love you." Her mother reached out for her and Carrie dropped Megan down lower so she could get a hug. "You two will have more time together after we get you transferred."

Carrie was glad to see Ms. Smith looking more alert than when she arrived. She often wished she got the whole story on some of these patients that came in to the ER. She had come in with an injured police officer and her daughter had a wild dog scratch her. Maybe she should have talked to Megan more about what had happened to her and less about school and other trivialities.

Kelly, one of her coworkers, came to the door, "Are you done with exam room eight?"

"I guess. I had Megan in there, but her mother's back. I could put them together now. What's happening?"

"Haven't you heard? There's been three explosions in the last hour and a half. The power plant was the first about an hour ago. Those injuries filled up St Luke and Teller's Regional. Judson's Chemical was next about forty-five minutes ago filling up St Joe's, Newton's Express Care, and cramming a few more into Teller's. Now it seems it's our turn. There's a six car pile up on the interstate and a big fire in the warehouse district. My girlfriend called and said that the word on the internet is the drivers going over the Porters Bridge saw the warehouse explode and some of them got rattled and caused the accident. Anyway, that's only a few blocks from us so they're coming here. Triage is suddenly swamped and we're now getting them back here. Everybody that can be discharged is to get out the door ASAP. They're calling in extra staff. I'll clean your room." With that he was gone.

"I guess I better see about your discharge instructions. I'll be right back."

Drago had been watching for the nurse to leave. This hospital emergency room was notoriously slow and his phone call earlier had confirmed that, but he almost missed his chance with the girl and her mother. He entered the room fully prepared, knowing he had little time and had to work fast. "Mrs. Smith, I have your instructions and a shot of penicillin." He was wearing a stolen white lab coat over his street clothes and carrying a small tray with two small pre-filled syringes. Each was filled with a sedative. A long sleeved lab coat, a small mustache, and an authoritative air was all the disguise he needed.

As Sheri was pushing herself up into a sitting position, he jabbed the needle into her neck.

"Ow!" Sheri exclaimed grabbing her neck just as her eyelids fluttered shut. The fast acting sedative was doing its job.

"Who's the other one for?" Megan asked with a little tremor in her voice. "Did that make my Mommy go to sleep?"

"It sure did."

"Why? You lied."

"Because you two are going for a ride and it's a surprise." To Drago that did not make much sense and he hoped she did not ask for a better explanation. His plan was simple. He wanted only Megan, but thought it might be safer to take her mother, too. They would be his bargaining chips.

He wondered if his own little girl would be as inquisitive as Megan. Drago quickly grabbed her and jabbed Megan's neck. Megan gave a tiny squeak that faded quickly as she went limp in his arms. He laid her beside her mother on the exam table and put up the side rails.

Drago was smart enough to make it look like Sheri Smith had been given her discharge instructions. He signed and dated the instruction sheets for both mother and daughter altering his signature so it looked like two different people at a quick glance. He took the patient copies with him and left the hospital copies on the clipboard in the exam room. He did not want anyone getting suspicious too soon.

After covering them with a sheet, he peeked out the exam room door. There was Sam, looking like an EMT, with a stretcher and a big smile. Hospital staff were hurrying past and not paying any attention to them, most were trying to reorganize and regroup.

Drago put an oxygen mask on Sheri after they transferred her to the ambulance gurney. They wheeled her out through the emergency waiting room without incident. At the outer doors they were stopped by a security officer.

Laughingly he asked, "Aren't you going the wrong way?"

Ready with an excuse, Drago answered, "She's being transferred to Teller's. Got to run." They kept on moving.

Sam was in the lead. There were four ambulances crowded near the entrance. Sam went to the one farthest away. They quickly loaded their kidnap victims and disappeared into the night.

When Carrie finally returned, she was surprised to find the instructions already done. The employee signature was hard to read, but she shrugged it off, glad that someone helped out since the rest of the evening was going to be crazy.

When Megan woke up she forgot where she was. It was not her house and it was not the hospital. The room light was dim and shadowy. While she rubbed her eyes with her fist, she looked around the unfamiliar room and saw a man lying on the couch. His arm fell over the side and she gasped; a dragon on his arm stared at her.

Silently Megan sat on the blanket with her back against the wall watching the man and his tattoo. She looked at the white gauze covering her arm. It hardly hurt at all now. On a piece of tape there was a blue fairy sticker. That made Megan smile. She had a fairy to protect her.

Megan kept quiet and remained still as she surveyed the room. There were newspapers and magazines scattered on the chairs and floor. Cups and paper plates were sitting around, most partially filled with various colored liquids. She thought about how her house never looked this messy or smelled so odd. The smell reminded her of when her mother had packed things in a box that had gotten wet. Her mother called it musty.

Megan had to potty really badly. She did not think she could hold it long enough to wait for the big man to wake up and decided she should be able to find the bathroom on her own. Softly, she padded across the worn carpet in her bare feet, keeping her eye on the dragon the whole time. The dragon's eye seemed to follow her until she reached the cool tile of the kitchen floor when it disappeared from view and a loud voice boomed at her.

"Where do you think you're going?"

Megan froze. *Was that the dragon talking?* Warm urine trickled down her thighs forming a small puddle between her feet during her few seconds of indecision–the table or the blanket. Megan raced under the table, her normal refuge of safety and it was closer.

"I'm sor-wy. I didn't mean to do it." Instantly her newfound strength and independence vanished, replaced by the shy, insecure abused little girl of old.

Harry Drago, surprised by Megan's reaction, was at a loss with what to do. She was such a little bitty thing and had hardly weighed more than a feather in his arms. If he had not been dozing, he would have realized she was not trying to sneak away but merely going to the bathroom.

He decided to handle the ransom exchange quickly so his life could get back to normal. Maybe he should call his sister to come help him for a while. Immediately changing his mind, knowing that would not work. He could not think of a plausible story to tell his sister about Megan. Besides, Megan was so feisty she would tell his sister the whole truth in no time. His normal voice was a loud bass. His first wife had left him because she claimed he scared her. He needed a loud, commanding voice to demand respect. If it scared people, that was too bad.

He chuckled. "Listen, I didn't mean to scare you." Drago found some paper towels and threw a handful onto the puddle of urine that was slowly coursing its way toward Megan. "Come on out, and I'll show you where the bathroom is."

"Are you going to hit me?"

"No, why should I hit you?"

"I peed on the floor," she whispered. She crept to edge and looked up at him with uncertainty mixed with fear in her pale blue eyes. Very few men were kind. Megan had learned to be wary of all of them.

"That wasn't your fault. Now get out from under there." Trying to encourage her, he waved his arm, not thinking of his dragon tattoo, "Are you hungry?"

"Yes," Megan answered, but she still did not come out from under the table. The dragon worried her.

Impatiently Drago boomed, "Now what!"

Megan ducked back farther under the table. Drago tried to reach her, but she was too far back. A bit of light caught on the silver of the dragon's eye. Megan was not sure her tiny fairy was enough to protect her against such a fierce dragon.

"Don't make me pull the table away from the wall. I thought you said you were hungry."

"I am," she said barely above a whisper.

"Then what's stopping you?" Drago bellowed. "I ought to shoot you and be done with it."

There was a pause. Drago looked under the table to see a whimpering Megan. *Why did I think this would be a smart idea? Maybe I should drop her and her mother off somewhere and come up with a better plan. I don't want to complicate things and wake the mother up. I thought a child would be simple to handle. It seemed like such a good idea–hold them until the police found Lisa and my daughter. Maybe I'm no smarter than Rico and Sam put together.*

"The dragon," Megan pointed.

"What about the dragon?" Drago looked at his tattoo, not seeing anything different with it. "Will it bite me?"

Drago roared with laughter. He plopped down on a chair and wiped the tears from his eyes. "No, it doesn't bite."

Satisfied, Megan enthusiastically ran out from under the table. "What's for supper?" She did not want to believe the big man or his dragon would hurt her.

"This is breakfast. You slept all night." He got her a towel and washcloth out of the cupboard. "Wash the stink off then go sit on your blanket."

Megan took off her wet underpants after using the toilet. On the counter was a small stack of paper towels with a handful of little bars of motel soaps scattered in front of it. She took her time washing off and looked around. The window was big and tall, but frosted so she could not see out. She spoke in whispered tones, "Mary Alice, if you were here, I'd tell you this pw-lace looks like the bathroom at the movie theater. There's one–two–three–four toilets. Nobody has four toilets in a house."

Megan put her underpants inside the towel and carried it into the hall. She looked around. There was a door with M-E-N, another one with S-T-O-R-A-G-E. Again Megan talked to her absent doll. "I know MEN means a bathroom for boys. S-T-O-R is what store starts with, but I don't know the rest of the word." Hanging high on the wall was a tattered and worn banner. Its once proud colors of purple and gold now faded to a dull eggplant and dirty yellow. Megan looked at the aged sign, but was not sure what it spelled. She knew most of her letters and could spell simple words, but that whole word was too hard for her. The first word started with an H–Heaton, but it was too hard to figure out. The second word was not any easier for her. That word began with a C–Cotton. She knew the third word–MILLS because that was in one of her stories. She was wondering about going down the hallway to explore when a booming voice startled her.

"Better hurry! Food's ready."

Megan raced back the way she came.

As she ate her scrambled eggs she chatted, "Where's my mommy?"

"She's still sleeping. She'll eat later."

"She doesn't have to work today?"

"No."

"That's good."

Drago gulped down a huge mouthful before the next question. He had not wanted to keep Megan doped up, uncertain how much was safe for her, but now he was having second thoughts. He was not used to children, not even his own. He did not like being a babysitter, and this was his idea.

"Do you have any little girls?"

"I have a little baby girl and a teenage daughter."

"What's their names?"

Drago thought for a moment and wondered if he should make up a name since he did not know his own baby daughter's name. It was not fair of his ex-wife to keep this from him. Angrily, he answered, "I don't know. Shut up! Eat!"

His rough tone scared Megan so she was quiet the rest of the time. She thought to herself that his niceness had not lasted much longer than Tom's. She looked around for beer cans and did not see any.

When he stretched his arm out, the dragon was revealed in all its glory. Megan's eyes widened in terror when she saw how much bigger the dragon was. Its red eyes glared at Megan. It was blue and green with a long tail that curved all the way up his arm ending with a vicious spike dripping a few drops of blood. The dragon truly scared her. It was not a friendly dragon like in her story books. This one had a long pointed red tongue and sharp fangs. It looked like it would bite her if she got too close. She was not sure if she believed him that it would not bite. Megan worried that the dragon might spit fire at her. Every time she saw the dragon its red eyes were looking at her.

She thought about it and decided to ask, "Does the dragon hurt you? It's scary."

He snorted and rolled his eyes. He looked at her and wished he could laugh, but he was in too foul of a mood right now. People were afraid of him, but not dear little Megan. She was afraid of a tattoo. "It's supposed to be scary," he rasped.

Drago's phone rang. He grabbed it quickly off the table, answering with an abrupt, "What?"

Megan finished eating as he talked. She did not like scrambled eggs that much, but she knew not to complain. The toast and sausage were good. The milk was not real cold and tasted a little odd, but he snapped at her to finish it when she left some in the glass.

Drago finished his phone conversation with a "Fine," flipping the phone shut as he said it.

Afraid, Megan was trying to curl up on her chair to hide. She tucked her legs under her and scrunched down. She did not know if she should go to her blanket or try to find her mother.

"Are you done?" He looked at the glass of milk to make sure it was all gone. He had slipped a small dose of sleeping medicine in it to make her more cooperative.

"Yes, sir," Megan answered barely above a whisper.

"Good. Put your plate in the sink and go get on your blanket."

Megan carried her plate across the room and carefully dropped it in the sink, the plastic clattered on top of the others. She hesitated a moment, deciding if she should include the Styrofoam cup. When she heard his footsteps, she threw it in too. After doing that simple chore, Megan ran to the safety of her blanket and lay down. She did not close her eyes. Drago turned on the television and watched the news. She wanted to ask if she could go see her mother, but was afraid to. In a few minutes, her eyelids felt very heavy.

She did not fall completely asleep. Someone knocked at the door— one sharp rap followed by a pause then two sharp raps. Drago got up and answered the door.

"Did you get everything I need?"

"Of course. Come on into the other room."

Megan could not hear everything they said. Drago picked her up and carried her through the room and down a hall. She kept her head resting on his shoulder. She did not fuss or try to get down.

The other room was bright, clean and smelled like bleach. Surprised by the sudden brightness, Megan dared to peek around. It reminded her of her doctor's office except it was missing the colorful letters and numbers on the walls. She wiped her nose on the Dragon man's coat and hoped he did not notice. She did not like the smell of smoke on his coat. Drago put Megan down on a table that the other man covered with a paper tablecloth.

The chill of the metal table came through the thin paper. Megan started to whimper and sat up. Then she saw the other man. Suddenly she felt very afraid and screamed. The other man had a very ugly eye. It was red where it should have been white and stuck out farther than the other one. Drago had to come back to her side. She quit screaming and buried her head in Drago's shirt, no longer able to see the funny-eyed man.

"You gave her the drug?"

"Yes, I guess it hasn't kicked in." Drago was a little surprised by the sudden tender feeling he felt, but he could not let it show. He put his hand on Megan's back with a gentle, not restrictive pressure. He was eager to hold his own little girl.

Megan, happy not to have to look at the funny-eyed man, stayed still.

The man handed Drago a large paper bag. Drago reached in and took out a rag doll which he gave to Megan. "Go on and take it. I got it for you. It's like your other one."

Hesitantly, Megan accepted the doll. This one had big blue stitched eyes with black lashes instead of black button eyes like Mary Alice. She had on a pale pink dress and pink silk slippers to match. Megan held the doll tightly, but right now it did not give her the same comfort that Mary Alice gave her. She squeezed the new doll tightly and considered names for her, but did not know if it was hers to keep or not. Some toys had to stay behind like at her special school. Maybe this doll had to stay behind for his little girl.

She stared at the big man. Tears formed in Megan's eyes, but she blinked rapidly so they would not fall. Tom always laughed when he made her cry. She did not want the big man to laugh at her. Would the dragon laugh, too?

"I want my Mommy." Silent tears started to fall and a soft whimper managed to escape.

"Whatcha crying for? I gave you a doll, didn't I? That was supposed to make you happy," he said to Megan a little harsher than he intended. Looking to the other man, Drago gave an exasperated sigh, "Let's get this over with."

The few tears Megan shed were nothing like he expected. He had to admit that Megan was doing ninety percent better than he ever anticipated. He expected she would have been fighting him and crying her eyes out for her mother the whole time.

Megan watched the funny-eyed man closely to make sure he did everything the way she saw her mother do it when she had to fix a cut. He washed his hands in the large double stainless steel sink along the wall. Then he opened a large envelope and unfolded a sterile white sheet on the table in front of them.

He reached for Megan, but she pulled away. "Now, Girlie, I need to look at your arm."

"No!"

He looked over Megan's head and spoke to Drago, "Feisty little devil."

"You got that right! Smart, too." Drago declared with a hint of pride as though Megan were his own child.

"Listen, Kid, I would rather do this the easy way and have you cooperate. Do you know what that means?"

Megan's blue eyes shone with defiance, but her lower lip pouted out with uncertainty, "No. The nurse fixed my arm already."

"The hard way is that I sew your arm without anything to numb it so you feel all the pain. The easy way is I give you one little shot, maybe two, and you don't have any hurting. Which way do you want it?"

Megan would not look at the man while he explained. She did not want to hurt, but she did not know if she could trust him. Her daddy was the only man that had ever made her feel safe and he was dead.

"This kind of wound needs looked at every day. Let me take a look. That's all I want to do right now. Okay?"

Megan faced him, trying to look at only his good eye. "Okay, just look."

He quickly cut off the dressing on her arm and briefly examined it. "They did enough in the ER. It'll probably leave a scar. Nothing big. You'll have a great story to tell your kids when you grow up." He looked at Drago, "I don't need to do anything. I thought you said they didn't treat it?"

"I wasn't sure what was done. Since I didn't know how long this little standoff might take I wanted to make sure it didn't get infected."

"I'll redress it and I brought enough supplies for you to change it again tomorrow."

"Me?"

"You can have the mother do it. This is simple, not rocket science. Hell, even the kid can do it."

Megan interjected before Drago had a chance to say anything, "That's a bad word. You're not supposed to say bad words."

The funny-eyed doctor glared at Megan. She backed into Drago's chest as far as she could go which was not far since he was holding her arm. "Little girls aren't supposed to say cuss words, but grown men can."

Drago, unaware of the little drama going on around him and how terrified Megan was, went on with the conversation. "I'm trying not to have the two of them together. That might cause more problems than I care for."

"Well, I can't take a chance on being seen or followed by coming back every day, and neither can you by taking her to a doctor's office or clinic."

"I guess I have no choice. What do I need to do?"

The red-eyed doctor explained the simple directions to him, leaving a week's worth of supplies before he departed.

CHAPTER 10

Rico was happy that Drago trusted him to do the phone. He was so excited he had gotten a hard on. He felt uncomfortable in this police uniform. He ran his finger around the collar again and rolled his neck as he rode the crowded elevator to the third floor. Visiting hours in ICU were limited, but a fellow officer should get to visit any time Drago had reasoned.

"Rough night?" a young nurse asked as they were getting off on the third floor.

"Huh, yeah," Rico worried he might blow it by appearing too nervous. Sweat was beading on his forehead.

"Are you here to see someone?"

"Ah, Officer Morgan. I have a card to drop off." Rico smiled and hoped he came across as friendly and not too stiff. He was not sure if she was hitting on him or interrogating him. His hard had wilted, but maybe she would be interested in reviving that later.

"She's in ICU for observation. You've missed visiting hours, but they might let you in. I'm headed that way. Follow me."

He did not mind following the cute little brunette and watching her hips sway. Maybe he would ask her out later. Would Drago get mad if he did? Would Drago even find out? Probably. That man seemed to have an uncanny sense of knowing everything that went on around him.

As luck would have it just as Rico walked past the nurses' station, they called a Code Blue. The entire staff became too busy to pay attention to one single, quiet police officer. Quickly he glanced around. The curtains had been drawn between her bed and the ones on either side of her.

He entered silently. Dana was sleeping peacefully. Her restful profile entranced him and Rico, knowing he was taking a huge chance, pulled out the stub of a pencil that he carried with him for times like this. Slipping on his gloves he quickly sketched her while she slept, focusing on her head and slender neck. He had honed his natural talent, so it took him only about forty-five seconds what might take the average person over five minutes.

He placed the ransom note with his sketch under the tray for her water pitcher on the over bed table and quietly exited. Dana never opened her eyes. Rico was glad she was sleeping since that made this step easier. He had a cover story ready and had planned to distract her while he slipped the note unnoticed under the tray if she had been awake. He had not known how he was going to pull off acting like one since police officers made him nervous and worried she might realize he was only acting. He heaved a huge sigh once he reached the hallway, glad that he could get out of this outfit after one more job.

Next he had the phone to place. Everyone was running around like crazy because of all the chaos that Drago had created. A police officer was considered trustworthy, so no one was going to stop him and question his presence or what he was carrying in his little bag. He could not get used to the uniform and again ran his finger around the collar, trying to relax some of the stiffness in the new fabric and the uneasiness he felt.

Rico took the stairs this time to get to the kitchen on the basement level. It was slow going to keep out of the security camera's view. It was late enough the staff were gone for the night. He cased things out yesterday. He made out with a shy dietary aide while pretending to be interested in working there. He had worked in the kitchen in a hospital in Texas so he knew a little bit about hospital kitchens and the food carts. She answered all his questions so helpfully, never suspecting he was up to no good. No one would be returning until four-thirty in the morning and he knew there was a guard that made rounds every two hours.

The kitchen lock was easy to pick. It took him ten minutes to move some of the carts around. He found a corner with a slight indentation that a cart would tuck in to and a pipe running down from floor to ceiling that he thought was perfect, but he still said a prayer that he would do a good job. He wanted Drago to be proud of him. He laughed softly, wondering if God would answer that prayer.

He opened his tool kit and got busy. He securely taped the phone to the inside of one of the cart doors. Rico figured it would easily be found there.

Footsteps in the hallway caught his attention. He turned off his flashlight and waited. *The security guard must be making his regular rounds.* Rico looked at his watch. The guard was thirty minutes early. *Was there a reason for the odd time?* He listened patiently as the man rattled doorknobs making sure they were locked. *Did I lock the door behind me? Yeah, I'm sure…almost sure.* Rico huddled behind a food cart, sweat beading on his forehead as he waited.

The doorknob jiggled, but remained closed. He hoped the guard was not terribly thorough and would take the extra time to look in any of the four large rectangular windows making up most of the wall to this section of the kitchen. If he noticed the carts shuffled around, he might decide he needed to check on things and that could mean big trouble. The footsteps shuffled past. Rico exhaled slowly, staying on the cool tile floor until his nerves calmed down which was long after the echo of the guard's footsteps faded away. Rico checked his watch before standing. He had not wasted too much time, only eighteen minutes. He had plenty of time before the guard would be back around. *Unless he decides to surprise you by coming at an odd time.* Rico decided he had better hurry.

He applied a bead of industrial strength glue all around both doors on the cart and shut them. After waiting a few minutes for the glue to dry he tried to open them. The whole cart moved. Rico smiled, satisfied. Next he cut a chunk out of two rubber tires so the cart could not be used. He damaged a few more tires after he moved the carts into place to make it hard for anybody to move them around.

Everything had gone smoothly. Eager to be gone before his luck changed, Rico checked his watch. He had twenty minutes before the guard was due back around. Again staying out of view of the security cameras, he took the stairs two at a time to reach the main level quicker. He blended in with the others as they were exiting occasionally offering a brief return greeting to those passing by. He wanted to run, but knew he should not. The front door was slowly getting closer.

Finally, Rico was outside, free, and breathing the warm night air. He knew he had done a good job even if it was slightly different from his original orders. It was better and he knew it. He felt good. He got on his bike and roared out of the parking lot back to their hiding place.

Local News: *Late last evening an ambulance was stolen from the East Side Hospital emergency room. We were finally able to interview the two EMT's who were driving it. Here's the update with John Powers.*

John: *Thank you, Lynda. I'm with Greg Matte and Lynn Grabowski who were assaulted by a young male who acted like he was injured. Lynn can you tell us what happened.* He put the microphone in front of Lynn.

Lynn: *Greg and I were at the back of the ambulance when this kid came up to us. He approached me and started to ask a question when he fell against me hard, pushing me against the open doors of the truck. Greg pulled him off me. He acted kind of faint.*

John: *I understand you're pregnant.*

Lynn: *Yes, four months, but the ER doctor checked me out and thinks everything is okay.*

John: *What happened next?*

Greg: *He apologized, talked like he was drunk or high on something then fell into me, grabbing me around my waist. We had to get our patient out of the back to take into the ER. This guy said he was feeling better and took off into the ER.*

John: *Did you see him again?*

Greg: *No, we were busy with our patient in the ER for nearly fifteen minutes because of the backlog. I thought I saw him leave with a patient on a stretcher, but I decided that I had to be mistaken. Then when we went to leave and neither one of us had the keys and our ambulance was gone, we figured he had picked my pocket when he fell against me.*

John: *That's it. At this point we have no idea why he stole the ambulance. Back to you, Lynda Razz.*

Nick got out of bed and winced with pain. Antsy to get busy, he was having a hard time waiting for the doctor to discharge him. After his surgery last night, he had been in no shape to go home, but now he wanted to be working on this case. He had wasted half of the morning impatiently waiting. He had a little girl and her mother whose life depended on him and he prayed it was not too late.

He showered and dressed, putting on his old jeans and yesterday's socks. It was still a little too tender to maneuver his arm and use those muscles, so Nick slipped on a clean hospital gown that was left with a fresh towel and washcloth. Since his own shirt was torn and covered with dried blood he decided he would put it on when he was ready to go out the door after being discharged. He did not want to scare everybody when he walked down the hallways.

An elderly silver-haired volunteer came by wearing a green vest. "Good morning, Sir. Here's a paper. Would you like anything else?" She placed the newspaper on the over-bed table. Smiling pleasantly she continued, "Of course, the everything else comes with a price."

"No, thank you," he stated as he picked up the paper then he thought of one thing. "Oh, any deodorant?"

She smiled, "Certainly. We carry two different brands I'll bring them in for you to choose."

Nick completed his purchase when one of the nurses walked in. "Good morning, Mr. Coburn. The doctor wants another x-ray of your arm. Jarrod will be here in a minute to take you to x-ray. We'll have you back before lunch arrives."

Just as she finished speaking a young black man walked in pushing a wheelchair. "Yo, Mr. Coburn, may I see your name-band?"

Nick held out his right arm with the band in view. "Could I walk instead?"

"It's policy," Jarrod stated as he looked questioningly at the nurse.

She responded, "I don't see why not. It's just your arm and you're in good shape."

The words *good shape* were said with a hint of sexual innuendo which Nick did not mind. He caught the twinkle in her eye. He needed a little humor now to help him feel better. He smiled, flexed his right arm biceps and said, "Thanks."

Before meeting Dana he might have hit on the nurse for her phone number. Today, however, he was not interested. He had to smile to himself. Never before had a woman so enthralled him as Dana did. He wanted to get to know her better. He wanted to feel her in his arms. He wanted to kiss her and make love to her. These feelings baffled as well as surprised him.

It did not take long for them to do the x-ray and Nick was escorted back to his room by a different orderly. Jarrod had hummed a rap tune as they went and talked a little. The one coming back remained stone-faced silent. He sat in a chair to read the newspaper and had gotten to page three when a short article caught his eye. It was about a mother and daughter, no names were given, missing from the hospital. *Interesting. I need to talk to Dana. First, something for pain.*

Nick went to the nurses' station to get something for pain when the lunch cart rumbled off the elevator. The station was empty so he went back to his room. He waited until they delivered his lunch tray before pressing the call button and explaining his need to the scratchy disembodied voice that answered. He hoped the doctor would come right after lunch.

He ate the mashed potatoes with gravy and the cup of chocolate pudding. The rest of his lunch tray he left untouched. Mystery meat and over done broccoli he could do without.

An older black nurse brought his pain pill a few minutes later. "Mr. Coburn, I've got bad news. Your doctor just had an emergency. He'll be in surgery for most of the afternoon."

"Is there anyone else that can discharge me?"

"Sorry, no. It has to be him. Is it so bad to stay with us for a few more hours?"

"I'd like to visit my partner and get busy on this case."

"Where's your partner?"

"In ICU."

"What's his name?"

"Her—Dana Morgan." Nick noticed the brief look of surprise on the nurse's face when he mentioned the name.

"Let me see if I can arrange for you to visit. I'll be right back."

Nick's eyes lit up. "I'd appreciate that. Thanks." Nick hoped she'd be able to arrange it.

About ten minutes later a different nurse entered. She was as broad as she was tall with unflattering straight black hair. "Miss Morgan's allowed visitors now, but you have to keep it short."

Nick fairly flew out of the bed, gave her a quick kiss on her cheek. "Thanks." He was at the door before he realized he had forgotten the newspaper and he did not know where to go. He turned back around. She was still standing at the bedside looking pleasantly dazed.

"Where's ICU?" he asked. His long stride easily covering the distance in the time it took for her to answer, Nick retrieved his paper and kept going.

"Third floor," she answered as she slowly walked towards the door with a silly grin on her face.

The elevator was crowded and stopped forever on the fourth floor while most of the people got off and another crowd got on. The next floor was his stop. He politely pushed his way to the front and followed the signs to ICU.

Nick walked into the unit and stopped at the desk. A young girl with spiked black and purple hair wearing a blue scrub suit sat talking on the telephone. Nick looked around while he impatiently waited for his turn.

"May I help you?"

"I'd like to see Dana Morgan."

"She's a popular person today. You have five minutes." She pointed with a many ringed finger and the clang of a dozen dangly bracelets. "Bed four."

"How about ten minutes? We have a lot to discuss." Nick recognized the look she gave him. It was the same one that petite old woman in Dana's building had given him, only this girl had a lot more attitude."

"I said five, cinco." She held up her hand, turning it and showing off her five perfectly manicured bright red fingernails, wiggling her fingers in goodbye. She returned to reading her magazine, muttering "Idiot" just loud enough for him to hear.

Nick bent over the desk, getting right in her face, amazed and a little annoyed that his good looks had not made any impression on her. "I happen to be an FBI agent." He pulled out his wallet and showed her his ID. "That little five-fingered wave is cute when you're a sweet little five-year old like Megan. Your cooperation would be greatly appreciated. I'm being polite and asking for ten minutes, or I may find a reason to have you arrested. The FBI generally doesn't hire idiots."

The girl looked up at him and gulped, not in a very feminine manner. "Okay."

"Thank you." Nick hurried off in the direction the girl had pointed.

She raised her hand as if in the classroom, uncertainly and only halfway up as if she was not sure of the answer. She said in a somewhat confused tone, "My name's Becky, not Megan." Nick did not bother to turn around. He acknowledged her comment with a two fingered salute as he went down the short hall toward Dana's bed.

His long stride reached Dana's bed quickly. He stood for a moment watching her sleep and wondered who all had visited her today. The oxygen tube hung on the wall. An intravenous line snaked up one arm, one finger was covered with a pulse oximeter, and multiple wires peeked out around her gown attaching her to a monitor that showed her heart activity.

Nick watched her chest rise and fall, steady and even. It was a comfort to see and hear the heart monitor's steady rhythmic beat. Nick walked to her side and placed a tender kiss on her forehead as he whispered, "Hello. A kiss to make you better."

Dana opened her eyes and smiled. Nick's heart skipped a beat. *This isn't right. I wasn't supposed to fall in love for real. I'm still not sure what I feel. I've never been in love before. Dana doesn't act like she loves me or even likes me. If I've fallen in love with her, shouldn't she be in love with me, too? How does this complicate our new assignment? Will it make it easier or harder? I can't turn the case over to another agent. What if she doesn't want to work with me? Cool it, Nick. There's no need to rush things. Then why do I feel like I want everything yesterday?* Nick smiled back, wanting to take her hand in his, but afraid to touch her and set off an alarm. "How are you feeling?"

"Quite well, all things considered," Dana sat up. "I've been working this morning and was resting a bit. I tried to call Sheri Smith to see how she and Megan were doing, but was unable to reach her. I had my friend at the hospital fax me a copy of the next of kin she listed which happened to be her mother. I called her and she has not heard from Sheri in a week." Dana coughed and got a drink of water.

Nick added, "She mentioned to me she had a boyfriend that she did not want to stay with, but maybe she changed her mind."

"Any name?"

"I think he works at the nursing home with her. Other than that, sorry. I didn't think to ask for his name."

Dana nodded her head. "It shouldn't be too hard to get it. I can't think there's too many male nurses working at the nursing home." She took another swallow of water and set the glass on the small plastic tray. "Anyway, on the news earlier there was a piece about a stolen ambulance. I started thinking and I called my friend back to fax over a copy of the chart on both Sheri and Megan." She grabbed some papers off the night stand and handed them to Nick. "Look at the signatures. Ms. Smith signed on arrival, but that is not her signature on discharge."

With barely more than a glance, Nick commented, "It's obvious the signatures are no match. You don't have to be an expert to see the difference."

With a grin, Dana added, "Ah, the best is yet to come. Look at the nurse's signature on the discharge form."

Nick looked and slapped the papers against his thigh. "I don't believe it! The balls of that man!"

"He's definitely got a big pair. I'm almost certain Drago kidnapped Sheri and Megan in the ambulance. My worry is why no ransom demand yet. He kidnapped them last night, I'm sure of it. He's had plenty of time to make his demands." She gave Nick a hard stare, "You know you can't tell anyone how I got the ER records. I'll have to come up with a story to cover my butt later."

Partly in frustration and partly in impatience, Dana slapped the bed linens with her free hand, "I can't wait to get out of here. I want to get to work on this case. I know the captain will insist I take some time off, but I see no reason to. I'm banged up a little, that's all. There's a rumor I get to go home today, but I think they're waiting for Social Security to kick in first. This hospital doesn't move fast for anything." Dana picked up her cup and noted it was empty. "Would you mind pouring me some water? I don't know why I'm so thirsty. Maybe it was that slice of ham I had with my eggs for breakfast. They told me if I eat well, they'll take out this IV and pull the monitor."

"I wanted to talk to…"Nick paused while pouring Dana a glassful of water. He handed her the partially filled glass as he stared at the folded paper sticking out from under the tray. A pencil sketch showing part of Dana's face was peeking out at him. He pulled out the note before setting the pitcher back down. Briefly he studied the sketch before asking, "Who's the artist?"

"What are you talking about?" Dana asked.

"This." Nick held the note so she could see it. "Did you pose for it?"

"No. I have no idea where that came from." She took the note from Nick and opened it. Her mouth dropped open.

"What!" Nick said, louder than he intended, as he edged around the table to see the note for himself. Several heads turned his way. One of the nurses put her pointer finger to her lips in the traditional *Be Quiet* sign.

Momentarily, Nick looked remorseful before softly apologizing, "I'm sorry." He did not want them throwing him out now. He turned his attention back to Dana and worked to contained his excitement and growing curiosity, but it was not easy. Finally he snatched the note from her hand.

On the left hand side of the paper was printed 'I want to see my little daughter by my second wife, Lisa. I will trade Megan and her mother for my daughter. I will contact you again at 4:00 p.m. to find out her location. Their safety depends on your answer.' On the right side the printing was not quite as neat. 'I have a cell phone taped to food cart number forty-seven, I will call on that. Drago'

"Your butt's already covered. Sheri and Megan Smith were kidnaped from the hospital last evening." Nick emphasized the word 'were' indicating that it answered a question. He went on to explain to Dana, "I read a small article in the morning paper. Here." He handed it to her, already folded open to an article. "There was so much confusion going on in the ER yesterday that the nurse wasn't sure if someone else had discharged them or they simply walked out on their own. The nurse that had taken care of Ms. Smith noticed the discrepancy in the signatures like you did and she didn't recognize the nurse's name on the discharge form so she went to her supervisor to show her the name and how the instructions had been checked wrong for that patient." Nick snorted a laugh, "Drago had some balls to sign his name on the nurse line. It took awhile to decipher his scrawling signature." He looked to Dana. "You were transported out by the time I found Tom Jenkins, the guy that Sheri and Megan were staying with, was murdered. Harry Drago did that also, I'm thinking." He added with a lopsided grin, "Apparently, Drago stole an ambulance to kidnap Sheri and Megan in."

"I think you're right," Dana agreed. "I need to get out of here. We don't have much time. He has an older daughter and a son by his first wife. I'll have to get his prison records to find out about any conjugal visits and birth records." Dana pressed her call light.

"I'm waiting to get out of here, too. How's your stomach feeling?" Nick lightly touched her hand. It felt cool to his touch. After an awkward silent moment, he withdrew his hand. "We were trying to let you rest, figuring you'd be back in the fight sometime today or tomorrow."

"Good, as long as I don't move, but that's not going to keep me here. You're hurt worse than I am."

"Nah, this is just a little bite. No big deal." Nick looked at his watch. "It's ten minutes after one. We have a little less than three hours to find out what Drago wants to know." Nick got on the phone, calling the precinct. "This is Officer Coburn, let me talk to Captain Wells." Captain Wells had stayed with his daughter half the night and had visited briefly with Nick before going home. He told Nick that he planned to start work about ten a.m. and work until three then come visit his daughter for a while, but he wanted to be called anytime there was a new development.

"Captain, Dana got a ransom note from Harry Drago. We're not sure exactly when or who delivered it…No, Sir, she was sleeping…I found it when I stopped in to visit…we both handled it before we realized what it was…I don't know if any of the staff handled it…I will, Sir…I'll put it in a bag…Not for money, for his little girl…I know, Dana said the same thing. He must know something that we don't. When was his last conjugal visit? Can I get a list of dates?…I want to know where, and I want to get them away safely before he has a chance to harm them." There was a lengthy pause while Nick listened to Captain Wells. "I can work from my room, or can you pull some strings and get me discharged faster? I'd rather be at the station. It would be a lot easier. Don't worry. I'll keep you posted on what's happening."

Nick continued, "We need another officer here at the hospital. If one had been here this morning, we might have caught Drago already." He moved the phone away from his ear at the explosive expletive that assaulted his ear. "No, I did not mean to imply you were incompetent. I meant that if we had thought ahead that Drago might do something like this, we could have been prepared. I never thought of it either." Nick figured he just blew his chances with the boss's daughter. Nothing like insulting the big man.

Captain Wells told Nick to do what he could from his room and that he would be in shortly. He gave his phone to Dana so she could talk to her father for a few minutes.

When she gave him back his phone, Nick grabbed it from her open palm and slipped it into his front jeans pocket. "I'm going to make copies of this note. Why don't you ask if anyone saw who was here, if they handled the note, when your water pitcher was last filled, you know the usual questions. I'm going to go get the phone. They're still reeling from all the disasters last night. It makes me wonder if Drago didn't have a hand in that, too. After I come back, I'll spend time studying the note for any other clues we may have missed. Maybe we can come up with something else. Captain Wells is sending out another officer to help."

"Drago likes explosives, but I don't see how he was involved. It was just a crazy night."

"What ages are his children?"

"Drago doesn't have any little children. All his kids are teens or older."

"He used the word *little*. I would think he was talking about ten or younger. Then there's the sketch." Nick turned it so Dana could see it.

"I don't think Drago did this. He's never done any artwork before. I don't like it." Dana gave a little shiver.

"I think it's good."

"It's not that." Dana rubbed a hand up and down her arm, "Whoever did it stood there and watched me while I slept. It makes me feel violated."

Nick wanted to hug her, but did not think she would appreciate it. "Do you want police protection arranged? I can stay with you since I'm here anyway," he offered with a devilish grin.

"No, thanks. You need to get that phone, and I don't think whoever it was will be back, if that makes any sense."

Nick took her *no* to apply to both of his offers. His was disappointed but did not want to push her.

The nurse came by to tell Nick his time was up. Before she had a chance to open her mouth he asked, "Hey, do you have a plastic bag I could put this in?"

"I'll get you a bag."

"The nurse came back with a large bag, and Nick slipped the note into it. "Thanks. Make sure security stays posted at the door." He pulled out his FBI badge so Dana could not see it. "Who do I need to talk to? Better yet, what's their number? Thanks." Nick called and explained the situation to them.

After hanging up, he turned to Dana. "I need to get going. Officer Stanton wants to meet me in my room in about twenty minutes. He doesn't want me to go get the phone without him."

While waiting for security, he turned his attention to the note. Nick studied the note through the plastic bag. He studied the picture first. The unknown artist had captured Dana's innocence and beauty while she slept. Nick wanted to make a copy of it and blow it up to keep for himself. He also wanted to yell in frustration. Instead he got up and pounded his fists on the window sill, regretting his foolhardy action instantly because of the roaring pain it sent up his left arm.

Nick sat in the nearby chair, cradled his arm and thought about his plight. *This was not supposed to happen. I was supposed to come down for twelve weeks, finish that class, get to know Dana and, hopefully, have her accept the Pittsburgh assignment. It's a tough way to break in a recruit, but I think Dana can handle it.*

I was not supposed to fall in love or whatever this feeling is that has my head in a turmoil. I saw that old grainy black and white picture of Dana and thought she looked kind of average, but in person, she's a knock out. Her smile makes me happy. I did not expect to feel this way about her after just one glance, one single glance.

It's more than just her looks. She has a sense of humor and a strength of character. Love? Maybe not yet, but whatever it is, it's playing havoc with my mind. I barely know her. You can't fall in love that fast, can you? That kind of stuff is nothing more than fairy tales. Then why can't I stop thinking about her? Why am I worried that Dana will not feel the same way about me?

Feeling the need to move, Nick got up and walked around the room, circling it twice, with his mind still in a turmoil, before sitting down on the bed. *Okay, Nick, pull yourself together. Focus on the case. There'll be time later to get to know Dana. Her smile says she has some interest in you, so there is some hope.* Suddenly, the thought popped into his head that she probably smiled that way to everyone. It did not mean anything special. *No! She has to like me at least a little. I won't let her not like me,* Nick argued with himself. *I'm a likable guy, aren't I?* Nick ran his hand through his hair, trying to concentrate on the case. He looked back at the picture. Now all he had to do was figure out what it meant. Did it mean anything? Was it a warning, like we're watching you? Did a friend happen to see her and draw her not realizing what he was drawing on? Wouldn't a friend have added some sort of note like *Get better soon* or *Hope you're feeling better* and then have signed their name?

Nick decided to look at the note for a while. Maybe a change would help. He saw a difference in the handwriting between the two sides. "Drago, were you having a problem?" He held the note closer to the light, studying the details intensely until he felt the beginnings of a headache.

There was not enough difference between the two writings to indicate two different people, Nick decided. He figured Drago wrote them at different times of the day or maybe was in a hurry when he wrote the latter part. Maybe he had no idea what the actual cart number was until later. Nick liked that idea. It made sense.

Nick's arm was really throbbing so he finally stopped to look at it and gasped in surprise at the blood oozing through the dressing.

Keeping his arm elevated and away from the note, he pressed his nurse call button. Tiny bright red drops of blood started dripping through the gauze. Nick ran into the bathroom and snatched a towel to cover it.

"May I help you?"

Nick hollered from the bathroom, "My arm's bleeding bad!"

A nurse was in his room within a few seconds. "What happened?" She peeked under the towel as she talked. "Keep the pressure on. I'll be right back."

Nick sat in a chair while he waited. The nurse returned in a few minutes with a dressing cart. "This is still your surgical dressing and Dr. Daniels has to take it off, but I can reinforce it." Quickly she opened the dressing supplies she needed and added more layers of gauze.

"What did you do to make it bleed?"

"Nothing that I can think of. I was working on a case on the bed, nothing more than reading a note when the pain wouldn't quit. I looked down and saw all the blood. Ah, look, it's on my jeans, too."

"There has to be a reason. Let me check your vitals." She finished cleaning up and putting away the extra supplies. She got out a digital thermometer and put that in his mouth. She slipped a stethoscope around her neck, while she wrapped the cuff around his arm.

The thermometer dinged and the nurse took it out. Nick asked, "Do I have a temperature?"

"No."

She checked his pulse and blood pressure. "Well, everything's normal. Call me if that bleeds through. My name's Gloria. I'm going to call the on-call doctor to look at your arm. I think Dr. Daniels is still in surgery."

Nick looked out his window and took a deep breath. "Thanks. There goes another flock of birds."

Gloria followed his gaze. "At least I know where my husband will be tomorrow."

"Oh?"

"Those are ducks. My husband loves to duck hunt, but for now, since it's not hunting season, he'll be taking pictures."

"Ducks?"

"Yes, ducks. Where are you from?"

"Up north."

"They have ducks there, don't they?"

"Yes," Nick laughed, "Gloria, my arm hurts. Can I have something for pain?"

"I'll bring your pain medicine before I call the doctor."

Just then the door burst open, and Captain Wells entered almost knocking Gloria over as she was leaving. Gloria darted around the big man without a *pardon me* annoyed by his rudeness.

"Let me see the ransom note."

Nick grabbed the plastic bag and handed it to the Captain.

The Captain read the note, flipped it around, saw the sketch, then read the note again. "Doesn't give us much time. What about the phone?"

Nick explained, "I'm waiting on security to get here. While I'm waiting I've been studying the writing. I think Drago wrote both sides of the note, just at different times. I think it was because he did not know the cart number until later. I doubt that he was under duress."

Captain Wells snorted, "Good thinking. I've got Sergeant Lorna Welby talking with Dana now. Let me go see what's going on with those two."

"I'll come with you. They're supposed to discharge me soon anyway."

"No, you stay put. It would make it easier if you came, but the doctor needs to check your arm, and I don't want him to have to chase you down. I'll be back in a few minutes."

Nick hated having to wait in the room, but he did not have long to pout. Gloria knocked on the door only a few minutes after Captain Wells left. "Mr. Coburn, the doctor needs you in the treatment room. Come with me."

Nick said a silent prayer that he would be able to get out of the hospital soon as he followed the nurse down the busy corridor to the treatment room. A young doctor with gold wire rimmed glasses greeted him with a hand shake and a warm smile.

"I'm Dr. Warholak. Let's take a look at your arm. I understand you had a wild dog bite you and Dr. Daniels did surgery yesterday evening."

"That's right."

As he talked, he got some supplies out of the cabinets and drawers. "Gloria, would you mind sticking around in case I need some assistance." He started washing his hands, "Gloria, would you mind getting his chart for me?"

Dr. Warholak put on a pair of gloves and removed Nick's old dressing. Bright red blood immediately started to run onto the floor. "Oops, I see what they were talking about." He quickly grabbed a handful of gauze squares and pressed them over Nick's wound to absorb the blood.

Gloria returned with the chart. While the doctor hastily scanned the operative report, Gloria placed the over bed table in front of Nick. She removed the few things the doctor did not need to have in his way then laid out the suturing kit, dressing supplies, and an ace wrap he would need. She put sterile a drape package on the over-bed table for him to open when he was ready. All that she did with quiet efficiency.

The doctor pulled up a chair and set it next to the bed. He readied the sterile field. "Sit down here and put your arm on the sterile paper." He arranged the light and another chair for himself.

Nick's wound was bulging at one end slightly. "I think you developed a blood clot. It's no big deal. We'll have you fixed up in a few minutes."

"I can still go home tonight?"

"I don't see why not. I'd like to observe you for a few hours," the doctor talked as he numbed the wound area. "You can go home after supper this evening. Dr. Daniels shouldn't object to that."

"Can you observe me while I'm in ICU?"

"You're not bad enough for ICU."

"I know that. Ouch!"

"That suture was a bit buried. I need to remove a few to clear the clot."

"Have we been that bad that you don't want to enjoy our hospitality for another night?" the nurse asked.

"No, it's just that I'm working on a case and I need to get out of here. There's a mother and her little five-year-old girl whose lives are at stake."

"Oh, I think I've heard about that on the news," the doctor commented.

Nick kept his eyes focused on a vision chart hanging on the wall. Anything was better than looking at his own blood. He did not mind the sight of blood, just not his own.

The doctor worked as he talked. Nick liked that he did not waste time. The mundane conversation helped take his mind off the discomfort. He felt the cold saline irrigation and heard a soft plop.

"That was bigger than I expected. I'd say a good tablespoonful."

The local anesthetic finally took effect and, since his arm no longer hurt, Nick dared to look. Swimming in a pool of light pink water in the emesis basin was a large dark red blob. Nick barely looked for more than a few seconds before his stomach started to revolt and he had to quickly avert his eyes.

It took Dr. Warholak a few more minutes to stitch and redress the wound. "Now, I still want you to wait for Dr. Daniels to discharge you."

"As long as I can do it from the ICU."

"I told you," Dr. Warholak sternly admonished, "you don't need to be admitted to ICU."

Nick laughed, "I don't want to be a patient in ICU. My partner's a patient there. I want to be with her so we can work together. She's getting a ransom call in a little while."

Dr. Warholak laughed. "That's all right then. Let the nurses know where you are. Dr. Daniels can see you there."

CHAPTER 11

Captain Wells was still there when Nick arrived. "I'll send Detective Charlie Danvers to help you while you're here," Captain Wells said. "When you're finally discharged, he can drive you around." He looked at his watch. "I need to get going. Bye, Sweetie." He leaned over and gave his daughter a kiss on her forehead.

"Bye, Dad. I'll see you later."

Nick and the Captain shook hands. "Thanks. I need to update Dana. I know she can't do much, but she's a target and a contact, all at the same time. She needs to stay in the loop. Let Detective Danvers know if I'm not in my room, I'll be in hers." Nick glanced at his wristwatch, "She'll be getting that ransom call soon."

He grinned from ear to ear when he looked at Dana. "You're looking better than a while ago. Ready for some action?" He meant job wise, but his thoughts were leaning toward the sexy side. Her smile was nearly his undoing. His mother was right. He knew he had found the right girl. His big problem was did she feel the same way?

"Your tone makes me think I may need to get a big, burly orderly in here to help fend you off since I'm certainly not strong enough right now to do it myself."

Nick's pleasant laughter echoed around the entire unit, making everyone smile. "No, it's just that you were so bloody and green around the gills back in the woods. This is a big improvement. You're recovering quicker than I expected from your beating." He did not add that her smile made him weak in the knees and sent his heart racing, or that her soft green eyes made him want to make passionate love to her until she had that well-loved, sated look, or that her full red lips made him want to kiss her over and over as his hands caressed her body, exploring every inch of her. He would tell her those things when she was home from the hospital and they were alone with nothing more than soft music and a bottle of wine for company.

"I've never been one to lie around. I grew up around two brothers and six male cousins. They offered little pity no matter how bad off you were." There was something about Nick that she found intriguing. Sure he had killer looks, but he also had a certain charm that she found irresistible. "I'm disappointed. I was hoping for another one of those kisses to make me feel better." *Where did that come from? The last thing she needed to do was encourage him.*

Nick grinned happily, raising an eyebrow as he stepped closer to Dana. Then, as he looked into her soft green eyes and saw a hint of desire, suddenly he became uncertain how well he could control himself. "That I can do," he swallowed hard as his voice cracked. Changing his mind about kissing her lips, Nick leaned forward and placed a light kiss on Dana's forehead.

As he slowly pulled away Nick paused, noting a look of disappointment on Dana's face. He had not moved very far before Dana grabbed the front of his shirt and jerked him down again. She kissed his mouth.

Nick, pulled off balance, quickly grabbed the side rails to keep from falling on top of her. His mouth already open in a partial exclamation of surprise made it easy for Dana's tongue to dart in for a brief exploration and fencing match with his tongue. She held on to his shirt, keeping him in place, not that he was struggling to get away.

After that startling, surprisingly passionate kiss, Dana pushed him away. "That's better!" She lightly licked her lips with the tip of her tongue. Her split lip was much better today. A tube of medicated lip gel someone had left for her had been a lifesaver. Kissing Nick hardly hurt at all.

Pressing his lips together, Nick stood speechless. He had kissed his share of women, but this was the first time he had really wanted to kiss a particular woman. Dana managed to surprise him.

That kiss had totally surprised him.

Keeping his lips tightly pressed together so no one could see, but not so tight that he could not lick the inside of his lips with the tip of his tongue, savoring the taste of her. When Nick released his lips a soft, "Wow!" escaped.

He could not stop grinning.

He had expected a simple lips touching, almost sisterly kiss. Dana's passionate kiss told him he may have a chance after all. He felt like he wanted to giggle and kept his lips pressed together to prevent any hint of laughter from escaping. Dana might not understand why he was laughing. Heck, he did not understand why he wanted to laugh and jump around.

This time Dana raised an eyebrow. "Don't tell me you're gay." She looked truly disappointed as she continued, "You've got such a pretty face, I should have known."

Pretty face? Nick was floored by that. He had always been called sexy, rugged, gorgeous or handsome, but never pretty. Did others think that he might be gay? Nick gave her a lopsided grin, "No, I'm straight."

He did feel like dancing around, however. To himself, he wondered if a guy should feel the way he did after that kiss. No, he decided he was being stupid, but Nick still could not stop from looking down. Yes, he had on a hospital gown, but he was still wearing jeans, not pink tights and a tutu. Casually he touched the front of his jeans. Yes, all was intact. He was still a man. His penis had not mysteriously disappeared.

He stuttered, "You just caught me off guard, that's all."

"Are you married? I thought you were supposed to be single."

"I am."

"Am what?"

"Single." Nick decided he needed to kiss Dana again. This time it would be on his terms. Maybe that way he could get his head back on straight and his brain back in gear. He had a job to focus on. There was a little girl to save and a bad guy to catch. He could not worry about any of this hormonal stuff now.

"I need to do that again." Nick spoke softly as he put his hands back on the side rails and leaned in closer to Dana.

"Do wh-," Dana did not get to finish before Nick's warm lips covered hers.

This time his tongue lead the attack, gently at first then deepening as Dana responded. Suddenly, Nick thought this might not be such a good idea. His mind said he should stop. His heart said no.

He did not stop. Dana's lips were warm and inviting, her breath had a hint of peppermint, cool and light. This was like a little taste of heaven.

Reluctantly, Nick finally ended the kiss. His theory worked. Somewhat. His mind felt back to normal, but the rest of him was not. His hormones were raging for release and there could be none now.

Breathlessly she asked, "What was that all about? I owed you a kiss for saving my life."

"Then I guess that was my *You're Welcome*," Nick stood up and moved to the window. He adjusted his jeans and took in a few ragged breaths to compose himself. He had no idea if Dana was as unsettled as he was, but he had to get back to business.

Feeling better, Nick turned and pulled a chair up to the bedside. "This may not be the best time to talk to you, but I want to do it while we have a few minutes alone. Captain Wells was not supposed to let you know too much until I got here, but then all this mess happened."

He put his hand up when Dana started to speak. "Wait a minute before you say anything. I have big news you need to hear. You should be receiving your letter in a day or two, so this will not be a huge surprise, but you passed your FBI testing."

He did not get the reaction he expected. Dana did not get all excited and happy. Instead she looked at him silently for a moment then starting hesitantly, yet finishing firmly, Dana asked, "How do you know that?"

"Because I'm not the novice you were lead to believe. I'm an FBI agent. *Special Agent, but he wasn't going to nit pick at this point.*"

Nick watched Dana's eyes widen as he continued. "The rest you may not like. I'm not really transferring down here. This is just a test to see how we get along. You are either taking a leave or quitting this job and accepting a position with the FBI, so you can work a case with me in Pittsburgh as an engaged couple."

"You're what? I'm what? There's got to be a hundred other female cops...ah, agents up north that could play house with you." Dana stated, anger evident in her measured tone. She felt like she was being used. "You make it sound like I have no choice."

"Oh, you have a choice. There were two main reasons you were selected. Primarily because you're fluent in French. There were only nine other possible candidates, but they've been slowly eliminated. I was working with another agent until she was badly hurt in an auto accident. There aren't that many agents that can speak French, more know Spanish, and, surprisingly, Chinese."

"That is odd And the other reason."

"The second reason, and it should probably be the main one, you were a sorority sister with Adaire Fontaine, right? She's involved in this."

"So." Dana crossed her arms. That move hurt, but it was the only show of defiance she could manage. She was liking this less and less. At first she had liked Nick. He had seemed so down to earth in spite of his gorgeous sexy looks. She loved his wavy brown hair and how that sexy grin made her melt. She wanted to get to know him better, then he throws this madness at her. She did not mind the part about being accepted by the FBI. That she wanted. It was the rest she just was not sure about.

She had liked it when she had kissed him, but when he kissed her, it was like the world started spinning in a different direction. Maybe that's why some of what he was saying did not seem right. She was not ready for a close relationship and that case would put them really close by the sound of it.

This was crazy, Dana decided. She could not be so instantly attracted to this man. It was too soon after losing Jim. All of these goofy feelings had to be due to some sort of hero complex. Maybe they would go away in a week or two and she would be back to normal. Somewhat unwillingly, Dana decided Nick belonged to her job, not her personal life. Besides, the last time she married a cop, that did not end well. She did not want to make the same mistake twice.

"So, am I an FBI agent now?" Dana asked, still a little puzzled.

"If you accept it. You passed all the tests successfully."

"I applied over four months ago, but I never heard anything after that."

"It takes time to do the background check. Someone made the connection somewhere along the line. We've been trying for nearly a year to get something solid on Mr. Maxwell Oliverio. I need an in with this guy and you're it. He has just announced his engagement to Miss Adaire Fontaine with plans to leave the country within a few months. They're putting together a hasty wedding and I don't think it's because his bride-to-be is having a baby. He keeps changing his plans. I think it's to throw the authorities off. I've done much of the preliminary work and can't get anything substantial on him. If I don't nail him before he leaves the country, he'll be gone for good. I want to be invited to the wedding. I think that's when whatever he is planning will happen. Miss Fontaine is arriving from France next month. According to the newspapers, they're having one wedding here for his family and another one in France for hers. I'll be done with my classes by then and we can head to Pittsburgh."

"What do you have on him?"

"Murder and bribery, maybe," Nick rubbed his cheek. "A woman came to me at my office, told me she worked in his office, but refused to tell me her name or what kind of work she did." He inhaled, blew it out sharply then continued. "She told me she accidently overheard Max Oliverio talking on the phone in French. He was telling the person on the other end that he would end their life the same way he did Senator Jeff Conley's for taking his bribe and not voting the way he promised. As you can guess, the unknown woman ended up dead. About two weeks after her visit to my office, she was killed in a hit-and-run accident. I haven't been able to prove his connection to that. It may truly be nothing more than a hit-and-run. I ran her fingerprints, but she came up clean."

As if she had not been listening, Dana's next question was a complete one eighty from the subject. "Did you mean that kiss or was that part of the act, too?" Dana asked, wondering why she cared when she had just told herself to let him go.

Gently Nick took her hand in both of his, but she hesitantly started to pull it away then stopped. Dana liked the warmth and gentleness of his hands, yet through the gentleness she could feel his strength.

"Please, Dana, you have to believe me." He leaned in closer. His voice took on an honest sincerity. "That kiss was genuine. I'd be glad to do it again to prove it to you." By the time he finished his last sentence, Nick was grinning devilishly.

Dana, ready to take him seriously, changed her mind with that last remark. He was certainly handsome and willing to face danger, but apparently not serious about developing a relationship. All she had to do was get her heart to agree with her mind. Why did her heart do flip-flops when he smiled a her? Why did she look forward to seeing him come through the door? Her mind said he was obnoxious, but her heart argued that Nick had a sexy smile that reached his eyes, making her feel wanted, needed and desired. At other times his eyes sparkled with mischief that she felt like a little girl stealing her first kiss.

A large burly officer walked in. "Don't you two look cozy."

"Hey, Uncle Charlie!" Dana greeted him warmly as she quickly snatched her hand out of Nick's light grasp.

Nick looked at Dana, "How many relatives do you have on the force?"

Nick liked the sound of Dana's merry laughter as it filled the tiny cubicle. If Dana could soften this fast at the sight of her uncle, maybe she was not too upset with him. He knew he was handling this all wrong, but everything he did just made it worse instead of better.

Dana explained, "He's not a real uncle. He just helped raise me, but I do have one brother, four cousins and three uncles on the force." She gave Nick a mock stern look, "Just so you know to behave yourself."

"Yes, Ma'am," Nick responded as he jumped to attention at the side of the bed.

Charlie Danvers stood beside Nick and took Dana's hand, the one that he had just been holding. Nick wished he had that hand back. Charlie patted Dana's hand. "You're looking good, Dana, Love." He leaned forward and planted a kiss on her forehead.

He raised up, turned toward Nick, and shook hands with him, introducing himself, "I'm Lieutenant Charlie Danvers. I'll be working with you on the Smith case." He looked at Dana, "Did you hear what I said? I will," he emphasized the words *I will*. "Captain says you are to stay in the loop, but that's all. Do you understand?"

Dana stared at Charlie then Nick then back to Charlie before questioning in a forceful tone, "Do I have to like it?"

"No, you just have to obey it, like any other order."

She looked down at the sheets and ran her hand lightly over a wrinkle, ironing it out with her fingers as she mumbled, "All right."

Satisfied, Charlie turned his attention back to Nick. "Let's go over the game plan." He glanced at his watch. "They'll be serving supper trays before you know it. Captain said the kidnapper will be making contact at four o'clock. Before I left the office, I made a few phone calls. Both of his ex-wives have disappeared. That might be why he's gotten us involved."

"Did you find out about his youngest daughter?" Dana asked.

"I did. He had a conjugal visit with Lisa about three years ago and that was the last time. She had a little girl which must be the one he wants. The birth certificate copy I got had the baby's name and year of birth blacked out. No father's name was listed. Who's got the phone?"

Nick replied, "It's still attached to the food cart."

"Why?"

"I'm waiting for security to go with me. He said it would be twenty minutes; it's been over an hour."

"I'm here. We can do it." Charlie waved his hand between Nick and himself. "I don't think we should waste any more time. Someone may find the phone before we do."

Nick made a soft guttural groan, "I hadn't thought about that. I guess my brains are on vacation."

They went out to the nurses station. Nick approached a man in a scrub suit and asked, "Where is the main kitchen?"

The man turned, scanned Nick up and down, wrinkling his nose ever so slightly as though Nick emitted a verminous odor. With evident disdain, he huffily stated, "How dare you address me in that tone! I am Dr. Lakely, Chief Medical Officer." With that he picked up his silver pen, put it in his pocket and walked down the hall.

A nurse came out of the med room, "Sorry about that. I couldn't help but overhear. Why do you need to go to the kitchen?"

"FBI." Nick and Charlie simultaneously held up their ID wallets. "We're working on a case and there's some evidence on one of the food carts."

She went to the intercom and pressed a button. "Tasha to the nurses station please." Within a minute Tasha arrived and the nurse asked her to take the two police officers down to the kitchen.

Out of habit, Nick started walking toward the visitors' elevators when he heard a sharp 'No!' He stopped and turned around. "Follow me. We need to use the service elevators. It's shorter this way." Tasha walked quickly toward the elevators.

The service elevator doors opened and they were met by the security officer. The man was not quite six foot, muscular build, around twenty-five to thirty, and not happy. He scowled at the trio then eyed Nick directly, "I'm going to take a wild guess, you're Officer Nick Coburn."

"Yes, Sir."

"Do you make a habit of not following orders?"

"Not usually. It's just you were late and we have a time limit."

"That still doesn't give you the right to break our rules." The elevator doors started jerking, demanding to shut. The officer moved aside. "I'm Sergeant Gilroy. You'll follow my orders." He looked at Charlie then Nick in turn, "Understood? Get in," he harshly ordered. He looked at Tasha and told her to return to her duties.

While they made their irritatingly slow descent in the aged device, Nick, standing next to the security officer, took a chance and quietly asked, "What made you think I was Nick?"

"Hmph, the good-looking ones are always the trouble makers," he answered while still facing forward.

The old elevator jerked to a stop with a loud clank. Before the doors were fully open, Nick started out only to by stopped by Sergeant Gilroy's forearm. "Follow me."

Nick stopped short once inside the kitchen when he saw dozens of tray carts all alike. "I don't think I expected so many. I need number forty-seven."

"I have to find the supervisor. She'll have the list." Sergeant Gilroy said and walked off.

Nick waited impatiently. He glanced around at the various employees. Some eyed them while pretending to do their jobs, others gave them hard glares, and some ignored them completely. No one was behaving suspiciously.

Sergeant Gilroy returned with a short woman who barely came up to Nick's armpits, "I'm Harriet Toddy, the Head Dietician. Ted explained a little of the problem to me. May I see some ID?"

Nick pulled out his ID wallet and flipped it open. She gave a curt nod, satisfied. "How can I help you, Sir?"

"I need to see the cart number forty-seven." *Will the phone still be attached to the cart after all this time?*

She continued talking as she walked. "It's over here, against the wall. I didn't use it today."

They wove their way between three short rows of various colored carts to another short row of five pale green food carts. Nick looked at the numbers clearly printed in bold black on each end of the carts. Number forty-seven was stuffed into the darkest corner they had. It was in the middle, flanked by two carts on each side, a tight fit even for Nick's nimble form.

Nick tried to pull it out a little further so it was under one of the fluorescent ceiling lights, but he was still going to need a flashlight to see underneath. He asked Charlie if he had one he could borrow. The top and front were clear as well as both sides and back. Nick squeezed his long legs into the narrow space between the rows of carts and lay on his back to look under the cart. Nothing glinted back from the flashlight beam. He was disappointed. He wanted to find the phone right away.

Nick got up and questioned the supervisor. "Did anyone talk about finding a cell phone attached to one of the carts?"

"No."

Nick got out his copy of the note. He slapped his forehead with his hand. "The inside of the door. He doesn't say which side." Before he touched the door he had a thought. Speaking softly to Officer Gilroy he said, "Maybe we should clear the room. This guy likes to use bombs."

Officer Gilroy cleared the room in record time, including himself. He was the last one out and pulled the door shut behind himself. Charlie checked the other carts. Nick let Charlie in on his secret–that he was an FBI agent and had some explosives training. Nick thought it might be helpful to have another person aware of his alter ego. He was good at sizing people up and knew from the start that Charlie was a trustworthy soul.

The cart doors were closed. After visually looking for a bomb Nick checked all along the edges of each door for a trip wire. No one spoke while Nick took his time feeling for a string or wire that might trigger a bomb. No signs of a bomb. If there was one, it was well hidden.

Slowly Nick tried to pull open the right-hand cart door, holding his breath the whole time. Nothing happened and he finally exhaled. It would not budge. Nick tried the left door and met with the same fate.

"Detective Danvers, let me borrow your light again."

The detective was one cart over. "Catch." He tossed the small but powerful light. "Call me Charlie since I plan to call you Nick."

Nick caught it with his left hand. "Okay and thanks." He shone the flashlight around the edge and finally noticed in one spot what looked like glue. "Great! He's glued the doors shut. Anybody got a crowbar?" Then a thought occurred to him. "Wait! Everyone be still." Nick checked around the doors again until he found a small blob of the thick gel he could carefully pick off with his fingernail. "I need something to hit this with." Nick gently placed the tiny blob on the concrete floor as far away from everything as he could.

Charlie offered, "Let me see what I can find." He returned quickly with a large rock. "This was sitting on a little wooden pedestal with a sign saying it was from the Grand Canyon."

"If it blows up, I'll replace it." Nick took the rock, tossing it lightly in his hand getting a feel for its weight. "Everybody move back." At the last minute he decided to use a food cart for protection and wheeled one into place. He stood to the side of the cart and reached out dropping the rock on the blob. It hit its mark without going boom. The room filled with everyone's softly exhaled sighs.

"Now, I still need some way to pry those doors open."

Surprising Nick, Sergeant Gilroy stepped up. They looked at each other as he spoke. "Let me try." He put his feet shoulder width apart, took a deep breath, put his left hand on the cart, grabbed the door handle with his other hand and pulled. There was a creepy ripping sound as the paint tore off the cart with the door opening.

It was empty on that side.

Nick asked, "Do you think you can do that again on the other door?"

"No problem." He wiggled his fingers and shrugged his shoulders before repeating the same steps on the left door.

Nick was relieved to see the phone this time. After checking for a bomb, he carefully removed it from the door.

He had not realized until then how tired he was nor how bad his arm was hurting again. Yet he could not stop. He and Dana still had a little girl and her mother to save and a bad guy to catch.

CHAPTER 12

"Stay in your room until I get back. I'll see if it's time for you to have something for pain. Dr. Daniels was looking for you to discharge you. He couldn't find you and was a little ticked off," the nurse dryly stated.

"Sorry about that." Nick went into his bathroom to wash up. He left the door open and, about the time he finished, heard a male voice call his name.

Nick came out rubbing a towel over his damp hair. "Hi, I'm Nick Coburn."

"I'm Dr. Daniels. I wanted to change your dressing and check your wound. I checked that second x-ray. You have a hairline fracture on your ulnar bone, but I can't put a cast on because of the wound."

"What's an ulna?" Nick held his arm out for the doctor to see. The dressing gauze was a bit mussed and dirty from his hunting for the phone.

Dr. Daniels frowned, "That's the bone that runs down the little finger side of your arm. Do I want to know what happened? Is this the way you're going to be taking care of your dressing on a daily basis?"

Nick chuckled, "I was looking for a bomb downstairs, and I don't handle bombs daily, so no."

Dr. Daniels raised an eyebrow. "Let's go to the treatment room."

"I need to be discharged so I can get back to work."

"What kind of work do you do?"

"FBI, Special Agent." It was out before he realized it. Dana, Captain Wells and Charlie were the only ones who needed to know. That ditzy clerk in ICU did not count as far as he was concerned.

Two quickly raised eyebrows this time. "That explains a lot. Are you a paper pusher?"

"No, field agent, and I'm on a case as we speak."

Dr. Daniels raised one eyebrow this time as he gave Nick a quick look before returning his attention to the wound. "I'd rather you not work for at least two days, a week preferred."

"No can do. I have a little girl and her mother who have been kidnapped, and I have the cell phone that the kidnapper will use to make his demands."

"I'll make you a deal. Will you promise to come in to my office in one week so I can check your arm?"

"I should be able to do that. I don't go back to Pittsburgh for three weeks. It's only for two or three days." *Will Dana make the quick trip with me?*

"Can you stay out of fist fights?"

"No guarantees on that. I'll try to watch from the sidelines when I can. I promise to take it easy once this case is over."

"You keep making my job harder and harder. You should be completely healed by six to eight weeks, however, you're in luck. I have a colleague in Pittsburgh that I can refer you to. He can be discreet about the reason for your injury if necessary."

"That would be helpful. Thank you."

After a brief examination of Nick's wound, he redressed it. "It looks like Dr. Warholak did a good job earlier. I'm going to put a splint on your arm which I want you to wear all the time," he emphasized the phrase *all the time*, "or the bone may not heal. You can take it off when you shower since you'll be changing the dressing then, too. I'd like to x-ray your arm again in about four weeks. Keep this dressing clean and dry. That was probably a waste of words, but I had to say them anyway." He added with a chuckle. "I'll have to tell my secretary not to take too many FBI agents as patients. I have a strong suspicion they'll be a lot of headaches."

They both laughed.

He opened a cabinet and read a couple of boxes before selecting one. "This is an arm sling. It's fairly easy to use." He fitted it on Nick as he talked. "That should be more comfortable."

"It is. Thanks."

"I want you to limit use of your left arm so it will heal. That dog did a ton of damage. I'll give you a list of limitations and an excuse for returning to work. Give me a few minutes."

"Thanks, Doc. I appreciate all you've done. Could I ask a favor?"

Dr. Daniels had reached the door by this time and turned around with another raised eyebrow. Hesitantly, and with a touch of annoyance, he asked, "What?"

"Would you by chance have an extra scrub top I could borrow? My shirt was ruined and I hate to leave in a hospital gown or my bloodied shirt."

Dr. Daniels smiled, "I think I can accommodate you. I'll send one around."

"Thanks. I really appreciate it."

Nick went back to his room and gathered up his belongings. The vase of flowers with the helium filled balloon he gave to the elderly woman across the hall. She was sleeping, but he expected it would be a pleasant surprise when she woke up.

He found a sheet of paper that was blank on the back and started making a list. He started with the phone. Charlie had already dusted the cell phone for prints. As expected, it was clean. The tape went back to the lab for more extensive testing. They did not expect the tape to give them anything either. Nick had the kidnapper's phone in a plastic bag. It was staying with him until both girls were safe. The CSI team was doing their best to investigate the kitchen without disrupting their schedule.

A different nurse came in, "Mr. Coburn, I have your scrub shirt, discharge instructions, and two prescriptions—one is for your pain med and the other is an antibiotic."

"Thanks." Nick grabbed the shirt and untied his gown. His right arm slipped out easily enough, but, with a sheepish grin he looked at the nurse, "I guess I need some help. This contraption's not easy to work with."

The nurse had been admiring the muscular show and had no desire to stop him. The fact that she was married did not stop her from appreciating the view. She stepped in closer to help. "My name is Nancy. I work for Dr. Daniels. I see his discharge patients and give them their instructions. We find that's better than leaving it up to the hospital nurses." She unbuckled the sling. "You must work out a lot," she commented as she worked.

"I have to keep in shape or I can't chase the bad guys," he said with his devilish grin.

"Oh, that's right! You're that police officer. I could never marry a cop. I would always worry if he'd come home at night. My husband works at Conner's Sporting Goods. They were robbed a few months ago, but it was when the store was closed. First robbery they ever had." She held the scrub shirt up. "Put your bad arm in first always."

Nick followed her directions and the scrub top slipped on easily. Nancy readjusted the sling. "Let me get these instructions out of the way so you can go."

Curious, Nick asked, "What did they take?"

"Not the guns and ammo like you would expect. It was a two-man tent, a coffee maker, a sleeping bag, and a lantern. Oh, I almost forgot, they did take a portable TV and radio combo."

Nick thought about that. *That connects those dots. Certainly would have limited the money trail to follow. They will have to widen their search of that area. Would he be back in that area now? I doubt it, but he may have moved to another spot nearby figuring he was safe there once.*

When Nancy shoved the discharge instructions in his face for his signature, Nick realized he had let his mind wander too long and missed most of his instructions. Not wanting to waste time going over them again, Nick smiled and signed his name. He promised himself he would read his copy later.

"Here's your Lortab prescription, and you didn't hear a word I told you about your wound care, did you?"

Nick inhaled and started to lie then thought better of it, "No," flowed out on the exhale, "but I really don't have time to go over them again. Your robbery made me think of the escaped con and kidnapping."

"You think they're related?"

"Maybe."

"My husband will love that. They've been making bets. He stands to win a hundred dollars now. He figures the guy was camping out down around Towers End, and if that proves right, his winnings are doubled."

Nick was floored that some schmuck from a sporting goods store could put things together so easily. "I hope he doesn't plan to go down there and check the area out. He might be putting himself in danger."

"No, I won't let him. Besides that's part of the bet. They each guessed a location, but they're not allowed to go near it."

"Good. I've got to go. Are we done?"

"All done. Your wound care directions are written down so you can look at them later. They're easy to do. Be sure to read the signs of infection. I'll walk you down."

"No, thanks. I'm going to ICU first. I have to get my partner and head out."

"I'll let the staff know you've been discharged. Since I'm breaking the rules do me a favor and don't get hurt on your way out."

Nick leaned forward and whispered in her ear, "Your husband's probably right, but keep that quiet for now." He grabbed his meager belongings and dashed out the door. He took the stairs down to ICU.

Dana, dressed in her torn uniform, was tying her shoes and looked up as Nick hurried through the door.

"It's about time," Charlie fussed. "We barely have any time before four o'clock gets here. The Captain sent over a packet of files for us to review." He pointed to a six inch pile on the over bed table

"Sorry, I had to follow hospital rules. How did you get discharged already?"

"They only had me in here under twenty-four-hour observation because they had no other monitor beds. I'm ready to go."

"Dana, here's the phone. We're probably breaking five rules regarding the chain of custody, but it can't be helped."

"Where are we going?"Charlie asked.

"I thought we'd go to my apartment. It's close by and I want a change of clothes and a quick hot shower."

"Sounds good to me," Nick agreed. "You know this area and are more familiar with Drago."

"Let's head on out. All my paperwork is done. The only time I care to see a hospital again is to visit someone."

The others chuckled as they hurriedly gathered up their things and followed Dana. In the lobby they were greeted by Captain Wells.

"I was just headed up to see you. I thought you might like a ride to the precinct. I brought my new SUV."

Dana smiled brightly, "Captain, that was very thoughtful of you, but we were going to my place. It's closer and I wanted to shower and change." Dana maintained her professionalism. She did not like to broadcast it about that Captain Wells was her father.

111

"Oh," he replied simply, looking a little disappointed. Then he smiled. "I'll play chauffeur. Everyone pile in. We'll grab take-out on the way."

Nick took advantage of getting a thorough shower, too, even though the garish pink bedroom was enough to make him want to vomit. He was going to have to ask her about this room. It did not fit with the rest of the tasteful decor.

Dana had told him to look on the floor in the closet for a plastic storage bag with some men's shirts that he could pick any he wanted. He found a light blue pullover that fit rather well. He did not ask the why or who about the men's shirts. After eating, the three of them hashed things out until Drago's cell phone rang.

They stared at the ringing phone until Dana finally leaned forward and picked it up on the third ring.

Megan sat on her blanket in the corner, afraid to move. When she first woke up from her nap, she was facing the wall and saw the plain pine paneling like she had at her house. Happy to be home Megan rolled over, ready to jump out of her little bed and go find her mother.

Instead of seeing her mother, Megan saw the dragon tattoo on the arm of the big man dozing in the chair. Then she remembered where she was. Megan sat up and picked up her doll, happy she had a new doll friend to talk to and gave her a hug. "I miss Mommy. I'm glad I got you now and you like hugs. Mary Alice liked hugs." She looked over at the man with the tattoo who was not disturbed by her quiet talking. "I need to think about a name for you." She pictured the name on the uniform badge and suddenly an idea popped into her head. She whispered to her. "I'm going to call you Donna May. That's close to Dana's name. Is that okay with you?"

The doll stared at her with her blue stitched eyes. "Good. I like it, too."

She needed to potty, but she did not want to scare Drago like the last time. She was sure he did not have a change of clothes for her and she did not want to stay in wet pants.

Megan still did not know what to make of the big man. He was kind to her most of the time. He had given her a blanket to sit on, a coloring book with crayons, and a doll. He was a big man with a fierce dragon on his arm, but he had not hit her. Yet.

"Mister," she called, in a soft voice. Megan squeezed her doll, wishing she still had Mary Alice. The new doll did not give her the same comfort, but she held on just the same.

She watched his large abdomen rise and fall with his heavy breathing. Megan watched the blue and green dragon with the red eye. It looked like it was watching her. She wondered if the dragon had a name. Maybe it would not be so scary if she could call it by its name. The man snorted and moved his arm, taking the dragon away.

Trying again, Megan called a little louder, "Mister!"

He mumbled a sleepy, "What?"

"I have to go potty."

"So go."

Megan raced to the bathroom. She did not care about the dragon. She knew she could run fast. She slammed the door and dropped the doll. She had beat the dragon. "Sorry, Donna May," she apologized to her doll as she hurried to get on the toilet.

When she came back, he was still sitting in the chair, but leaning forward. "I'm hungry. I think I napped through lunch," Megan told him as she held her doll and wiggled her hips.

"It's past lunch time and my friend did not show up with ours." Drago looked at his watch. "I need to see about putting more gas into the generator then I'll make us some sandwiches. I'm hungry, too." He coughed, "Go sit on your blanket and be quiet. I'll take care of the generator so we can have lights and then I'll make our supper."

Drago had just finished refilling the fuel tank when he heard a faint rustling sound. He pulled out his pistol ready to fire and crouched down behind the generator, hoping no one shot the generator and blew him up. He stared in the direction of the noise as he slowly stepped backwards towards the door. For being a large man, he was surprisingly agile, yet he regretted not keeping in better shape while in prison.

After a moment of intense concentration and worry that Megan would peek out the door calling *Mister!* Drago thought he saw a rifle outline. "How in the hell did they find us?" he cussed under his breath as he took careful aim. Drago fired a single shot at what he thought was the shoulder area.

No one returned fire. He heard a snort and more rapid rustling. He decided it had been a tree branch or a deer that he saw and not a man making the noise. *You're getting too paranoid in your old age. There's no way the police could have figured out where you're at—yet.* Drago looked at his watch. There was time to make a bite to eat if the boys did not return soon.

He was only a few steps away from the door where he had filled the generator and had not pulled it all the way shut, so it was easy to push it open to quickly get back in. Afraid to take any chances, Drago stayed low as he backed his way in.

Megan was standing there watching him come through the door in his squatting position. Giggling she said, "You look silly."

With the innate ability of children, she knew that the Dragon man would not hurt her, even if he did talk loud sometimes. Drago stood and grunted, suddenly not feeling so well. "I don't feel well." He placed the heavy wooden bar into the brackets and gave it a slap. The bar seemed heavier now than when he had opened the door and he got a little winded with the exertion. Drago sat in the closest chair to rest a minute.

"Maybe that's because we need to eat." After resting, he stood to make their meal out of whatever he could find in the cupboard and felt the room spin. He held on to the back of the chair, angry at himself for feeling weak.

"Maybe so," replied Megan solemnly with her five-year old wisdom. "I want to see my mommy."

Drago had been wondering when that demand was coming. "Later," he replied abruptly.

The mild dizziness passed and he hoped it had been due to standing too quickly. He had had some blood pressure problems in the past and probably should see his doctor when this was all over. To Megan, he said, as he patted his rounded abdomen, "I like to eat."

"So do I, but Mommy and me watch our weight."

Drago ignored the comment. He could argue that he was only thirty or forty pounds over weight, and at five foot eleven, he looked good. He did not feel like arguing with a child. "Do you like peanut butter and jelly?" Drago asked as he started getting the stuff out of the cabinet. They had stocked a few basics to last them a couple of days. He had not anticipated a long stand off. He figured the police would be able to find his ex-wife easier than he could. He should have given more thought to food.

"It's my favorite." Megan could not remember the last time she had eaten and was a little surprised that he said it was near supper time.

"Good, because we don't have too much else to pick from." He took a carton of milk out of the refrigerator, poured a small glassful, and set it down on the table. "I didn't plan on being here for long. I thought my friends would be able to bring us meals, or we would have the generator to use." Drago fixed their sandwiches as he talked. "I can't find my little daughter, and I asked the police to find her. I'm worried about my friend, too. He hasn't returned, and now we only had eight more hours of power left. I can't go back outside to refill the generator again."

She wondered what else they were having and got her answer a moment later when she could smell apples and cinnamon coming from the microwave. When he called her to come eat, Megan left her doll lying on the blanket. She hoped Donna May was not hungry.

"The police are supposed to help people find things. Dana was helping me find my stolen tea set when the bad man stabbed her."

"You like the police woman, Dana?" Drago appreciated the fact that Megan did not realize he was the one that knifed Dana.

Megan nodded her head. "She's really sweet and smart."

"Do you think I'm a bad man?"

"Yes, because you take little girls away from their mommies."

"Only for a little while. There you go, Missy," Drago smiled as he handed her a whole sandwich.

She simply looked at it and said, "My name's Megan, not Missy, and the sandwich is supposed to be cut in half and put on a plate."

Drago rolled his eyes. He searched through the cabinets and finally found an opened package of Styrofoam plates. "Will this do?" Impatient, the question boomed out.

"Yes, Sir." Megan cringed. She was hungry, but fear was slowly taking over because of his loud voice. She put her hands down to her side, tightly gripping the edges of the chair, and wished she had the safety of the blanket, or that she could hide under the table. She kicked her legs back and forth, watched the big man, and waited to see what she needed to do.

Drago sat in his recliner. He was worried. Their supplies were low and neither Sam nor Rico were answering their cell phones. Something had to be wrong. There was not much milk left either. He opened the last can of beer for himself. They sat in silence eating their meager meal. Happy to be alone, Megan gobbled hers down and returned to her blanket. Her fear quickly vanished. She ran her tongue along her teeth trying to clean the peanut butter off.

"The next time you steal a little girl you might want to think about a hairbrush and toothbrush, too."

Drago let loose with loud bellowing laughter.

A few minutes later Drago checked his watch again. Ten minutes to go. He wanted to be punctual. He had planned to call at four o'clock to find out what arrangements they had made for him to see his young daughter. Maybe he could ask them for an order of take-out, too. Drago flipped through a few channels looking for some news about him. After a few swallows, he put the beer down. It did not seem to be sitting well on his stomach.

He picked this location for several reasons. The abandoned Heaton Mills were fairly secluded, and since they closed, the neighborhood had vanished. It had a good view of the two roads accessing it. The building had at one end several offices, a small kitchen and dining area combo, and several conference rooms. One of the conference rooms was being used to hold Megan's mother. They had put in a fold-up cot since she was kept drugged most of the time.

All the doors were secure except for one in the front. Its lock was broken and they had made a bracket and bar set up for it like the side door. Only two windows had any glass in them, and they were high up on the second level. They boarded up only the windows in the area they were staying in. The best feature was a working generator.

Drago had been surprised at the amount of furnishings that had been left behind. He found a torn leather office chair that worked as a recliner. As it tilted backwards a small foot rest came out. The footrest was nothing more than a rusted bar–all the padding was gone but it was good enough for Drago. Megan was happy with a few blankets on the floor. They found two cots which had been stored under plastic tarps and were still in good shape. Sheri was tied to one cot in a conference room. Rico and Sam put the extra cot in a conference room next to Megan's mother. They took turns sleeping in that room while the other one was on guard.

He was unaware that Rico had lied to him. Bored sitting around with nothing to do, Rico had walked through the building starting with the cafeteria. He found a pinball machine, but knowing that used electricity which put too much drain on the compressor and Drago would definitely object to playing it, he told him it was a ping pong table and he bounced the ball off the wall. Rico played on it every chance he got.

The kitchen still had a refrigerator and microwave. Both of which smelled rather nasty. Everything had needed a good cleaning, but all Drago cared about doing was a quick wipe to get rid of the heavy dust and grime.

Drago was proud of himself that he was again eluding the police. This place was better than the tent, but not by much. It was certainly drier and the chair was more comfortable on his back, but after he saw his little girl he was leaving. He was going to enjoy a comfortable lifestyle like he had before. Maybe Lisa would change her mind about him and come with him.

"I want to see my Mommy," Megan declared with tears shimmering in her eyes.

Drago hoped Megan was not going to fall apart on him now. "She's working," he claimed.

"Oh," Megan looked at Donna May as if to verify Drago's remark. Donna May stared blankly at Megan. "What time is it?"

Drago looked at his watch. "Five minutes to four."

"Does she know where I am?"

"Of course."

"I hope she's not working late again. She's trying to earn money so we can move to a big house with a grassy yard. I won't have to pw-lay in the rain anymore and I'll have a little sister," Megan ended with a little excitement.

"That's good." Drago was still not feeling up to par and had no inclination or time to play nicey nice with a child. "I have to make a phone call. Go sit on your blanket and be quiet."

Before he had a chance to dial the number, Rico came in. His eyes still glimmered with excitement as he set three bags down on the table. He liked it when Drago trusted him to do things on his own even if they were small tasks. He reached into one of the bags and took out a white Styrofoam box. "Sorry it took so long. I brought back a Philly cheese for you and chicken fingers for the kid. I took care of all your errands. I'll go check on our other guest."

"Where's Sam?"

"He said he had some personal business to take care of and he'd be back around midnight. He said you told him it'd be okay when he asked you a couple of days ago," he answered as he got two sodas out of the refrigerator. "Did you take care of the generator?"

Drago was annoyed that he could not remember the discussion with Sam. That bothered him. He was not that old to be forgetting simple things unless they were both lying. Absently Drago rubbed his chest. He was tired, but there were things to do, and he could not be bothered with Rico and Sam right now. He waved his hand in dismissal and grunted an affirmative reply.

Rico gladly disappeared through a side door carrying the bag with both his and Sheri's meals in their Styrofoam boxes and two cans of soda. It was his job to keep Sheri sedated and he was late. He had found it easier to hide the small pill in her first bite of food. She usually gulped that down without too much fussing.

"Megan," Drago reached for the largest bag. "Here, this is for you. Wait until tomorrow morning to put it on. You can use the bathroom to change in." He pulled a frilly pink dress out of the bag, still on its hanger. "Look at that. It comes with a hat, too." He turned it around so she could see the hat. Drago huffed and puffed with that little effort even though he was sitting down.

Megan's mouth dropped open. "Oh, how pretty! It's a fairy princess dress. Thank you!" In awe, she took the plastic hanger in her tiny hand and gingerly touched the delicate lace that was on the bodice and sleeves. "Is it really mine?"

Attached to the back was a simple white straw hat with a small bouquet of pink and white flowers on a pink band. Megan gasped again. She looked up at Drago with amazement in her shining eyes. "It's so beautiful!" She giggled happily, "Mommy will think she has a new little girl when she sees me."

This was almost too much for Drago. He was not going to let some snip of a child turn him to mush. He shoved the large bag at her and gruffly ordered, "The rest of the outfit's in there. Go look at it on your blanket."

Megan did not care that his tone had changed again. She decided he was more bossy than mean. She was so enthralled with the dress she completely forgot about his gruffness and being homesick.

"I have to make a phone call. I want you to play quietly for a few minutes." Drago heard Megan whispering to her doll and was relieved that she was so easily distracted. Megan did not seem to mind his deep voice. He was satisfied that he could take care of his call and ignore Megan's whispered conversation with her doll.

Megan nodded her head and added a softly spoken, "Yes, Sir," for good measure. She knew how to keep quiet.

Drago got his phone out of his pocket and dialed the number. He was surprised when the phone rang three times, expecting that someone would answer it on the first ring even if Dana was unavailable. He smiled when Dana answered. Someday he hoped to hear the story of her rescue.

"Tell me Officer Dana Morgan, are you doing well?"

"I am, thank you for asking." She said with a smile in her voice. She was willing to play his game if it would keep the hostages alive. "How is everyone, that includes you, Megan and her mother?"

Drago continued with the niceties, "I'm not feeling well. What do you have to tell me?"

"How about the girls? Can I talk with one of them?"

"No, you're trying to delay things."

"How do I know they're still alive?" Her tone became more businesslike.

"You have to trust me. I've had no reason to kill them—yet." Drago coughed, "If you don't tell me what I want to know, you'll still get them, but no guarantees about what condition they'll be in. Now talk."

Dana inhaled deeply, knowing he would not like what little she had to offer, and was putting two lives at risk. "I don't have much to tell you. Even your first wife has disappeared. We've had no luck tracking down Lisa after she moved from Charleston. We've tried under her maiden name as well as Drago." Dana hesitated just a few seconds, "In the little time we've had…"

Drago interrupted, "Don't play games! You've had all day."

Dana inhaled another deep breath before continuing, "Not actually. You may have left the note early this morning, but we did not find it until late this afternoon."

Drago let loose a string of expletives. Dana moved the phone away from her ear. When he quieted she calmly reported, "There's a possibility she went to Mexico, but it was nothing we could confirm."

Drago was anticipating good news and was sorely disappointed when Dana had nothing to offer but a guess, and a bad guess at that. *Lisa refused to go Mexico with me two different times. Maybe that's why she went to Mexico. She knew it's the last place I'd look for her,* Drago reasoned. He had been sure Dana would find her. Anger bubbled up inside him which his weakened heart vessels did not need. He was not sure who he was more angry at—Dana for having no answers or his ex-wife for taking his little girl to Mexico. After a long pause he finally spoke, "You're guessing with two lives at stake?"

Megan had stopped playing with her doll and was staring wide-eyed at Drago. She may not be able to talk right, but her hearing was fine, and she had an understanding far beyond her five years. She knew Drago was talking about her and her mother and that he might kill them. Tom liked to watch all the police shows and she heard them. She understood the word kill.

Not knowing what to do, Megan continued to listen, never taking her eyes off Drago. She wished she had Mary Alice. She hugged Donna May and whispered very softly in her ear, "I don't mean to make you feel bad, but Mary Alice was smart. She was with me since I was three and I don't know you yet. Maybe you're smart, too. I promise I'll take good care of you, like I did Mary Alice. If you come up with any ideas to get us out of here, let me know. I won't leave you behind."

"Do you take me for a fool?" Drago yelled into the phone.

Megan cringed at his loud voice and squeezed Donna May tightly.

Calmly Dana replied, "No, Sir, I do not." She made sure she clearly pronounced her words, not wanting him to misunderstand anything. "You said you could not find her, and we had no better luck. Apparently, she does not want to be found. I assure you my fellow officers tried. We followed several promising leads that dead ended. Her name does not appear on any death records if that's any consolation. We could not find a record of her giving birth. She probably used a midwife and kept it under the table."

He snorted. Drago did not want to drag this out. He was tired and his stomach was still bothering him. Maybe he should call his doctor friend to come check him. He'd be mad since he was just here this morning, but this was important. He could spend the night and take care of Megan's wound tomorrow.

Dana waited through the long pause. She had nothing else to say and did not want to anger him further. She was sure the line was still open, but the quiet was unnervingly long. Finally, after a protracted silence of almost two minutes, she dared to ask, "Are you still there?"

"I'm thinking!" he gruffly retorted, "It's a nuisance having two hostages, especially a kid."

Megan scooted back against the wall, trying to make herself small and unseen.

"You could always give us one."

"I'm not sure which one is more trouble, the mother or the girl."

"Why not give us the child? We'll even come get her."

"Well, let me give you my address." He paused to drag in a ragged breath. "Dana, Baby, I took you for someone with some smarts. I guess I was wrong. Maybe I'll kill the mother and keep the child. I've grown kind of fond of her. What the…" The line went dead.

The air was filled with the ruckus sound of ducks. Just at that moment a huge flock of ducks flew in for a landing on the lake next to the mill. The quacking they made was deafening as it echoed around inside the empty mill.

Unmindful of orders to stay on her blanket and too excited by the excessive noise, Megan jumped up and put her hands over her ears to block out some of the sound. "What's that?" she yelled. Fear forgotten, she ran to a window and stood on a chair to look out the peephole. "Ducks! Wow! There must be a million ducks out there." She pointed and bounced excitedly, nearly tipping the chair, unable to contain her exuberance. "I remember feeding ducks with my daddy when I was little. I used to throw pieces of bread into the water and they ate it. I'd cw-lap my hands when they went under the water. There wasn't this many. This is a whole bunch!" Megan giggled and turned back to the hole.

Dana heard the noisy quacking before the line disconnected. "Well, that didn't go so well. I thought he might give up one hostage, but then he threatened to kill the mother and keep Megan. I'm not sure what he might do. He sounded short of breath. I heard ducks quacking before the line went dead," she paused briefly, "and I could have sworn I heard Megan's voice. It sounded like she said *What's that?*"

"Are you sure?" Nick asked anxiously. This was the first proof of life they had since the kidnapping.

She picked up her television remote and clicked on the TV, ignoring Nick's question. No, she was not sure, but she wanted to be.

Sharply Nick admonished, "We don't have time to watch TV."

"I need to see the news. I'm hoping they mention something about the ducks." She flipped around until she came to the local news channel.

Drago was doing the same thing, only he hated to waste the generator power by turning on the portable television. He kept only the fluorescent lights on since that type did not use much power, and they shed enough light in their little living area that he did not have to turn more lights on.

The local news had already started and had already covered several big stories including the kidnapping of Megan and her mother. The newscaster was finishing the story about the death of a prominent business owner, Mr. Harold Daniels, founder of the Daniels and Son Fine Furniture chain when he was handed a note. He quickly read the note, looked back up into the camera, and gave his award-winning smile. "Well, folks, the ducks have landed. The first sighting seems to be Willows Pond. All you duck hunters need to patient for the season to begin. We'll be back after this word from our sponsors."

As Dana flipped open her laptop on the coffee table and looked up about ducks she commented, "I hope they keep the stores open. My friend Myra and I like his line of furniture." She took a swallow of her soda, "What do you guys know about ducks?"

"Not much," the two men each said, practically in unison.

She found the file she was looking for and printed out three copies. "Charlie, grab those copies and pass them around. I made one for each of us. It's a list of last year's sightings. While you're up, would you get me a refill on my coffee? Thanks, you're a dear." She blew him a kiss. "This may give us an idea of where Drago's holed up."

Drago did not know that ducks could be so noisy. When his friend Harley had first looked at the place there had been no ducks. He got up and looked out one of the peepholes Harley had made in the plywood boarding up the windows. There were ducks all over the place. A few more were still landing, but they were quiet compared to the chaos of the others preceding them. He had no idea what he was going to do. Was it duck hunting season?

He was going to need more ammo if he had to kill the duck hunters as well as face a shoot out with the police. *Why was nothing going right? This was such a simple plan.* Out of breath from that little bit of exertion, Drago dropped into his chair leaning back as far as it would go. If Monday brought duck hunters, Drago decided he would have to have all this resolved by then or he would cut his losses and leave.

Dana phoned Captain Wells to let him know about the phone call. She discussed with him about the ducks quacking and that she had emailed him a copy of last year's locations. While she talked she crossed off a number of names on her list. He agreed with her line of thinking, but decided to send a team out to Hampton Lakes as well, heading it himself."

"Are you sure? You crossed those names off without really looking at them," Nick commented worriedly.

"People phoned in those sightings. Most likely Drago's not going to phone in his. All three of those are in developments. Drago wouldn't be hiding out anywhere near them, especially with hostages. River Ridge and Three Points are both very upper class. Any activity out of the ordinary and someone would be calling the police. Willows Pond is just that–a pond. Dobie Roberts lives in a shack out there and always calls in when he sees the ducks fly overhead whether they touch down in his pond or not." Dana nibbled on the end of her pen, "Hampton Lakes has possibilities, but I don't think it'll lead anywhere. Captain Wells is leading a team out there. I know the ducks were close to Drago. They were unusually loud with kind of an echo sound. Does that make sense?"

"What makes an echo?" Charlie asked.

"Mountain ranges," Dana offered quickly.

"Cathedrals," Charlie chimed in next.

"Reverb on a microphone." Nick snapped his fingers. "That's it. We have a flock of ducks flying around with their own sound system."

Nobody laughed. Dana gave him a withering look and Charlie snorted. Dana did not know what to make of Nick. One minute he was a serious, intelligent hero and the next, a blithering idiot. *How could she ever consider becoming serious about this guy? She did not mind a sense of humor. His was simply at the bottom of the barrel. Yet, she had to admit, he kissed better than any other guy she had dated so far. That had to count for something.*

"Please, Nick, do you have a reasonable or sensible idea?" Dana asked.

Nick did not seem to mind her chastisement. He gave her a wink and quick little smile which he knew some women found sexy. "In fact, I do. What about large, empty buildings? Any empty warehouses or mill houses nearby?"

"Good point," Dana said, reaching for her computer again, appreciative of his intelligent input. That little wink and smile worried her. She could not help but smile at his devilishness, yet she wondered if he had read her mind.

Nick was delighted to see a glimmer of delight in her eyes at his suggestion. He liked those 'Ah-ha' moments.

Charlie broke the silence while Dana was toying with her computer. "I'm going to call the precinct and see if anything new has come up about his ex-wife."

"Good idea. I wish I knew what Drago was thinking right now. It was obvious he was a little pissed at me. I hope he didn't shoot everyone after he hung up and take off. He had his number blocked or I'd call him back. Nick, how about if you use my desk top and look up mountain ranges and lakes under the DNR while I'm checking out empty warehouses and churches." She typed in her password and did not object to Nick watching. "Okay, I've put in my password so you can use it now. We need to narrow those empty buildings you suggested down to ones around water."

Dana took a sip of soda before continuing. "I can't lie to him if he calls again. I don't know what he'll do to his hostages if we can't deliver his little girl." The worry was evident in her voice, she added with a short wave of her hand in helpless frustration.

Nick said, "Frankly, if he hurts Megan. I might be tempted to accidently shoot him and save the justice system some trouble." No one disagreed with him. Nick stood up and casually asked, "Are they still trying to locate his wife?"

"Oh, yes. Officer Jenkins has been assigned to help now. The last I heard they were still drawing a blank."

"Do you think they're both dead?" Nick asked.

"Let's hope not," Charlie answered, heaving a heavy sigh. "They've checked death records and can't find either one listed. Of course, we're working blind with the baby. We know his ex-wife's name, but have no clue about the baby. We're having trouble finding any birth record."

"So she delivered at home and paid a midwife under the table to keep Drago from learning that he had a child. She must have recognized Drago's sister, realized she had been discovered and disappeared," Nick conjectured, talking more to himself than to the others. Suddenly he snapped his fingers and exclaimed, "She had the baby in Mexico!"

Megan fell asleep on the blanket holding her doll. Drago sat in his chair dozing. Around ten-thirty, Rico finally came back to the living quarters such as they were. He had watched Sheri while she ate and let her use the toilet. After making sure she got another dose of drugs again to make her sleep, he played the pinball machine for a little while. That was one thing he wanted to see if they could take with them when they left this place.

Rico wanted a beer. He had not thought about that when he had done all those errands earlier. "Drago, I want to run out and get a couple of six packs, maybe I should just make that a case." Drago gave him a half-wave and he took that as an okay. Rico never slowed down enough to take a close look at Drago to see the mild distress he was in. He never noticed the labored breathing, the sweat on his forehead, or the pallor under Drago's normal ruddy complexion.

Drago was not feeling well at all. His stomach pain had moved higher in his chest. His left arm ached fiercely and his fingers felt almost completely numb. His right hand was not much better than his left. His breathing was rapid and shallow because there was a heavy weight like an elephant on his chest. He swiped at the sweat beading on his brow with the back of his hand. Unable to speak when Rico had nonchalantly come through, he had tried to wave at him for help, but Rico had misunderstood, considered it a wave of dismissal, and had already slammed the door before Drago found his voice.

He managed to take his cell phone out of his shirt pocket, but he could not get his fingers to cooperate and press the numbers right. It seemed to him the buttons on his phone had suddenly gotten exceptionally smaller. His vision blurred. On the third try, he fumbled and dropped the phone. When he leaned over to pick it up, the pain worsened, and he became dizzy to the point that he nearly passed out; gasping for air, he slowly eased back up.

"Megan," Drago rasped before passing out.

Sleepily, rubbing her eyes, Megan woke up with the door slamming. Again she was hoping to see her mother. "Mommy," Megan called softly. She needed to potty and looked over at the Dragon man. He was sleeping. She padded in her bare feet down the hall to the bathroom. Megan finished her potty needs, washed up, and returned to the blanket. Fully awake, Megan sat quietly holding her doll and watched the dragon on the man's arm. After watching it for a while, she decided it was not so scary after all.

Everything was quiet. The bright fluorescent kitchen lights shed plenty of light in this area. She saw the cell phone lying on the floor and decided she could call her mother. Then she thought better of it. Her mother had told her she was not to bother her at work unless it was an emergency, like if she was hurt. "Donna May, now what?" I can't call Mommy cause I'm not hurt. Let me think. If you get any ideas, you tell me."

She had heard three things earlier—that he might move them, keep her, and kill them. She turned sideways and put her hand up against her dolls ear, "Moving us might not be a bad thing, but killing me and my mommy is very bad. I don't want to stay with him." She eyed Drago to make sure he was not listening then very softly resumed whispering to Donna May, "I won't let him kill you either. You know Donna May, I think he lied to me. I don't think Mommy's at work, but I don't know where she is. He called the police lady on that phone. Listen. I have a plan, but you have to keep it a secret, okay." She whispered her plan directly into the soft fabric of her doll's face.

Still in her bare feet, Megan tiptoed on the cool tile floor over toward Drago. Half way there she dropped and started crawling. Just as she stretched to grab the phone. Drago coughed. Megan froze for a second, grabbed the phone then ran as fast as her little legs could carry her down the hall and out of sight.

Rico had left the light on in the dining hall and Megan raced into the room. Breathless, she stopped and leaned against the wall. Then she spied the pinball machine and hid under its tall legs.

She looked at the phone searching for the button with an R. She did not know the police officer's number, but she knew about redial. There—R-E-D-I-A-L. Megan was not sure how to spell the word she was looking for, but this had the first three letters that sounded right. She hoped she picked the right one. She pressed her eyes shut and prayed to Jesus to help her as she listened to the phone ring.

It was almost midnight. They were tired, but they were not stopping. All three of them were still hashing things out, trying to narrow the locations down to a manageable number when the phone rang. Dana stared at the kidnaper's phone as if it were a venomous snake. Suddenly she reached out and snatched it up as if she was striking first.

Expecting Drago to be on the other end she spoke firmly but cautiously, "Hello, have you decided anything yet?"

"Dana?"

The timid tear-filled voice took Dana by surprise, "Megan!" Dana jumped up, "Where are you? How are you? Where's your mother? Is she okay? Are you okay?" She paced as she spit out her questions. Tears of joy filled her eyes just to know that Megan was alive.

The two men stopped what they were doing and paced with Dana. They waited in silence, but it was evident they were ready to race out the door as soon as they knew where they were racing to.

"I don't know where my mommy is. He said she was off then she went to work, but I think he lied." Megan started to cry. "I want to go home. I want my mommy."

Dana gulped, "Sweetie, can you describe anything about where you are so we can find you?"

"It's a big building and there's a bunch of ducks. Oh, it's a mill but I couldn't read the name. It was too big a word for me."

Hopeful, Dana asked, "Do you remember the letters? Can you spell it?"

"It had a big letter C. I can spell just a few words—'I love you' and my name, but I like to put an 'M' inside a heart. I think it looks sweet. Mommy says I'll learn more in school this year. Let me go look."

Dana talked softly, "You're being very brave, Megan. We're going to get you home. You and your mother. I promise. Where's Drago?"

"He's sleeping."

"Is there anyone else there?"

"I don't see the sign. It's gone."

Dana could hear Megan crying. "Honey, don't cry. We'll find you. There aren't that many mills." *Liar, liar. Can you find her before Drago kills them?* "You gave us a big clue with that name. Can you tell me if there is anyone else there?"

"He has two other guys, Sam and Rico. They're both okay. Rico brought me a beautiful pink princess dress with a hat."

Dear, sweet Megan, Dana thought. *She's in dire trouble and still she rambles on. Must be nice to be five years old and so trusting.* "Do you know where they are?"

"No." She sniffled.

"Where are you at now?"

"I'm hiding under the pinball machine in what they said used to be the cafeteria." Megan stuttered over the word cafeteria. "It's a secret. Rico said not to tell Drago it was here."

Dana scribbled on a piece of paper and handed it to Charlie. She simply listed 'C' mill, ducks, pinball, Sam, Rico. Nick looked over his shoulder and took the names 'Sam' and 'Rico' leaving Charlie with the rest.

Charlie went to work looking up the mill. Depending on how far out they had gone, they could be in any one of fifty cotton mills. Charlie started the process of eliminating while Dana kept Megan on the phone.

"When you look out the window what do you see?"

"All the windows have boards on them. We have little holes to look out. Do you think it would be all right if I put on my dress tonight so when you come get me you can see how beautiful I look? Drago said I shouldn't wear it until tomorrow."

"I think that's a splendid idea. I can't wait to see you in your dress. Can you look out a little hole now?"

"These windows are high." Suddenly her voice was louder as she exclaimed, "I see a hole!"

The line went dead.

CHAPTER 13

Dana was at a loss. She called Captain Wells, waking him up to let him know the latest development in the case. Secretly she wanted some reassurance from him that she was doing everything she could. She did not have to ask for it. He gave it by telling her she was doing everything humanly possible. The three of them would get this figured out. He knew Dana was tough, but she cared too much for kids. That was her undoing. She should have been a kindergarten teacher.

He offered to help out, since he was now wide awake, by letting Jenkins and Travis know what was going on. That way Dana could add her head to the clues and solve them faster. Maybe one of the other guys might know something. Dana thanked her dad and hung up after apologizing again for waking him.

Fatigue forgotten, Dana made a fresh pot of coffee and Charlie whipped up a large batch of scrambled eggs. They sat together at the table, this time to eat as well as work on the clues. Charlie had pulled up mills in their area only with a 'C' in it, somewhere–front, back or middle. There were five.

"That's not bad," Nick said a touch sarcastically. We send five teams out chasing around in the middle of the night."

"I don't like the amount of time and work force we'd waste and then what if they're not in this area? I wish Megan would call back. I wish I knew why the phone went dead." Dana got up to make another cup of coffee. "Anybody want a cup?"

"I'll take another one," Nick replied. "I like your coffee. Are there any eggs left?"

"None for me, thanks. I'll have heartburn so bad there'll be fire coming out my nose if I drink any more," Charlie commented. "Do you have any ginger ale?"

"I keep extra sodas in that closet beside the refrigerator if you want to look for something else. I'm not sure what all is in there," Dana answered Charlie first. "Nick, hand me your plate. I think there's a spoonful or two left."

He handed her his plate with a thank you and went back to work. A second later it dawned on him Dana would have two coffees and a plate to carry. He stood up and went into the kitchen. "I thought you might need a hand."

"I do and thank you." She turned to hand him his plate. Nick took the plate from her hand and set it on the counter. He enveloped her in his arms and kissed her, letting his mouth and tongue say what his brain could not seem to. He released her, picked up the plate and left.

When Dana came out of the kitchen a moment later with the two coffees, Nick was hard at work, as if nothing out of the ordinary had happened. He was comparing his earlier list with the one Charlie was working on with the names with the letter C. "I don't think we'll have to waste any time at all." Nick, with a huge grin, exclaimed happily as he waved his paper, "I know where Megan is!"

Charlie and Dana looked at Nick expectantly. The room was eerily quiet except for the quiet ticking of the clock in the living room.

"She's at the old JC Heaton Cotton Mill. There's a large pond there that the ducks would have landed on. The building's empty so it would echo. The best clue was," he stood and waved a form, wearing a cocky grin, "One Sam Hawkins got a ticket for speeding earlier this evening. He gave his address as 2799 Old Mill Road, and I see here that the Heaton Cotton Mill is on Old Mill Road." Nick rocked on his feet, knowing he was right, but it was Charlie's or Dana's call. "Some criminals are plain stupid."

When neither said anything he pushed, "I think we should call for back-up and head out that way. I don't think I'm wrong."

"Good thinking. You're probably right, too. I'm just amazed you came up with it." Dana finally spoke up. "Charlie, do you agree?"

"Sounds good to me."

"Thanks. I'm sorry I've given you a bad impression of me." Nick grabbed his jacket and slipped his shoes on. He checked his pistol. "Okay, I'm ready."

Dana and Charlie went through the same routine. "Let's head out. I'll call the other guys on the way."

Megan could not get the phone to work and did not know what was wrong with it. She gave up trying. She decided the Dana would find her and she needed to get ready. She was glad Dana had said she could wear her new dress tonight. She wanted to look beautiful when they came for her and her mother.

Megan was careful with her new clothes. She kept everything on her blanket since there was so much dust everywhere. The paper bag was almost as big as Megan. She kept the dress on the hanger and laid it down carefully. Next, she really had to stretch to reach the bottom of the bag and nearly fell in before she managed to pull out a three-pack of underwear. Megan grabbed the bag and dumped out the remaining contents. She talked softly to Donna May the whole time. "Look at this. There's a new slip, white socks with lace, and, ooh, white sandals."

She walked barefoot to the bathroom, carrying the large bag with the panties and slip inside. She splashed cold water on her face and dried off with the front of her dirty dress, wanting to make sure she looked her best. "Donna May, I wish I had a toothbrush. How do my teeth look?" She bared her teeth for Donna May to see them then turned her head to look in the huge hazy, cracked wall mirror. "This mirror makes them look gray. I don't think my teeth are gray, but I can't remember when I bw-rushed them. I guess they'll do."

Megan worried, "How long do you think it will take them to find us, Mary Alice? Oops, I'm sorry, Donna May. Too bad I can't change your dress into a fancy one like mine. It won't take me long."

She had never had such fancy clothes before and, not wanting to get her new dress dirty, she left it on her blanket. Standing naked, she shivered in the chilly bathroom as she worked to rip open the plastic bag holding the new panties. She put her old clothes in the bag as well as the extra new panties.

After putting the slip on, Megan tried to check herself in the mirror but it was all too high up. The slip did not look right. She twisted around as much as she could and saw some lace on her back. She wanted to cry and wished she had her mother to help.

Megan took the slip off and put it on again. This time she paid attention to the lace and kept it in the front. The slip looked and felt better this time.

Megan returned to her blanket to put on the dress. She took it off the hanger and sat down on the blanket to admire it. "Donna May, I've never worn anything so beautiful before." She fingered the wider white lace and traced the pink satin ribbon running through its center. "I'm going to keep this dress for my little girl."

Megan dressed but could not tie the bow in the back. She was sure her hair needed combing, but hoped the hat would hide that. That left just her shoes and socks to put on. She liked sandals because they did not have buckles or laces. She thought she looked so beautiful and went back to the bathroom to see herself in the mirror. The mirrors were high enough that she could see only from her shoulders up. She could not wait to show her mother and Dana.

She turned to her new doll, "Am I beautiful?" Megan giggled. "I agree. Mommy will be so happy to see me." Her smile faded, "I wish I knew where she was."

Returning to the blanket, Megan took off her hat and shoes. She played with Donna May for a while and soon fell asleep.

Rico came back with his case of beer and one bag of pretzels and another of chips. He dropped the case of beer noisily on the kitchen table.

"Do you want a beer?" he called to Drago.

Drago mumbled no.

"I'm going to play pinball for a little while before I go to bed. Megan's sleeping. It looks like she couldn't wait until morning to wear her new dress," Rico chuckled. "Do you want me to check on her mom or will you do it this time?"

Rico snapped opened his beer just as Drago mumbled something that sounded like he did it already. He could not make out exactly what Drago had said, but he knew better than to ask him to repeat it. That always caused Drago to get mad and retaliate with some type of punishment.

He kept it cool, "Okay, thanks. I'll get her first thing in the morning." Going out the side door, he headed down the hall to the pinball room with his beer and pretzels, not giving Drago another thought. He hoped Drago did not check on him or catch his slip-up with saying pinball instead of ping-pong.

Dana, Nick and Charlie reached the mill they thought was occupied by Drago and his victims. They used lights and sirens until they got close then switched to silent and dark. One back-up team arrived two minutes later. Joe Jenkins positioned himself so he could see the back door and Bill Travis took the right side and buddied with Joe. Charlie got the left side with Dana as a buddy. Nick got the front. There was another team coming, but they were tied up at another crime scene and it was uncertain how long before any more assistance would get there.

It was eerily quiet. An owl hooted and a few crickets chirped but other than that you could not hear the sounds of the city. All seemed peaceful, a beautiful summer night.

"The windows are boarded up and I don't see any cars," Charlie commented.

"Travis, go scout around the perimeter," Dana ordered.

"Are we at the right place?" Nick worried.

"There are two cars parked in the woods back of the parking lot," Travis informed Dana over the radio.

"So we must have two kidnappers inside," Dana deduced. "I wish we knew what kind of fire power they had."

"Let me scout around the building," Nick offered. "Maybe I can find an opening to see into a window."

"I don't want anyone to get too close and trigger any alarms," Dana argued.

"I know how to be careful," he retorted sharply, annoyed that Dana was treating him like a rookie.

Before he had a chance to say anything else, she agreed. "On second thought, go ahead. Travis you're in charge here at base. I'm going with Coburn. We'll stay in touch by radio only when necessary. I want us to be as quiet as possible."

Removing his arm sling, Nick slipped away easily into the night. Dana followed in his shadow. The unkept landscape was to his advantage. The tall grass and untrimmed shrubbery shielded them from view. Nick easily crawled foreword to hide behind a battered, rusted fifty-five gallon drum. This gave him a better view of the front and side doors, but he was still adequately hidden.

They moved slowly, silently, like living shadows, taking their time, checking anything suspicious that might set off an alarm or explosion. They reached a narrow open area that offered no protection. Staying low, with nothing more than a few padded footfalls, Nick and Dana reached the corner of the building. Nick took a moment to search for any signs of alarms; seeing nothing, he signaled Dana that he was moving forward.

They decided to start along the front. They had about twenty feet of plywood to check before they reached the glass entryway. All that was left of it was the frame. Nick peered around the corner. The inner door was boarded up. So far they found no peek holes that he could tell. Dana had double checked a couple of places and shook her head. Nick could not believe these guys had themselves sealed up tight. Some of the wood looked old and weathered like it had been there a few years, and some looked brand new as if it had been put up in the past few weeks.

He moved down and found a board with a piece that moved, but when they looked in, it was an empty room. According to the plans, Nick remembered there were several offices along the front of the rectangular shaped building. He moved down to a door and signaled to Dana. She approached cautiously as he had instructed.

"Look, this door is being used," Nick whispered. Dana nodded and, shining her light down, looked on the ground, noting fresh foot prints. Drawing their weapons they positioned themselves and Nick turned the doorknob.

The knob turned silently. Nick pushed. The door stopped with a sudden jolt and thunk. They froze and waited for some sign that they had been discovered.

No one on the inside heard them. Drago was dozing. The noise of the pinball drowned out the soft thunk the metal door made against the wooden bar.

"We don't know where they're keeping them. I hate to break down this door and find they're at the back of the building. Let's keep checking. We might get lucky," Dana suggested.

Nick nodded and they silently moved on. Just because they were using that door did not mean they were staying near there. Maybe it was the only door that worked. It did suggest that all the culprits were probably inside since the bar was across the door.

The front of the building was the short end of the rectangle, but there was still maybe a hundred feet of boarded up windows to check before they reached the corner to go down the long side.

They turned the corner before they got lucky and found a large circular opening. Nick looked out at the view and determined that whoever was looking out the hole would be able to see anyone coming up from town along the curved uphill road. Now he had a new worry. Had they already been discovered? Was their element of surprise totally gone?

He used hand signals to tell Dana what he had found since voices would probably carry into the large opening. The hole was simply a jagged opening, but it was as big as one of his Aunt Dale's lemon cream pies. By the soft whitish blue glow emanating through the opening, it was obvious the room was faintly lit with fluorescent lights.

Dana came close enough to see the hole and sign, 'I'm going to look inside.'

Nick shook his head no emphatically, but it did no good. He worried that anyone showing their head in that hole might get it blown off.

Dana had her mind made up. She edged slowly and quietly to the opening and peered around. Quickly darting back out of view, she grabbed Nick's shirt and they dashed around the corner out of sight.

Both of them could hear the faint sound of running footsteps. Nick stayed low on the ground and saw a face appear in the hole. It was a young man. The face turned as it searched in the darkness for something that it was not sure it saw. It took a minute for him to recognize it was Rico Regales that he had checked out earlier on the computer. The face disappeared.

Nick signed about checking the rest of the building and Dana nodded agreement. They moved a little faster this time. They found another peephole not too far from the other one. Nick vetoed looking in it and this time Dana agreed.

As they hurried along, the ground became uneven and rocky. Not the best surface to try walking on in the dark. Suddenly, Nick yelped and disappeared from view.

Meanwhile, inside, Rico ran into the main room. He was thankful that he had gotten the beer and returned quickly. He might get some kudos for saving the day. "Boss, they found us!" He had not seen anyone, but he knew someone was out there. He stopped in surprise when he saw Drago. "Are you all right? He touched his arm to wake him up. "Drago, wake up." He pulled his hand away and looked at it before wiping it on his jeans. "You're all sweaty."

Drago coughed and gasped in a breath before getting out the words, "Call for help. I'm dying." He gasped again as he dropped his head back against the chair. That action opened up his airway a little bit more, making it easier for him to breathe.

Rico hesitated. The last thing he wanted was the police. It did not matter that they were most likely right outside the door. He watched Drago's chest go rapidly up and down as he fought for air. His face was an unusual color of blue and red, kind of purple "Okay."

He had another plan. Quickly he dialed Sam. Rico was ticked off that Sam did not answer and it went to voice mail. He left the coded message, "Daddy came home and caught the boyfriend in Betty's bedroom." If Sam was smart, he would listen to his voicemail before he headed back to the hide out and know not to come here.

Drago was not feeling well at all and considered his death imminent. Unable to speak, he looked up at Rico, gave him a thumbs up, and passed out again.

Dana stopped in surprise when she saw Nick disappear and dropped to her knees. She softly called his name. There was no reply. Cautiously Dana crawled, inch by inch, carefully testing the ground's solidity, to the spot where Nick had vanished, testing her weight to make sure the ground did not give way and she did not fall in as well.

What she expected to be a small hole turned out to be much larger, something her car could have easily fallen into. "Nick," she called softly again over the rim of the small crater as she shone her light into the empty darkness. *Where did he go? Maybe he crawled out while I was crawling towards him.* While she was peering around above ground, her flashlight started flickering and clouds covered the pale moonlight. Dana was relieved to hear Nick's quiet voice echoing from inside the hole.

"I'm okay. I hurt my ankle, but it's not too bad. Come on down. Just be careful where you land. I think I found a way in."

The hole was not much of a drop, about eight to ten feet. Dana swung around so she could slide down a short but very steep slope. A sturdy gnarled tree root helped to stop her rapid descent. She saw a rusty metal bar protruding not two feet away from her. Considering that right below her was a small pile of jagged rocks, Dana opted to jump out to the bar and pray that it wasn't too rusted to hold her weight. She gently pushed off the tree root and caught the bar in the crook of her elbow. She could feel tiny flakes of rust grinding into her skin. She hung there only a second before dropping the last foot safely to the ground. After brushing off the loose dirt, she ran to the large opening where Nick was standing. The corridor was tall enough to stand up and walk around in. There were fluorescent lights in the ceiling, but they decided not to try turning them on.

"Are you okay?" Dana asked.

"When I fell in, I landed on a broken rail. I think my high tops will help for now, but it still hurts."

"Do you remember seeing this on the plans? That hole looked like an elevator shaft for loading rail cars."

"No, I don't think it was on the plans," Nick answered honestly.

"Are you up to walking?"

"Don't have much choice, do I," Nick flatly stated as he gingerly took a step.

"Let's get going," Dana ordered.

Nick hobbled as they ran up the long tunnel. "I hope this stops before we reach the next county."

Dana noticed he got slower the more they ran. "You're limping. How bad is that ankle?"

"It only hurts when I put any weight on it."

"You're hilarious."

They came to a three-way intersection. Their flashlights told them another long corridor headed to their left, but down a short hallway on their right was a door marked 'STAIRS'.

"I opt for the stairs," Dana suggested.

Somewhat reluctantly Nick agreed.

Dana jerked on the door. It refused to open. Nick pulled and was met with the same resistance. He swept his shoe along the floor in front of the door and Dana checked the hinges. Nick found a small piece of wood jammed under the door and was able to get it out. The door opened willingly, but with a small groan. At that moment, they heard a gun shot.

Briefly Dana and Nick froze and looked at each other. Each wondering the same thing–were they too late to save the hostages? They drew their weapons and headed up the metal stairs, as quietly and as quickly as they could. Dana took the lead. Nick was having more trouble walking than he cared to admit.

Rico grabbed Megan, startling her awake. He held both her arms at her sides. "Listen, Drago's dying. I'm going to let you out. You go tell the police that your mommy is sleeping in one of the rooms down that hall," he pointed in the direction he meant, "and that Drago is dying."

Megan rubbed her eyes, "Where will you be?"

"I'm staying here with Drago." *Like hell I am. I'm looking for a back way out.*

After Rico unlocked the door, he picked Megan up, holding her in his right arm when he opened the door so that no one would shoot him. He felt protected on his left by the metal door and on his right by Megan.

"I'm sending Megan out," he hollered into the darkness." He caught glints of reflective moonlight shining off at least two cars, he guessed. They were parked well back behind a row of decorative trees that lined what once was the management's parking lot.

An authoritative voice called back, "Who are you?"

"Don't worry about me. Megan and her mom are safe. Drago's dying of a heart attack, I think. I'm going to set her down. She can tell you where her mother is." To Megan he said, "When I set you down, I'm going to shut the door. You count to ten then run to the police over by the trees. Okay?"

Aroused by the voices, Drago pulled out his .357 which he kept hidden along side the chair cushion. Megan, still in Rico's arms, saw Drago point the pistol at them. Her eyes opened wide with fear, knowing he was going to shoot her. With tears streaming down her face she squeezed her eyes tightly shut and held her doll in front of her face. She prayed her little heart out to Jesus the only prayer she knew, yelling at the top of her lungs so she would not hear the sound of the big gun, "Now I lay me down to sleep…"

Rico had no idea why Megan was praying a bedtime prayer. He was just ready to set her down when a bullet penetrated his left lung and aorta. He was dead before he knew it.

Charlie yelled, "Hold your fire! Who fired?"

An officer answered back, "No one from this side."

Megan fell with him and, fortunately, had been missed by the bullet, but Drago was aiming for a second shot. Crying and screaming, Megan scrambled to get out from under Rico just as an officer arrived to help her.

Travis had already worked his way closer towards the door when another shot rang out. Travis used himself to shield Megan, as he hurried to get her legs out from under the body. The bullet flew wild.

Gasping for air between the words and rubbing his chest trying to ease the pain Drago ordered, "Don't take her. She's mine."

Dana pushed open the door at the top of the staircase, sending a silent prayer of thanks that it was not locked. She and Nick started running down the hall, in the direction of the sound of the gunfire, just as the second shot rang out. They arrived just in time to hear Drago say—"I hope my little girl's like you."

Drago did not sound or look like he had any energy for anything, but he raised his arm and pointed the pistol. Dana had no idea if he was aiming at anyone in particular. From her viewpoint she could not see his target and his arm was shaking so badly, his chances of hitting someone were slim. It was a lousy angle and there was no time to try for a better shot. Before Drago had a chance to fire again, she fired.

Drago collapsed back onto the chair. His pistol dangled from his lifeless hand.

Limping badly and cussing under his breath with pain, Nick finally caught up to Dana after all the shooting was over. Warily, weapons poised to fire, Nick and Dana cautiously approached.

Dana's shot had hit his upper right chest and probably would not have been a kill shot. They did not see any chest movement to indicate breathing.

Nick checked the jugular vein and did not feel a pulse. He looked at Dana and shook his head no.

Harry Drago was dead.

Epilogue

Sam approached the police station hesitant to do what he knew he had to. Drago was dead. Rico was dead. He felt like he had lost his family all over again. Everything was planned out–had been since he had started with Drago. All he had to do was give Officer Dana Morgan this envelope. He looked at the wrinkled and dirty business envelope Drago had given him his second week on the job with very precise directions.

The envelope had been safely stored all this time behind a loose brick in the men's bathroom of St Michael's church. Every two weeks he and Drago would go to the church and, after Drago said his confession, they would go to the restroom downstairs to make sure the envelope was still there. Sam did not think anyone else would ever bother to look for it, but Drago always wanted to check.

The basement restroom used to be used only for the school until it closed. It was rectangular with high barred windows which were frosted so pedestrians could not peek in. There were four toilets along the wall opposite the windows and four urinals across the end wall. Six sinks were nestled in the long counter below the windows. Sam had to climb onto the counter and stretch to reach the first row of bricks above the large gray and yellow tile squares just to the right of the last sink. It was tricky to maintain his balance while trying to pull that brick out. Drago kept watch for anyone coming in; however, this out-of-date bathroom was used very seldom. Most of the worshipers preferred the newer restrooms upstairs.

Sam had to ask Drago how he knew about the loose brick. He was surprised to learn that Drago had gone to that parochial school. He had found that loose brick back then and used it to hide their contraband–cigarettes, marijuana and girly pictures. They had managed to break part of the back of the brick off to make more room for their stash. Looking at Drago that day–forty pounds over weight, old and balding, Sam had a hard time picturing him lithe enough to capably handle the task.

He shoved the folded envelope into the back pocket of his jeans and leaned against the wall of the building across the street from the police station. Drago had made it sound simple. He was under age and would be treated as a juvie. So what that he had used a fake ID and passed himself off as twenty-one so he could drink and play with the girls. It felt good to be treated like a grown up.

Sam started walking up the street, away from the precinct. He was having second thoughts. Rico and he had been told to split up if anything happened to Drago. If they were not sure if he was dead, they could go into hiding until he could get in touch with them. If he was killed, they were to completely break up and go their separate ways. Neither one knew enough, but together it made for bigger trouble for them. Rico was to disappear, preferably go back to Mexico for a while.

Sam, on the other hand, was to turn himself in. For the first time since meeting him, Sam argued with Drago. Drago explained that since Sam was under eighteen he would get off with a lighter sentence. Also, he could swear he did not know where all the money was. Drago stressed the word *all*. He had split up their accounts so there would be no fighting or stealing from the other, hopefully. If one or the other of them died, the other got it all. Sam was sorry Rico was gone. He had really liked him and almost did not want his share of the money. Almost. It would be great to be wealthy, but now he was back to having nobody again. Money could not make up for that.

Drago had repeatedly gone over how it was supposed to work with the lie detector. 'They're going to ask you if you know where the money is. You think in your head no. Why? Because you only know where your money is, not all the money. It will come across as the truth because you don't know where all the money is,' he stressed his point by jabbing him in the chest with his finger. Sam rubbed across his chest, trying to ease the remembered soreness of Drago's strong finger drilling into his chest.

'You keep thinking that and it will make it easier when the time comes. Maybe if you're lucky, you won't have to do one.' Drago had looked at Sam closely. Sam had not been sure what to make of that look and still did not, but he did not think he would forget the hardness in his eyes, mingled with what Sam did not know. Curiosity? Regret? Love?

Sam kept walking, trying to decide if Drago was right. Maybe he did need to grow up more. Prison would do that or kill him—most likely kill him. When he was with Drago, it had seemed like the right thing to do. Now it did not make any sense.

Rico had been like a big brother to him. Sure he hated those hard slaps on the back Rico loved to give him, but now he missed them. Rico had always been encouraging. He still could hear him say *Keep strong,* and was sorry Rico was gone.

Sam had no idea how much money he was getting, if any. Drago always talked like there was a lot. Drago had him over a barrel. When he turned himself in and gave the police the envelope, there was a name of a lawyer to call. That lawyer had the information to the location for Sam's share. If he did not turn himself in—no info and no money.

Finally Sam walked into the police precinct.

Dana wondered why everyone was eager to have the horror of those days rehashed. She felt the need to change the subject and took in a deep breath. "I'm sorry Drago didn't live to make it to trial. He got off too easy. It's still hard to believe that after all we went through he simply died of a heart attack and never got to see his own little girl." Dana patted Nick's shoulder. "You got a sprained ankle, and Travis got a dislocated shoulder when he rolled protecting Megan. The only good thing is that young kid, Sam, went to jail. Maybe that'll help to straighten him out."

Dana opened her next present. It was a coffee cup with the word HERO printed in pink on the side and stuffed with packets of hot chocolate.

"I'm glad it's all over," Nick commented.

She read the card and gave Charlie a hug. "Thank you. You know I love hot chocolate next to coffee." Before she grabbed another present, Dana commented, "I thought it was rather weird that both his ex-wives were hiding out in Mexico. His first wife told the police when she read about his death in the newspaper, she felt safe to come back home."

Charlie added, "I heard he left Megan and his newest daughter fifty-thousand, each."

"He certainly got a lot done for being on the run," Travis commented as he adjusted his shoulder sling. "I hate desk duty."

Dana planted a kiss on Travis' forehead. "A kiss to make you feel better. Now quit whining. You're not alone. I've still got to wear my thumb splint for two more weeks."

"I've got three more weeks," he said grumpily.

"You're not getting another kiss," Dana teased. "Oh, I just remembered! I got a letter from Megan yesterday. Her mother married a nurse named David Porter. She gave me her address so I could write to her. Wasn't that sweet? They moved to North Carolina." Dana unwrapped as she talked. This time it was a shimmery pastel blue tank top. "Oh, how lovely!" Dana looked under the tissue paper for a card. Finally she found it. "Nick? It's beautiful! Thank you."

"I hope you have something to go with it." He was a little disappointed he didn't get a hug. He almost let it slip that he knew of two things in her closet that would pair with it beautifully.

"I do." She put it with the others. "Thank you all for this send off, but you shouldn't have gone to all this trouble. I'm coming back."

Nick was sorry to hear Dana say that. He was hoping she would like to stay and work with him permanently. He wanted to see where their relationship might lead. He was happy that she had agreed to do this assignment with him. That might give him enough time to change her mind.

After the last present was unwrapped everyone slowly wandered back to their duties. Nick hung back reluctant to leave.

"Oh, Nick," Dana said very seriously, "before you go I have something I'd like to discuss with you privately if you don't mind."

Nick picked up on her tone of voice and slight frown and became worried that something was really troubling Dana, "Sure." He worried that she changed her mind at the last minute and was going to tell him in private. He was not going to let her change her mind. She was going to Pittsburgh with him even if he had to bind and gag her.

"Follow me. I need this to be a private conversation." Dana led him to an old storage room at the far end of the hall. She quickly removed her thumb splint. "Remember I owe you this…"

Before he had time to realize what was happening, Dana landed her right fist square on his jaw enough to rattle his teeth and cause a few stars to twinkle in the middle of the afternoon. He fell against a stack of plastic crates.

"Wow!" Nick rubbed his sore jaw, "You sure pack a wallop."

Dana grabbed his hand and helped him straighten back up. She did not move away. "Now I get to give you a kiss to make you feel better." Slowly tenderly she placed butterfly kisses along his bruised jaw until she came to his mouth. Dana traced his lower lip with her tongue then nipped him ever so gently.

Arms at his side, Nick stood still, enjoying the kisses. Each one was truthfully making his jaw hurt less and less. Repeatedly Dana's tongue darted into his mouth, explored briefly, and retreated leaving him wanting more. His breath quickened. He tried to catch her lips with his, but she turned her head. When he tried to hold her, she pushed his arms away.

Finally he could stand it no more and held her head between his two hands, "My turn." Nick enveloped her in his arms and kissed her with a passion he could no longer contain.

Having Dana for a partner was certainly going to be interesting.